I'll Be Home for

CHRISTMAS

WHEN I FALL
IN LOVE

I'll Be Home for

CHRISTMAS

JULIE L. CANNON

summerside
PRESS™

Summerside Press™
Minneapolis 55438
www.summersidepress.com
I'll Be Home for Christmas
© 2010 by Julie L. Cannon
ISBN 978-1-60936-018-4

Scripture references are from the following source: The Holy Bible, King James Version (KJV).

All characters are fictional. Any resemblances to actual people are purely coincidental.

Cover design by Chris Gilbert | www.studiogearbox.com

Interior design by Müllerhaus Publishing Group | www.mullerhaus.net

Summerside Press™ is an inspirational publisher offering fresh, irresistible books to uplift the heart and engage the mind.

Printed in USA.

DEDICATION

For my dear mother-in-law, Marion Weltner Cannon,
who was twenty years old in 1944 and allowed me to
mine her memories as I was bringing Maggie to life.

ACKNOWLEDGMENTS

I would like to acknowledge the extraordinary debt I owe to the following people, whose encouragement and/or critical response helped me at every stage of writing this book: first and foremost, my tireless agent, Sandra Bishop, who urged me to move past the familiar and never lost faith; my editor, Susan Downs, for your ideas, your guidance, and your outstanding good humor in bringing this story to life. Every single correspondence I ever got from you was upbeat, and your enthusiasm gave me the courage to keep typing. And Ellen Tarver, who copyedited this book with enormous skill, warmth, and precision through numerous rewrites; and all the folks at Summerside Press. I admire your vision and your commitment to bring inspirational stories to readers.

I would not be able to write anything if not for the continual support of my enduring husband and best friend, Tom. Thank you from the bottom of my heart for sacrificially allowing me what I needed most—many hours to write, dream, edit, and edit again. You've always believed in me, and you can still make me laugh so hard I forget my troubles.

I have to applaud my three children. Iris, our frequent phone conversations and your encouraging, "So, how's the book going,

Mom?" never fail to lift my spirits. Gus, you're a brilliant technological guru who didn't complain when I needed hours of computer help and who didn't call me a moron (out loud) when I couldn't ever figure out how to attach the right version of a file. Sam, you're great about not complaining when I ignored you and turned the house upside down to write this book, realizing even at the young age of twelve years that it's just your crazy story-telling mom trying to live her dream.

Finally, the biggest thanks to my Heavenly Father, who always leaves the light on for me. I'm so grateful for the ways You've blessed my life.

CHAPTER ONE

December 1943

The world might be at war, but on Margaret Culpepper's little piece of earth, Christmas spirit filled the air.

"Looking pretty festive for war time, huh, Maggie?" William asked, navigating his father's 1940 Lincoln Continental through the streets of downtown Athens, Georgia. "I believe everybody in Watkinsville saved up their gas ration stamps to drive into the big city for Friday night."

"Mmhmm," Maggie muttered, pulling her chin even farther down into her coat's luxurious fox fur collar until most of her ears disappeared. From this safe little cave, she peered out at red ribbons wound around street lamps so that they looked like giant peppermint sticks. This gave the place a magical look and made the war overseas seem far, far away.

William fiddled with the radio dial and tuned in to Frank Sinatra singing "Have Yourself a Merry Little Christmas." He began singing along in a silly, melodramatic voice. Normally a happy, optimistic guy, tonight he seemed even more upbeat than usual.

"You okay?" he asked after several stoplights, turning his

shining eyes on Maggie. "I don't think I've ever known you to be this quiet for this long."

"Guess I'm just tired. Mother wasn't feeling well again last night, and Father had to call Dr. Elder to come over." Maggie managed to swallow the lump in her throat.

"I'm sorry," William said, turning on the Lincoln's blinker. "I'm sure she'll be just fine. Finer than frog's hair."

Cruising along Washington Street, Maggie tried an unconcerned laugh at William's little joke, but it stuck in her throat. She attempted in vain to block the image of Dr. Elder's concerned face in the soft glow of her mother's bedside lamp at three o'clock this morning. "Bob," he had said, turning to Maggie's father, "let's think about getting her into the hospital." Her father nodded, standing there in his pajamas, with his terrified eyes fastened on his wife's face. He loved her so deeply. Maggie could see it in the way he leaned in to stroke her cheek. With his other hand, he'd reached for Maggie's, and she closed her eyes to hold back the tears when she remembered the way he shook.

I'm eighteen, she reasoned. *I shouldn't be feeling like I'm five years old and needing to go hide in my blankie.*

Finally, Maggie managed to allow the anticipation of a chili dog with her best friend and next-door neighbor, William Dove, to take over her thoughts.

Good old William. She looked at his familiar profile in the dashboard's light. She always felt comfortable in his presence. Even the hardship of her mother's illness seemed to ease when she was with him. Plus, William was good to rest her eyes on.

Tall, with golden brown curly hair, soulful brown eyes, and those curvy, full lips that were almost... What was the word? Classic, that was it. A Roman nose and a chiseled jaw that put her in mind of Michelangelo's *David*.

William pulled into a space on College Avenue behind a battered coupe, and Maggie was out of the car before he could even get his door open. Waiting on the sidewalk, she glimpsed a gift the size of a jewelry box resting on the backseat. A little question niggled at her mind. Did William have something special planned tonight besides a chili dog and a frosted orange? Christmas was still a week away, and her gift to him, a Swiss Army knife, was back at the house. Anyway, he wasn't the jewelry-giving type. Or was he? She shook off the silly thought and walked down the sidewalk beside her friend.

The windows and the glass doors of the Varsity were decorated with snowdrifts made from what looked like shaving cream. Maggie's mouth watered when she smelled clouds of sizzling grease and frying onions, trademarks of the restaurant.

Behind the order counter, a tall, pimply-faced boy with a blond buzz cut beneath his white paper hat grinned, leaned forward, and sang out, "What'll ya have?" as the pair stood staring at the menu board on the wall.

When the attendant produced a tray piled high with their food, William picked it up and Maggie walked beside him as he carried it to a table. "This okay with you?" he asked, standing much closer to her than usual. In fact, it was a bit unnerving, the way his lips, level with the top of her forehead, were only inches away. Did he just lean in to graze his lips across her skin? Shock waves raced down to the soles of her feet.

Nah, she convinced herself. *I only imagined that. I'm so exhausted I'm imagining weird stuff.*

"This is fine," Maggie said, removing her coat to hang it over the back of the bench. She'd chosen to wear her green cashmere sweater since it brought out her eyes, a camel-colored pleated skirt, and her black loafers. She'd even splurged and worn a pair of nylon stockings. No one could argue her devotion to the war effort, but every so often, even a patriotic girl like Maggie needed to feel feminine.

William had dressed a bit fancier than usual too—creased navy slacks and a white button-front shirt. He folded a blue and gold Oconee County High letterman's jacket on the seat beside him.

Maggie picked up her chili dog and took a nibble off one end, savoring the tang of mustard mixed with diced onion and meat.

William watched her, smiling. When she'd swallowed, he raised his eyebrows. "Mind if I say grace?"

Maggie's hand paused midway on its mission to lift her frosted orange to her lips. "Oh, sorry," she said, not at all self-conscious the way she would have been with almost anyone else. "I skipped lunch today and I'm about to cave in." In fact, she'd skipped breakfast as well. Her stomach had been too nervous from hearing her mother's moaning to keep anything more than a Budwine soda down.

William reached across the table and took her hands in his. After a gentle squeeze, he looked deep into her eyes before bowing his head. "For these and our many other blessings, Lord, we give Thee thanks. Amen." He kept his head down a bit longer, as if he were having some extra, private conversation with God.

Maggie felt no thankfulness at all toward God today. When was the last time He'd answered any prayer of hers? Despite her intense devotion to prayer in recent months, the war still raged on, and her mother's physical condition was worse than ever. Instead of giving thanks for their food, she let herself muse on the gorgeous sound of William's voice—that slow, smooth, Southern cadence with the dropped *R*s.

When he lifted his head, she quickly snatched her hands away, reaching for her frosted orange. She took a long pull from the straw so that the icy, creamy, citrus concoction chilled her throat and made her tonsils ache in a good way.

She could feel William's amused gaze as she sank her teeth into the crunchy outer shell of a golden-fried onion ring. The heavenly coating gave way to the perfectly tender piece of sweet Vidalia onion inside, and an involuntary "Mmm" escaped Maggie's lips.

"Mmm to you, too, Maggie Jane," William said, one eyebrow raised playfully. "You look really beautiful tonight, you know."

Maggie had no idea how to respond. She and William had known each other since they were both seven years old and had spent plenty of time together. But never on an actual date.

Though she couldn't deny the definite chemistry between them, they'd never ventured into the realm of romance, and the complications this would bring were definitely not welcome at this point. She needed to keep their simple, pure friendship just the way it was. At least until life returned to normal—at home and abroad.

Maggie searched her brain for something ordinary to talk about. "Uh, how are sales, with the war going on and everything? I heard folks might be spending their money on war bonds instead of Christmas trees." She surveyed the Varsity's modest attempts at holiday decorations.

"Sales are okay. Dad says folks still want trees, even if they can't have big hams or figgy pudding."

"Even if they can't have real snow?" she teased. This was a running joke between the two of them, because it rarely snowed in Georgia, except for maybe a few half-hearted flurries in February that melted quickly in the Southern humidity.

"Yeah," he said, a big smile lighting up his face. "Speaking of snow, I'm still counting on that promise we made to each other the Christmas we were twelve."

Maggie's heart skipped a beat. "Promise?"

"You remember, the day you got that Christmas card from your uncle up in Vermont and he'd put a photograph in it of him standing outside his house? There was snow piled in mounds taller than him, and we went crazy. We said that one day we'd go on a trip up north together to see some real, honest-to-goodness, knee-deep snow."

Maggie could feel her pulse accelerate as she vividly recalled William and herself that December day making pretend snowdrifts from tufts of spun cotton for hours on end, making impassioned plans to see the real thing. But she didn't answer.

"You know, I think I'll carry my camera along and get somebody up there to take our picture standing in the snow," William added after a bit. "Then, when we get home, I'll write a caption for the photograph that says something like, 'Two Georgia Crackers in a Winter Wonderland.' You think Mr. Byrd would let me put it up on the wall at the cabin?" He threw back his head and laughed.

Maggie brightened as she thought of Tyronious Byrd, the ancient caretaker of Dove's Tree Farm. He always made her feel special, calling her Magpie and sometimes giving her an arrowhead he'd found in the dirt after a hard rain. "How is Mr. Byrd?" she asked.

"Oh, he's good," William said. "Carries his Bible around in the bib pocket of his overalls and doesn't miss an opportunity to tell folks that Christmas trees and presents are nice, but that they need to make sure they store up their treasures in heaven. If the customers will let him, he'll even open his Bible up to Luke and read the Christmas story to them."

"Do they let him?"

"By and large they do. He's kind of become, well, for lack of a better word, he's like this sort of tourist attraction at the tree farm. I don't know if the customers take him seriously or if they just want to see what everybody's talking about."

"And what about you? When you cut a tree for folks," she teased, "are you preaching at them?"

William looked thoughtful. "Ought to," he said at last. "Too many people look like they sure could use a big dose of divine peace when they come to choose a tree. Even in ordinary times, the holiday season puts lots of stress on folks, and with the war going on, the majority of them have a loved one fighting over-seas. Cut a tree for this woman last Saturday, and she looked near tears the whole time. Finally she told me her son was off fighting, and she hadn't gotten word from him in…I think she said it was six weeks."

Maggie swallowed a lump of sadness in her throat and closed her eyes for a brief second to think of all their classmates who were fighting in the war—especially Will's best friend, Ernie Haygood. Nothing, absolutely nothing, had been the same since that momentous Monday, back in December a couple of years ago, when the entire Oconee County High School jammed into the library to listen to President Roosevelt's words over Mrs. Cooke's little Philco—the first time in Maggie's memory a radio broadcast had been played during school hours.

The war had levied a huge toll on the educational system of Watkinsville, Georgia. As war efforts grew, all able-bodied men—teachers, coaches, bus drivers, custodians, even students at the tender age of eighteen, boys she'd known all her life—were drafted to fight. Erasers for blackboards and coal for the potbelly stoves were in short supply, along with gas and tires for the school buses.

"Too bad *I* can't go and fight those Nazis," William said, his face frustrated, wistful.

Maggie knew this expression well. The two had shared many conversations about William's childhood battle with polio. The illness attacked nerve cells in his spinal cord, causing paralysis of the muscles that controlled his right arm and leg. Through therapy, he had recovered some degree of muscle function over the years. Still, he walked with a pronounced limp and dealt with a hand that wouldn't always obey him. But William, being a natural athlete, had been able to overcome much of his disability, and this, added to the fact that he was left-handed, meant he was able to live a somewhat normal life.

His disabilities had rendered him 4-F, or medically unfit for service in the U.S. military, and this rejection hurt him deeply, Maggie knew. Though totally willing—eager in fact—to go and serve his country, he had to express his patriotism by pouring his energies into all manner of war-relief efforts on the home front. Both he and Maggie did, actually. Whether by collecting used tires, paper, tin, and recycling oil or by writing letters to their friends and former classmates now serving in overseas assignments, they looked for every opportunity to show their devotion to their country and support for the men in uniform.

He gazed at her with such an odd look in his eyes, she had to turn away.

Maggie focused her eyes on a small Christmas tree sitting on a newspaper box in the center of the Varsity. Silver garlands draped the tree and a handmade tinfoil star perched on top.

They ate in silence for a minute or so, and when Maggie looked up at William again, he still stared at her in that peculiar way even while he chewed a bite of his chili dog.

She squirmed in her seat and focused on her food. "Heard from Ernie lately?" she ventured.

"Got a letter from him two weeks ago. Sounds like their October raid on Schweinfurt, Germany, was somewhat of a disaster. Lost so many lives, so many planes…" William's voice trailed off, and Maggie noted how he slumped in his seat a little.

"Knowing Ernie, he'll be okay," she offered, the words sounding hollow amidst all the happy chatter going on around them. She tried not to think of the horrible newspaper account she'd read the previous week of the terrible losses suffered by the U.S. during an assault on Germany. She'd literally bawled all night over the reports of the large number of dead soldiers, their young bodies sacrificed for freedom.

"Well, guess there's something good about having polio, huh?" William uttered after a bit. He even chuckled.

Normally, Maggie would make a snide comment at what she thought was William's self-pity, his sarcasm. But now she wanted to laugh just a little too, in hopes of defraying her mounting fears. "Yeah," she said with a little smile, "like getting to use Ernie's letter jacket till he comes home?" Secretly, she loved the way William treated the basketball letter jacket that Ernie had left in his care like it was a royal robe.

"Yep, that is nice," William admitted, patting the jacket next to him. "And whenever I wear this, I think of my best buddy out there fighting for us. But the silver lining of this cloud is I get to stay here with my Maggie Jane. The love of my life."

"What?" Maggie's heart hammered like crazy.

"I love you," he said, "and I want to spend the rest of my life with you."

Maggie found it hard to breathe. "You're silly, William Dove," she said when she could talk, swatting at him with her free hand.

"I'm not joshing. I counted it up and we've known each other for over eleven years now. Been through a zillion skinned knees together, played a million games of I spy and hide-and-seek..." He paused, waiting for her response.

Maggie stiffened.

"Think about it," he said. "We've grown up together. We understand each other. We have so much in common. We both love the outdoors and board games. We both like reading biographies and watching Westerns. I like managing the basketball team, and you like watching the games. Right?"

Maggie still could not move.

Leaning forward, he placed his free hand on her cheek. In a gentle voice, he said, "I want more for us than being best friends who walk to Harris Shoals together when our chores are done."

Maggie blinked at last then turned her eyes to the big white V and the silhouette of a football player painted on the wall of the restaurant. Her throat tightened and cut off her air supply. She forced her thoughts to a soft, hazy place where memories lived—the two of them playing in the creek together when they were seven, building a tree house when they were ten, his laughing at her monopolizing the hammer, her telling him that just because he was a boy didn't make him any better at using it, roasting marshmallows at twelve, and being at the fair when they were sixteen. In rapid fire, she saw these safe images as if they were pages in a well-loved scrapbook, filled with innocent pictures of Margaret Culpepper and William Dove—her childhood best friend, her ally, this boy who was all at once becoming a man.

How simple things used to be between them. How pure. *I don't want anything to change.* She felt like standing up and screaming that out loud.

But obviously, William was changing. What was wrong with her? Lots of girls Maggie's age had been going steady since they were sixteen. A good number had moved from going steady to getting engaged, and some were even married at eighteen. The girls getting engaged or married were mostly those with fellows being shipped overseas. Her friend Eugenia insisted that a lot of girls said yes to engagements simply because they felt sorry for their boyfriends having to go to war. They worried their men might get themselves killed and then they'd live with loads of guilt if they'd said no.

At least she didn't have to worry about saying yes to William before he went off to fight. He wasn't asking her to marry him, was he?

If only she could talk to her mother about all this. But any heart-to-heart conversations with her mother would need to wait until she was well. Dr. Elder had warned them to keep her calm.

A deep tug of confusion and wistfulness started in Maggie's

chest and worked its way up, where it tangled her tongue. She could only sit there with her eyebrows lifted and her mouth open. She must look like an idiot.

William didn't seem to notice. "I've got an idea," he said, leaning forward, touching her wrist, his eyebrows raised in urgency. "We could make our own commitment to each other tonight. A private little vow, you know? I might even be able to rustle up some symbolic piece of jewelry."

Vow? What kind of *vow*? And a symbolic piece of jewelry? Maybe he was trying one of those sly maneuvers girls were warned about—where the guy gets her off alone somewhere, says they can be married in the eyes of God, and then takes advantage of the girl. No, that definitely didn't sound like the William she knew. But then again, everything else in life seemed to be changing, so why not William, too?

Before she could answer, William rose and moved to her side of the booth to sit beside her. "Listen, Maggie Jane," he said, leaning close and whispering in her ear so that the warm puffs of his words sent shock waves radiating through her. "What do you say we finish this conversation out in the car?"

"But—but aren't you hungry?" she asked, her gaze resting on William's half-eaten chili dog. She'd never seen him leave so much as a crumb on his plate.

He shook his head.

Maggie's stomach was becoming a tighter knot with every second that passed. "Uh," she said, "I—I've got to go to the ladies' room. Excuse me, please."

She hurried to the restroom, locked the door, and leaned her sweaty palms against the cold white sink. After several long, deep breaths, she lifted her head to peer at herself in the mirror. The drawn, startled, and fearful expression, that totally vulnerable and stricken look, belonged to someone Maggie didn't know—someone who wanted to run away from here, escape all these scary changes. Escape the intensity of William's eyes.

* * * * *

Inside the Lincoln, Maggie folded her hands in her lap and watched William as he carefully twisted the key in the ignition just to the point where he could turn the radio on. Rudy Vallee's voice filled the car, crooning "As Time Goes By."

William turned to the back seat as if to get something. "Close your eyes and hold out your hand," he said over his shoulder.

Maggie tensed, wondering if that tiny box she'd spied earlier held a ring. After his declaration in the Varsity and his talk about a vow, she wouldn't be surprised. Part of her thought of the round, cool, realness of the nickel she had in her purse, how she could make a run for it and call home for a ride. But, with her heart booming in her chest, she closed her eyes and held out her hand.

William leaned in close, and she could smell the tang of mustard over his aftershave as he placed a light object on her palm. "Okay," he said. "Open your eyes."

Maggie gazed down at the little package.

"Go ahead," he urged. "Open it."

Hesitantly she used her fingernail to slit the tape on the fancy paper. Inside was one of those pebbly white cardboard boxes, the kind department stores put jewelry in. With her heart in her throat and her hands trembling, she lifted the lid and placed it in her lap.

Resting on a square of white cotton was the golden head of an enchanting reindeer. No bigger than a silver dollar, its delicate antlers were encrusted with tiny winking rhinestones. Two faux-emerald eyes glinted in the dusky gray. Maggie lifted it out and held it on her palm so that it caught light from the street lamp. She stroked her forefinger along the sparkling red jewel at the nose.

"It's a brooch," William said after a bit.

"Yes," Maggie said, releasing a great lungful of air she'd been holding in.

"I planned to give it to you at Christmas. But then I thought you might want to wear it to Christmas parties and stuff. Do you like it? Really?"

Maggie looked at his hopeful eyes and smiled. "Yes, William. I really like it."

"I named him Rudolph." He cocked his head and smiled. She thought she saw something vulnerable in his smile.

"Really?"

"Mmhmm. After that character in the children's story. I like old Rudolph. Guess it's because we're both misfits."

"Oh." Maggie didn't know what else to say.

"Promise you'll think of me every time you wear it?"

Maggie hesitated but at last nodded her head. This gift obviously held more meaning than the rocks and feathers William presented to her on their nature walks.

"May I pin it onto your sweater?"

She paused to think if this act was too intimate. "Okay," she said finally, and before she could even blink, William's left hand slid behind the collar of her sweater to gather a pinch of cashmere and guide the pin through.

The sensation of his fingers against her skin sent a ripple of confusing signals up Maggie's spine. She had a fleeting thought of a poem by Robert Frost about the earth's ending, one where he asked, "Is it ice or is it fire?"

When he had accomplished his mission, William gave the pin a small pat, and Maggie felt the hard coolness of it against her chest. He leaned his face close to hers.

She pulled away, bending forward to grope around on the floorboard until her hand found her pocketbook. She didn't need anything from it, but she had to do something to break the tension.

"Wear it whenever you go to parties so you won't forget me when all those fellas come clamoring around, wanting to dance with you." William laughed as he said this, but she heard a note of seriousness running through the words.

This request posed the least of her concerns. What things were leading up to now—*that* was the matter at hand. How could she maintain the distance needed to keep this conversation from progressing to that vow he'd mentioned inside the Varsity? Some people might say that friendship made a great foundation for a romantic relationship, a marriage, but what if she wasn't ready yet to transition from friendship to romance?

She scooched over snug against her door. She had to get a hold of herself. It was so easy to be moved by the moment—to be caught up in the spirit of romance and not think before she reacted.

"Maggie?" William's voice was husky as he leaned close to her again. "Like I said earlier, I don't want us to be just *friends* anymore." His eyes matched the intensity of his words. She could tell, from the way his mouth seemed to soften, that he was preparing to kiss her.

Maggie's insides fluttered. Would her first kiss be with the proverbial boy-next-door, her best friend in the world?

When long moments passed and she still had not answered, William moved so close the fine hairs on her cheek sensed him. He reached out with both arms to draw her to him until she could feel the booming of his heart on her chest. His right hand, the one affected by the polio, was certainly obeying him now. She could feel him stroking her back. She left her own arms at her sides, but she didn't pull away as he tenderly grazed her cheeks, her eyelids, the bridge of her nose with his lips.

A million tiny impulses filled Maggie. She could feel her center melting. She bit her bottom lip hard as a mental image of her mother's face appeared. "Stop, William!" She snapped her head up and her shoulders back.

William didn't seem to hear her. "Maggie, I want to spend my whole life with you. I knew you were made for me the very first time I saw you." He moved in closer, to that sensitive area of her neck right below her earlobe.

Maggie's stomach leaped. She let out a puff of air. She couldn't think of a word to say. The feeling of William's lips, his nearness, was powerful. If she hadn't been seated, she knew she would be a mere puddle on the floorboard.

"Don't you love me, Maggie Jane?" William asked, gently stroking a finger along her cheek. "Don't you?"

When she still didn't respond, he looked as if he were in pain. "I love you, and it's more than physical passion," he said. "Don't you believe me?"

Maggie's mind traveled backward in time again. She saw the two of them, at eleven years old, running zigzag through rows of cedars at the tree farm. Her red scarf was flying behind her like the wind as she tried to lose William amongst the fragrant boughs, casting quick backward glances as he gained on her, then laughing breathlessly at the way he finally reached out and grabbed the fringe on her scarf, followed by their laughter as they both tumbled to the ground.

Maggie looked deep into William's eyes, trying to see what pushed him to this turning point, because if they went the direction he wanted, they could never return to their former relationship.

"Hey, you're trembling," he murmured. "Don't be scared. You

know me. We've shared everything, from our fears to our dreams. What more is there?" He pulled her close again and just held her a minute, the warmth of him working its way through her sweater.

There was one thing Maggie hadn't shared with William. Something about putting her anxious feelings about her mother's health into words would make the situation more real.

At last, William pulled back and raised one brow, looking suddenly more like a shy, pleading schoolboy than the confident Casanova he'd been a few moments ago. "Won't you be mine? I'm begging you now, Maggie."

"But how do you know what we have is true love?" she ventured in a shaky voice.

William reached for her hands and pulled them into his lap. He used his thumbs to rub gentle swirls on her palms. "I have no doubt this is real. I trust my instincts, and it's almost like I know it's… What's the word I'm looking for? It's like our love was foreordained."

The physical sensations Maggie felt were powerful, as were the thoughts that perhaps she could see herself loving this man forever. But foreordained? She swallowed hard. She wasn't ready to admit such a thing. It felt too much like falling into a deep, black, bottomless pit. Too much like losing control.

"What are you afraid of?" William spoke into the darkness.

I'm afraid of these intense feelings I have for you. I don't want to lose myself to this powerful force. I don't like to feel so out of control. I don't like it when things change.

William leaned in again, and he kissed her eyelids tenderly, his honey-chestnut hair falling forward to tickle her forehead. His breathing was ragged when he pulled back to whisper, "Don't be scared, Maggie Jane. You can trust me to take care of you."

Just at that moment a new song began, Bing Crosby's unmistakable voice singing "I'll Be Home for Christmas." The crooned words, the music, danced in the air around Maggie, and in the blink of an eye, the sound of a note, something took over, a powerful force beyond her reason, and she sank into William's embrace, putting her lips on his as she fell and fell, tumbling until there were no rational thoughts left inside her. Until there was nothing but the music's melody pouring over them.

"I'll be home for Christmas, if only in my dreams."

At this moment, Maggie wanted nothing more than to be in William's arms forever, to be wrapped in this tenderness laced with physical passion. "I love you, William Dove," she said into a curl behind his ear. "I truly do."

"Then promise we'll spend every Christmas together from now on, Maggie," William whispered back, lightly stroking her hair. "This is our song. Every couple has their song, and this is ours. Whenever I hear Bing singing 'I'll Be Home for Christmas,' I'll think of this night, this moment we kissed, our new promise, and our old promise, too, that one day we'll go see that real snow he's singing about."

As Maggie nodded, small glints from the jewels in the reindeer pin danced like stars in a night sky. She knew she'd never hear this song without thinking of William Dove and remembering the night she fell so hard and so fast.

CHAPTER TWO

April 1944

Three months. Had it really only been three months since Maggie'd knelt at the altar inside that very church on the corner, her knees aching on the polished oak, her hands pressed palm-to-palm beneath her chin? Three months since she'd believed God loved her and wanted good things for her? The memory of those long hours spent in hopeful prayer made her shake her head in wonder and at the same time blink back painful tears.

Quickening her stride, Maggie walked past the parsonage, trying her hardest to resist the image of Reverend Peterson sitting at his desk, writing a sermon for the upcoming Sunday. After the funeral, a short two months ago, when she had questioned him about why God didn't listen and didn't heal her mother, he'd assured her that God actually did listen and He had a plan for Maggie to have an abundant and joyful life. Somehow Maggie couldn't quite envision this abundant life without her mother in it.

Main Street in downtown Watkinsville was lined with American flags rippling in the spring breeze, and Maggie's heart felt as if it rolled over within her chest for the soldiers serving overseas.

How naïve, how gullible she'd been, to think that prayer made any difference. She clenched her teeth and walked even faster as she made her way to the old red brick schoolhouse-turned-collection center.

A recruiting poster on the wall caught Maggie's eye as she poured a jar of used cooking grease into the large recycling barrel. She looked hard at the image of a no-nonsense female, at the bold words printed below her that read WOMEN—JOIN THE ARMED SERVICES AND FREE A MAN FOR COMBAT! The woman was wearing a plain white blouse and white gloves, her hair tucked beneath a tomato-red kerchief sprinkled with white polka dots. She brandished a wrench while glancing over her shoulder at the cloud-enshrouded silhouette of a soldier holding a gun.

Maggie stood mesmerized by the poster gal's determined, compassionate face. She hugged herself, scarcely breathing. Did the woman use the wrench to work on those hulking military vehicles in the background of the picture? How did a woman know how to fix army tanks anyway?

Free a man for combat. The idea struck a chord within Maggie. No matter how many old newspapers she collected or how much cooking grease she recycled, she never felt she did enough to make a real difference. As she listened to nightly radio broadcasts about the war, she was forever questioning what more she could do to help. When Mother was still alive, they'd often paused to join hands and pray for the servicemen, but since Maggie no longer believed in the effectiveness of prayer, what better way to show her patriotism than to give herself—100 percent—in service to her country? Plus, Maggie had to admit, a change of scenery could really do her some good. Since her mother's death, her hometown held too many reminders of what she'd lost.

"Got any questions, miss?"

"*Eek!*" Maggie startled as a man's voice yanked her from her deep thoughts.

"Sorry, sorry, I'm really so very sorry!" The plump man raised two pink palms and began backing away from her, tripping over his own feet. "Please forgive me. I really didn't mean to scare you, miss. I was just—I was just wondering if I could answer any questions you might have about enlisting." His eyes bulged, and the flesh on his cheeks jiggled as he shook his massive head. "You see, I'm supposed to… I mean, part of my job here at the collection site is I'm supposed to talk to people, to women, when they're in here, and see if…"

"You didn't do anything, sir," Maggie managed after a deep breath. "It's okay. I'm okay. I guess I was just lost in my own world or something."

She dipped her head toward the wall. "That's a great poster." She studied the wrench-toting gal again. "Certainly has set me to thinking. In fact, I'm giving some serious consideration to enlisting. I want to free a man for combat. Do you think they'd take a ninety-eight-pound, nineteen-year-old girl like me?"

"Well, you wouldn't qualify for the Marines. They've got a hundred-and-fifteen-pound weight requirement, but I reckon we can get two pounds added on to you to meet the Navy's one-hundred-pound requirement."

"Great!" Maggie clapped her hands. "The Navy's fine with me. I didn't even know a recruiter for women had come to our little town."

"Been here going on a week now," the man said. He stood beside her, his arms crossed over his chest. "Women all over the United States are enlisting for service. Army, Navy, Marine Corps, Coast Guard—they all have women in their ranks. Very patriotic thing to do, I say. Though that aspect of patriotism's been a little slow catching on here in Watkinsville." He looked disheartened as he shook his head slowly from side to side.

"I'm sorry," she said.

"Well, you strike me as the spunky, independent sort."

Maggie pulled herself a bit more erect at his words.

"I suspect you're open to new adventures, aren't you? If you sign up today, they'll send you to New York for your eight weeks of basic training—boot camp, if you will. Doesn't that sound exciting?"

The man stepped a bit closer to Maggie, his florid face practically lit up. "Navy women are known as WAVES," he said, "which stands for Women Accepted for Volunteer Emergency Service. Great name, don't you think? They've converted Hunter College in the Bronx into a training center for WAVES."

"Is that right?" Maggie smiled, her imagination already zipping ahead like a runaway horse. She could easily picture herself in uniform. What that poster offered, what she wanted to sign up for, would be so meaningful.

But when she paused to give the idea more thought, the

reasons why she shouldn't enlist—why she couldn't possibly—rose to the top like cream in a milk pail. What would her father say? What kind of a daughter would she be if she were to leave him so soon after her mother's death? On the other hand, since her mother's passing at the end of January, Father had poured himself into his work, and days would go by without Maggie even seeing him, much less having a meaningful conversation with him. Still, she was all he had left now.

Next there was Maggie's best friend, Eugenia Peterson. Each girl was an only child, and they were devoted to each other. In fact, they were closer than most sisters, spending countless afternoons talking and laughing and sharing affairs of the heart.

And then there was William.

William.

Silence hung over Maggie as William's gorgeous face swam into her consciousness. Her heart pounded like a jackhammer, and she couldn't keep from biting her lower lip. The muscles in her throat tightened, and she found it hard to manage a breath.

Since her Mother's passing, she'd come to the conclusion that loving *anyone* the way she loved William was entirely too dangerous—a recipe for future heartache if she were to judge by what her father was going through.

"Umm, how long would I be committing myself to?" Maggie asked.

"Oh, just for the duration of the war," he said, "plus six months. That's all."

Maggie grabbed an application form and a pen from the

card table below the poster. With trembling hands she filled it out quickly and thrust it at the man.

"Your country thanks you, miss," he said, beaming and tipping his shiny, sweating head.

Maggie could only nod in return.

* * * * *

Well, that's one way to plan your future. Maggie stood outside on the sidewalk in the early spring sunshine. She had merely volunteered to drop off some newspapers and used grease for her housebound neighbor, Mrs. Webster.

The elderly widow slept with her radio on all night, just in case a warning was broadcasted about the Nazis or Japan invading. She adored President Roosevelt, along with General George Patton, and was constantly looking for something, anything, she could do to help the war effort.

Maggie's heart went out to the decrepit old woman, and every day she walked next door to check on her. She'd relished the big smile on Mrs. Webster's face this morning when she told her that, yes, she'd be glad to carry her items to the town's collection site. Now, Maggie felt doubly rewarded as she realized her good deed had set the course for her own life.

Maggie whistled a bar of "Yankee Doodle Dandy." For the first time in a long time she was as excited as a kid at Christmas. Not only was she doing something noble, something good and patriotic by anyone's standards, but she had a ticket to adventure as well.

She stood on the street corner, waiting for two cars to go by. With their windows down, the air they left in their wake smelled of cigarettes, and Maggie recognized the hair of one driver. It was Mrs. Morgan Bray, president of the Stitch and Chat Club. That got her to thinking that by nightfall every single person in the tightly knit city of Watkinsville, Georgia, population seven hundred, would know what she'd just done.

She decided she'd better go ahead, bite the bullet, and do her explaining to those who needed to know. She didn't want those closest to her to hear the news from anyone else. She was thankful that, in her father's case, she could put that unpleasant task off until suppertime. With William, the more she thought about telling him, or rather, the more she tried *not* to think about telling him, she just didn't know if she'd ever have it in her to break such news to him face-to-face. Not after all the hints he'd been dropping about an official engagement lately.

Right now, the only person she actually wanted to tell in person was Eugenia. Genie would probably pitch a fit when she first heard the news. But in the end, when Genie saw how important this was to Maggie, she'd calm down and come around.

Maggie turned on her heel, took a deep breath, and headed in the direction of the Petersons' house. She could walk this whole town, this whole county almost, with her eyes closed. She wondered what it would be like when she was living up north, in a busy city where she didn't know every nook and cranny.

As she passed the courthouse, Maggie smiled at the daffodils and crocuses blanketing the strip of grass between the sidewalk and Main Street. She couldn't resist stopping and burying her nose in the warm center of a yellow daffodil. It smelled like the sun.

On down the road, she noted four pear trees flowering like giant snowy lollipops. It seemed Watkinsville could hardly wait until everything was in full, glorious bloom. Her own sense of urgency grew as she headed toward the Petersons' house still two blocks away. She soon found herself running. Maggie ran headlong into life as a general rule. The memory of her, mother's gentle, calming voice constantly called after her, "Slow down, Maggie Jane. It's not ladylike to run. There'll be time enough. Things have to happen in their own good, sweet time." But hadn't Mother's early death proven her words wrong?

Maggie sped along, barely aware of the twittering birds in the trees, scarcely noting the stray chickens on the sidewalk or the backyard lines of laundry glowing Clorox blue in the morning sunlight. She spied Ashford Memorial Methodist on one corner of Main Street as she made her way up Harden Hill.

Downtown was quiet today. New York would certainly be a change. She'd seen photographs of the milling crowds of people in New York, and behind them, skyscrapers housing all sorts of businesses. Oconee County had more turkeys than people, and if you asked most men in Watkinsville what they did for a living, they'd tell you cotton, sorghum, wheat, corn, or poultry. There was even a two-acre field of cotton in downtown Watkinsville.

Maggie and Eugenia met during their seventh-grade year, when Genie's father transferred to Watkinsville to manage the nearby cotton mill. Boys were drawn to Eugenia like bears to honey. With her blond hair, blue eyes, creamy skin, and voluptuous figure, Eugenia had been sought after and fought for from day one. She giggled easily, listened with interest to fishing and hunting stories, and often touched the arm of the boy she was talking to, drawing them in even closer with her mysterious power.

Because Eugenia was both popular and lovely, Maggie had struggled with jealousy at the beginning, thinking her too vacuous to even be considered friend material. But then Eugenia chose *Maggie* to be her best girlfriend, and all of that envy evaporated. Maggie's next humbling discovery was how wrongly she'd judged Eugenia. Genie was the best friend a girl could wish for. Maggie could tell her almost anything. In fact, only Genie had heard the uncensored version of William and Maggie at the Varsity.

Eugenia sat with Maggie in St. Mary's Hospital as Maggie's mother lay dying from lung cancer. And it was Eugenia who'd insisted on staying at Maggie's house that entire week after the funeral, "Just to be there. You know, to take all those phone calls and casseroles so you and your papa can rest." Only after all was said and done did Maggie realize what a wonderful gift Genie had given her. Being in her friend's presence was great therapy for Maggie even now. When waves of sadness engulfed her, when the vacuum of her mother's absence left her angry and depressed, it gave her comfort to inhale the signature fragrance of honeysuckle-rose that followed Genie everywhere.

Maggie arrived out of breath at the Petersons' brick house, slipping through the white wooden gate right off Jackson Street, down a stone pathway, and up the steps onto the front porch.

She turned the doorknob but found it locked, so she pounded the brass knocker until the gathered curtain along the glass strip running beside the door moved a bit and she saw Eugenia's blue eyes peering out.

Pretty and fresh in a white blouse and a blue skirt, Eugenia opened the door. She looked hard at Maggie's face. "You're sweating like a field hand!"

"I've got something to tell you."

"Come in and sit down and I'll fix you a Coca-Cola. Then you can tell me."

Maggie followed Eugenia across Oriental carpets scattered throughout spacious rooms. She knew the inside of the Petersons' imposing home as well as her own. Lately, she'd spent more time there than ever. Her own house felt too empty.

Eugenia deposited Maggie at their favorite hanging-out spot, a screened porch off the kitchen that held a white wicker sofa and ottoman covered in purple corduroy cushions. The floor was made of roughhewn boards, and on the wall hung a framed picture embroidered by Eugenia that read HOME IS WHERE THE HEART Is, the letters intertwined with small forget-me-nots.

When Eugenia returned with a Coke, she handed it to Maggie and settled herself on the sofa. "Tell."

Maggie paused her pacing to take a long, fizzy swallow of her drink. She set the glass down on a side table and turned to Eugenia. "I just joined the Navy."

Eugenia's eyes widened and her mouth dropped open for so long flies could set up housekeeping inside.

"Did you hear me? I said I joined the Navy."

"But, Maggie," Genie squeaked at last, "they *cuss* in the military."

Maggie laughed. "I imagine they do. But I'm a big girl."

"Jeepers. Tell me you're joking."

Maggie shook her head. "I've already filled out the papers."

After a minute of bug-eyed silence, Genie asked, "Have you told your father?"

"No. I'll tell him over supper."

Eugenia shook her head slowly. "You're all he has left."

A wave of sadness swept over Maggie, but she was ready. "He'll hardly miss me. He's been working nonstop. Even weekends. I bet we'll communicate more through the U.S. mail than we do now. I'm planning to write him at least once a week."

Eugenia looked down at her feet. "Well, I've never really thought of you as the military type."

"But I want to do my part, serve my country. I want to make a difference."

"Well, I think you're wonderful and noble, but couldn't you just be a seamstress and work on flags and banners?"

Maggie laughed so hard she bent double. "Don't you remember that horrible mess I made out of that apron we made in home ec?"

Eugenia smiled.

The Petersons' pug, Laney, pranced out onto the porch to sniff her.

"Hey, pretty girl," Maggie crooned, running her hand across the fur on Laney's ribs until the dog's back leg began working excitedly and her eyelids closed in rapture.

"What's Laney going to do without her best pal?" Eugenia asked in a playful voice, though Maggie could easily read between the lines.

"Why don't you sign up too, Genie?"

Eugenia gave a disbelieving little snort. "Can you see me in the military?"

"Not really," Maggie admitted. "Listen, I promise I'll write you. But you've got to understand, I can't not go. Don't you ever feel like there's something bigger than yourself you need to pour yourself into?"

Eugenia didn't answer. Her voice was teary as she reached for Maggie's hands. "What about William? Have you thought of William?"

Maggie flinched. She'd been thinking of William constantly since her decision at the recruiting center. Kind, funny William, with his All-American smile and his soft Southern drawl. A boy, actually a man, who treated her like a princess and was eager to make a lifelong commitment at the tender age of nineteen.

In fact, she thought of him every hour of her life. Maybe even every single solitary second if she counted those thoughts that just barged their own way in, that lined her life like wallpaper. And that, she acknowledged to herself silently, made her much, much too vulnerable.

"This," she said finally, laughing uneasily as she formed the words of an argument that came to her as she was speaking, "will be like a test for us."

"A test?"

"Yeah, you know, to prove if our love is true."

"True? Maggie, I remember the night you said you were one hundred percent sure you wanted to marry William and have his babies! Remember? We were sitting right here, wearing our nighties and eating popcorn, and you went on and on about how you two have chemistry? How you have to catch your breath every time he gets near you?" Eugenia paused to sigh. "That kind of thing doesn't happen twice in one lifetime. You said that what you and William have together is so honest and real that nothing will ever change it. I can repeat what you said word-for-word."

"No, please don't." Maggie tried a playful laugh. "I just wonder sometimes, what if I'm too young to know real love? What if it's just youthful infatuation? You don't really think the very first person you fall for is *The One*, do you, Genie? I mean, it might just be a matter of geography. Sheer convenience. Ever thought of that? William is that proverbial boy-next-door. I mean, how would you ever know if you just hooked up with the very first fellow you're with?" She paused for a quick breath. "You'd be forever wondering if there wasn't someone else out there even better. The perfect soul mate or something. And just because you settled for the first fellow who came along, you're stuck."

"Stuck? Really, Maggie?" Eugenia's tone reflected a disapproval Maggie had never heard from her before.

Surely Eugenia didn't think Maggie was referring to William's disfigurement from polio, that Maggie thought he was somehow less than desirable. "This has absolutely nothing whatsoever to do with his limp!" she said in a loud voice that shocked even herself. "I don't even notice that anymore, and I don't care that his hand does funny things sometimes! This is about putting a bit of time and space between us so I can sort it all out and decide if he's really the one for me." Maggie turned away, crossing her arms.

She thought for a moment then added, "Think about it like this, Genie. If it is true love, then William will still be available when I decide to come home. See? Ultimately, this is going to be in his best interest too. He wouldn't want to commit his heart and his life to someone who had doubts, would he?"

"I think you'll regret this, Maggie. Lots of girls marry their high school sweethearts, the boys-next-door, and they're perfectly happy."

Maggie went to stand at the window looking out over the Petersons' backyard, focusing on a trellis covered with blue flowers. She tried to reach down deep into her center, into that part of her where truth lived, but the mere effort was making her queasy. "I won't leave William hanging," she said at last, turning back to Genie. "I'll talk it all out with him, explain everything."

"You make it sound so easy," Eugenia said, hands on her hips. "Just remember, William's a good-looking guy, and he's going to be in hot demand here at home with all the other boys off fighting." She scooped Laney up like an infant and buried her chin in the dog's neck. After a bit, she looked Maggie straight in the eye and said, "Who says he'll even take you back if you do decide you want him?"

Maggie couldn't answer.

CHAPTER THREE

William Dove frowned and hoisted himself up from the deep pocket of a leather wing chair in the study. The enthusiastic announcer was right in the middle of a report on Allied fliers destroying railroad yards across Belgium and France. William hurried across the rug to the roll-top desk and twisted the radio dial to OFF.

God, please protect Ernie, he prayed as he made his way to the mud room off the kitchen to pull on his work boots. His heart, like the rest of his body, felt heavy.

After gulping a glass of sweet tea, he grabbed a hunk of ginger cake wrapped in paper from the breadbox, opened the front door, and stepped outside into the clear spring day. He paused on the stoop to dig the truck keys out of his pocket. From force of habit, his gaze was pulled in the direction of the Culpeppers' house next door, and he smiled as his thoughts turned to Maggie.

He pictured her face, so beloved to him—her dancing green eyes, her pert nose sprinkled with freckles, and that playful, slightly mischievous smile. She had mentioned to him that this was the day she was planning to devote to their elderly widowed neighbor, Mrs. Webster. The woman needed help with errands as well as someone just to sit and chat with her.

William almost laughed aloud as he thought of Maggie's comical face when she described the way the old lady sometimes sat in the rocking chair out on her porch at 5 a.m., singing the national anthem in a loud, quivery soprano.

William had spent his morning working on the financial ledgers for the family tree farm and now it was time to go make his rounds, checking soil moisture and the general state of the trees, making sure things were good before the weekend.

"Weekend's almost here. Just hang on," he said aloud to himself as he walked down the brick steps and out to the garage, concentrating on the fact that tomorrow he had a date with Maggie.

He'd had to plead with her to accept his invitation, and he was looking forward to their picnic on the banks of Harris Shoals. In fact, ever since Wednesday when she'd finally said yes, William daydreamed constantly of this event. It was like the scenery on a movie set, the backdrop of his life as he went about the rest of his duties.

Since January, since her mother's final days, Maggie had seemed skittish, rejecting all his attempts at romance. He understood that she was going through a lot and knew instinctively to just give her time. And so for a while, he took it easy, though he did keep going next door to see her, kept calling her to see if she wanted to take a walk. Every now and then he'd ask her on a date, and each time she'd say, "Maybe later, okay?" and then he'd kiss her cheek and walk back home alone.

Time ticked on and he began to worry he'd lose her. He

couldn't quite figure out why she was holding him at arm's length. Wasn't this Maggie, his best friend?

He determined to keep their love alive, even if it cost him his pride, and so one day he resorted to begging. He took her hands in his and said, "Maggie, babe, please tell me what's going on in that head of yours. I feel like you're running away from me."

"I am not running," she said, pulling back her hands.

"You've got one foot out the door then."

"I don't."

"Prove it," he'd said, pleading with his eyes so that she finally said yes to the picnic at Harris Shoals.

When he'd had time to plan his strategy, he thought, *This is the perfect opportunity. I'll let her know, again, just how much I love her.*

He kept trying to reassure himself that Maggie was ready to make things final.

Since Maggie was not, to put it kindly, domestically inclined, William told her he would take care of everything for their picnic, from planning the menu to convincing his mother to prepare it. Mrs. Dove happily agreed to make her special fried chicken, homemade pimiento cheese, and hard-boiled eggs.

William had gathered other items they would need. In the corner of his bedroom was the picnic basket filled with cutlery, plates, and napkins, and on top of that was a quilt to use as their picnic cloth. To get this quilt had taken a lot of begging and pleading with his mother, promising that he would protect the family heirloom.

His grandmother had made the quilt when she was young. She was gone now, but he'd heard her reminiscing about it often, about the fact that she'd made it for her hope chest, in a pattern called Wedding Ring. William had a brilliant plan to casually point this fact out to Maggie as he spread the quilt over one of the wide, flat rocks in the shoals.

Musing on just how he would bring the name of the quilt pattern into the conversation, William climbed into his truck, placed the ginger cake on the seat next to him, and leaned across to roll the passenger window down. He rolled down the driver's window as he turned onto Harden Hill then adjusted the sun visor as he turned onto Main Street, cruising past Will Henry Hodges' Hardware and Mrs. Effie Veale's Tea Room.

It wasn't till he was on Highway 15 that he got going fast enough to feel the breeze lifting his hair. This road meandered through countryside and rolling farmland, past pastures full of Charolaise and Angus, lakes full of catfish, and chicken houses full of clucking hens.

March had been a wet month in Oconee County, and William saw evidence of this everywhere. Trees were full and the pastures on either side of the highway stretched lush and green between long lines of fence posts strung with barbed wire. Barns and silos dotted the farmland, looking so pastoral it was sometimes hard to imagine the country was at war.

His great-grandfather, William Jennings Dove I had purchased three hundred acres, half of which lay in Oconee County and half in Greene County, when real estate was dirt cheap. The land had lain fallow until William Jennings Dove II, otherwise known as Billy, or Dad to William, had decided to plant Virginia Pine, Cedar, Leyland Cypress, and Fraser Firs—a regular smorgasbord of Christmas trees. The trees were sold throughout the Southeast, and the farm had served as a good source of income for over thirty years now.

William loved the feel of the wide open country. A breeze smelling of fresh-mown grass and springtime itself called to him. The curve of his elbow resting on the open window felt the kiss of sunshine. A pair of geese flew through blue skies overhead, honking and flapping. If the weather was this nice tomorrow for their picnic, he couldn't ask for anything more.

This hope filled William's mind as he spied the roof of the old log cabin at the entrance of the tree farm. On November 1 each year, William's father transformed the cabin into a roadside business called the Yule-Tide Shoppe. He stocked it with fresh wreaths and boughs and garlands and filled the shelves with various ornaments, silver icicles, tinsel, and tufts of spun cotton to look like snowdrifts.

William eased up off the gas as he approached the huge wooden sign reading DOVE'S TREE FARM stretched between two tall timbers just off the highway. He turned and puttered down the dirt road, past the Yule-Tide Shoppe, pulling to a stop on a little patch of gravel just beyond it.

William cut the engine, climbed out, and shut the door. He drew a long breath of fresh air smelling like sunlight on cedar as he walked toward the first row of trees. The ground felt springy beneath his feet, and the only noises were soothing ones—the occasional rustles of a small creature in the grass, the calls of birds flying overhead.

Most of the time he found total peace out here amongst the trees, but today his mind was cluttered with a million different thoughts. Mixed emotions about the picnic tomorrow, the war, family finances, and a recent letter from Ernie. After several minutes of struggle, William managed to push them all away except for images of tomorrow's picnic with Maggie. He imagined her slipping off her loafers and her bobby socks and stepping into the water with no hesitation. Most girls would just sit demurely on the rocks, fearful of the possibility of snakes and crawdads, not to mention the thought of a little mud on their skin.

That was one of the many things he loved about Maggie—her spunk, the way her eyes lit up at the mention of any kind of outdoor adventure. When they were younger, in grade school, she was often the one pulling him to the rope swing hanging from a stately oak in her backyard, daring him to follow her as she used it to propel herself into the creek just beyond.

He'd been taken with Maggie Culpepper since the very first time he laid eyes on her. But it was an innocent love, pure childlike devotion.

Now things were a bit more complicated. The girl could be a mystery sometimes, and her rejection of late hurt, but now that she'd said yes to tomorrow, somewhere in his heart a voice kept whispering she was ready to take their relationship to something more committed.

It had been a long time, close to four months since that night at the Varsity. A long time since their declarations of love, followed almost immediately by Mrs. Culpepper's intense battle with cancer and then her death at the end of January. William constantly reminded himself to give Maggie time, but still he was unnerved by the anxiety he felt today.

He stopped walking, shut his eyes, and lifted his face to the sun. Warmth cascaded down on him. *Didn't she tell me she loved me, God? Didn't You hear her confess her undying love at the Varsity?* He let the short prayer infuse him with hope before he opened his eyes and walked on.

Up and down three rows everything looked strong and healthy. The trees were free of insects, their trunks thick and straight, with no dead limbs. Stopping now and then to rub a robust bough or needle between his thumb and forefinger, William was pleased. The green on either side of him was familiar and enfolding. After a bit, he began walking more briskly, his eyes expertly surveying the trees as he had been taught from his youth, pausing only to remove a single bough that drooped from its trunk. Digging the pocketknife Maggie had given him for Christmas from his trousers, he made a clean slice, removing the dry, splintery branch.

William checked his watch. Almost two o'clock, still nearly a full twenty-four hours until the picnic. Patience might be a virtue, but it sure was a hard one to appreciate.

When William reached the end of yet another row, he heard the sound of shuffling footsteps behind him. He turned.

It was Mr. Byrd, in his signature overalls and chocolate-colored brogans, his hair sticking out in woolly white tufts below a bill cap that read ATHENS SEED CO. "Hey, my man!" Mr. Byrd raised a wrinkled black hand. "How ya doin'?"

"Hi, Mr. Byrd. I'm fine. Yourself?"

"Doin' good." The old man nodded. "Every day the Lord see fit to let me see another sunrise, I be doin' good."

William chuckled.

"Care for some comp'ny while you do yo' rounds?"

"Sure." William waited for Mr. Byrd to reach his side then adjusted his gait to match the older gentleman's as they began a new row.

Mr. Tyronious Byrd claimed to be just seventy-five years old, though he said he didn't know his actual birth date, and his wrinkled face had always looked like he was nothing short of a hundred to Will.

The man had literally walked into their lives in 1928, when Will was only three years old. It was on Thanksgiving Day, and everyone in the family was stricken with the flu. Even William's father, who boasted about never being sick, was feeling poorly, but he was dragging himself around to check on things at the tree farm when the black man walked up with nothing but a beat-up leather satchel in hand, offering himself as a professional gardener/caretaker in exchange for living rent-free in the small cabin.

William loved to recall what his father told him was Mr. Byrd's rationale: "When I seen the sign that says Dove's Tree

Farm, I know I ain't got to travel no further. See? A Byrd at Dove's Tree Farm?"

William's father, for lack of any other solution, hired the man on a temporary basis. But it took just two weeks for him to discover that Mr. Byrd knew the soil better than anyone he'd ever known, even the county agent who had been to school for it. Mr. Byrd could grow anything.

When William's father would come home crowing about Mr. Byrd's green thumbs, William pictured the man with literal green thumbs, and when he accompanied his dad out to the farm on Saturdays, he would stare hard at Mr. Byrd's thumbs, wondering why they didn't look green to him, if his eyes were somehow defective.

From the very beginning there was a special bond between Mr. Byrd and William. William was inexplicably drawn to the old gentleman, and he followed him around the farm, fascinated as he watched the man's hands trim boughs to shape the trees, listening as Mr. Byrd told stories of a childhood spent picking cotton.

Mr. Byrd was a fount of practical information from the Good Ol' Days. He taught William to keep a dish of Indian cornmeal on the sink to rub on his hands after soaping, to cleanse and soften them, keep them from chapping. He taught him how to attract toads to the tree farm—sturdy little hoppers, each able to eat a hundred pesky slugs in a single night.

Race had never been an issue between Mr. Byrd and William. All William saw when he looked at Mr. Byrd was a steady, faith-filled man who was one of the warmest, most generous, and wisest individuals he knew.

Today Mr. Byrd smelled strongly of Vick's VapoRub, and William noted as they went along that the old gentleman's erect figure was going just a bit slower than usual. He figured his rheumatoid arthritis was acting up. Mr. Byrd would never complain of the pain, though William often saw his face contort as he rubbed his gnarled hands together.

Instead Mr. Byrd made his affliction sound like a blessing. He liked to brag that he could sit right inside the cabin with the shades down, and just by the feeling in his knees he could tell it was going to rain. Sometimes William could tell the man's knees and shoulders got to aching too. He knew by the way Mr. Byrd rubbed them as he set his teeth and squinched his eyes together tight. Mr. Byrd claimed the best remedy, the best way he knew to keep his mind off bothersome problems like rheumatoid arthritis, was to keep busy.

"Anything going on today, Mr. Byrd?" William asked after a bit.

"Naw. Everythin' been mighty quiet."

"Well, good. Looks like we're still doing fine on the water level."

"Mmhmm. Ground still good and tender."

They walked along not talking, side-by-side, for a long stretch. Mr. Byrd finally broke the silence. "How yo' folks?"

"They're fine. Dad's working on the draft board today, and Mother's at a church circle meeting."

"Well, good. I know they enjoyin' this pretty spring weather. Yo' brothers?"

"They're fine too. Getting itchy for summer."

"Don't have too long to go 'fore summer." Mr. Byrd looked over and smiled at William. "Rest of April and then May and they be done."

"That's a long time to a kid, Mr. Byrd!" William laughed.

"You right. Bet you glad you finish with school. Graduated with honors, yo' daddy say."

William didn't know how to respond. He knew Mr. Byrd had never had the chance to go to school. He told William this was because August was the time to pick cotton. William was thankful someone had taught Mr. Byrd to read.

"I'm glad to be done, I guess," William said after a minute. "But it's kind of hard, too, because all my buddies are either off fighting or getting ready to go fight."

"Do seem like all our young men gone. I know you told me yo' friend Ernie fightin'."

William nodded. "Got a letter from him Tuesday week."

"That right?"

"Yep. I was sort of scared to open it, because I knew he'd been assigned to fly this dangerous combat mission. I mean, you see them in the newsreels and you hear about them on the radio and you read about them in the paper, Mr. Byrd. About all these different battles, you know, where soldiers lose arms, legs, their lives. But it just never seems real. Not somebody like *Ernie Haygood*, my best friend, could be in the middle of all that. Anyway,

I'd heard he got wounded back in October, during an Air Force assault on Schweinfurt. His plane got shot down and a bomb fragment went into his arm." William paused to swallow the lump in his throat.

"He okay?"

William nodded. "Bad wound."

"Sho' do hate to hear that."

"Yeah. His mother told me that they'd sent him for surgery to an army hospital on the Welsh border because he'd gotten some kind of secondary infection. It's a bacterial bone thing that's killed thousands of soldiers. Mrs. Haygood said the doctors thought Ernie's arm would have to come off." William jingled some loose coins in his pocket. "But," he continued, "in the letter Ernie said he's still got his arm. Something called penicillin can wipe out a lot of stuff, and now he's back at it."

Mr. Byrd gave a nod.

"Wish I could be over there!" William said, louder than he meant to, swinging his good arm in a fist.

"Now don't go pityin' yo'self, son. Seem ever' day I hear about some mama or daddy gettin' a telegram say their baby ain't comin' home."

"Yeah, yeah, I know. But you got to understand what it feels like to be 4-F."

"4-F?"

"That's what they call it when you're medically unfit for service. Sometimes it feels like I've got this big stamp on my forehead that says, 'Only half a man.'"

Mr. Byrd stopped walking and put a hand on William's shoulder. William stopped, too, and Mr. Byrd turned him to look into his face. "Son, don't be gettin' jealous of nobody over there fightin'. Besides yo' limp and a hand what gives you trouble, you an able-bodied man. Got this nice family business just waitin' for you to take it over someday."

Mr. Byrd rubbed his chin. "I'm gonna tell you somethin'," he said after a long spell. "You already fought yo' very own war. We was all scared you was goin' die when you came down with the polio. Fact, I remember yo' daddy out here on his knees in the middle of the trees, pleadin' with the Lord not to take his boy. You know good as anybody it takes a lot to drive yo' daddy to his knees."

William blinked. He'd never heard this story. He knew more than anybody what a proud man his father could be, and the thought of him on his knees touched William deeply. The truth of the matter was that memories of his struggles with the illness had dimmed to only a faint haze in William's mind, and if he didn't consciously pull them up, it was hard to be grateful that he'd pulled through and that all it had left behind were atrophied muscles.

"Ain't no tellin' what kind o' enemies been conquered as a result of yo' battle with the polio." Mr. Byrd's voice interrupted William's thoughts. "You know the old sayin', 'Clouds got silver linin's.'"

William knew the old man's words held wisdom, because his silver lining to being 4-F was that he didn't have to leave his Maggie. This realization was just one of a thousand different times when the man's insight had helped William see the light or gotten him through a hard time.

They finished one long row of trees and turned to head down another, and a few minutes later they reached the end of yet another row and were in view of the truck. "Hey, remind me before I go, Mr. Byrd, I've got something to give you. Mother sent some ginger cake."

Mr. Byrd gave a grunt of delight. "Way they been rationin' the flour and sugar to help our boys, it feel like Christmas to get some cake. 'Course, it always feel like Christmas 'round this place." He chuckled at his own joke. "Your mother a good woman, Will. You tell her I 'preciate it."

"I'll tell her," William said, smiling.

For the next half hour, they walked, with Mr. Byrd musing on everything from his small vegetable patch to how he'd been taking regular doses of blackberry tonic for stomach distress. He told William about a pair of bluebirds he'd found in an abandoned woodpecker hole in the white oak along the farm's eastern border.

William listened and nodded, making a few grunts here and there, his mind on what was still left to do before tomorrow's picnic.

When they got to the end of the final row, William went to the truck and retrieved the ginger cake. Handing it to Mr. Byrd, he said, "Guess I'll be getting on back to the home front."

"Don't hurry off. Come on in the cabin and I'll fix us some coffee."

"Uh, sure." William hated to say no. Though he'd never liked coffee, never would, he always accepted a cup of the bitter brew when Mr. Byrd offered it to him, just so he'd have the excuse to visit.

When they were inside the cabin, Mr. Byrd removed his cap and hung it on a peg. He shut the door and pointed to a rickety wooden bench. "Have a seat."

William sat and took a look around as he waited for Mr. Byrd to make coffee. Mr. Byrd kept a tidy little place inside the cabin. One corner served as an office for the tree farm, and here a crude desk and stool were centered on a braided oval rug. In the corner diagonal to that sat Mr. Byrd's cot. A nightstand next to the bed held a well-worn Bible and a goose-necked lamp that bent out over the bed.

The kitchen was in another corner. The bench William sat on ran along a table with a lazy Susan in the center that held all sorts of things, from matches to toothpicks to a jar of sorghum syrup. On a short stretch of Formica countertop, there was a tiny icebox, a bread box, and a hotplate with two burners.

Mr. Byrd pulled a silver percolator from a cabinet above this. He measured coffee from a tin can, ran some water from the sink, and set the percolator on the hotplate. As the coffee gurgled, Mr. Byrd produced two chipped mugs and a Mason jar with a bit of sugar in the bottom. He set these on the table with great fanfare and, when the coffee had finished percolating, poured two cups of the steaming brew, arranging two slices of the ginger cake on a plate.

William clenched his teeth together as the first stream of bitter black liquid went down his throat.

The pair sat in silence for several minutes, but Mr. Byrd had been a part of William's life for so long, William could be quiet in his presence without feeling uncomfortable. He watched Mr. Byrd as he drank his coffee, head back, eyes closed, and a smile on his face. The picture of serenity.

William's mind, however, was running a mile a minute. He leaned forward and gently touched Mr. Byrd's wrist.

The old man's eyes flickered open.

"Do you think nineteen's too young to ask someone to marry you?" William felt his heart rate accelerate.

"You talking about Miss Magpie, ain't you?" Mr. Byrd asked, his left eyebrow raised high and a twinkle in his eye.

William nodded.

"She a feisty one."

William couldn't help smiling as he pictured Maggie's wild tangle of red hair glinting in the sunlight, almost hearing her impetuous laughter. "Yes. That she is. Do you think she's too young?"

"I be married at sixteen."

"Really?" William could hardly imagine this. Sixteen sounded much too young. At sixteen, he himself had been three inches shorter than he was now, and all he could think about then was having fun—certainly not anything as serious as marriage.

"Mmhmm. Met Hattie Johnson at church and we knowed right away we meant for each other. We run off and find us a justice of the peace." His soulful eyes looked off into the distance as he remembered. "Livin' on love." He laughed softly. "Love about all we had. After a spell, we come back home, tails tucked 'tween our legs. Lived on a small cotton farm near my fam'ly. That where our chirren be born. I be seventeen when they come. Twin boys. Fine, strappin' boys. Pride o' my life, until…" Mr. Byrd caught himself and his voice trailed off.

The silence after that was full. Mr. Byrd had never mentioned any sons to William before.

"Then I guess nineteen isn't too young," William said finally, carefully choosing each word. "I want to share my life with Maggie, and I feel like we were made for each other. Does that sound crazy?"

"No." Mr. Byrd's expression softened. "Anybody can see you love that girl with all yo' heart."

"I do!" William was sitting on the edge of the bench now. "So, you think I ought to ask her tomorrow, Mr. Byrd? Do you think she'll say yes?"

Mr. Byrd looked hard at William. "I ain't God," he said at last, "so I can't tell you what Miss Magpie gonna say. But I do know the way she look at you when you bring her out here. She think you hung the moon."

William smiled. "Hey, would you mind asking God if she'll say yes tomorrow?" This request just popped out of him, but after he considered it, William didn't think it sounded far-fetched at all, the way Mr. Byrd walked so close to God. He sat, waiting expectantly, as Mr. Byrd remained motionless for quite a while. He didn't bow his head or close his eyes to pray. The air in the little cabin seemed charged with something.

"You wantin' some divine wisdom, ain't you?" Mr. Byrd said after a bit. William nodded and the old man reached for his Bible. He flipped open the front cover and William could see lots of jottings—words scrawled here and there in a very distinctive handwriting.

"Let me see," Mr. Byrd mused, ruffling through well-worn pages until he reached a certain place. "Here we go. James 1:5 tell us, 'If any of you lack wisdom, let him ask of God, who giveth to all men liberally, and upbraideth not; and it shall be given him.'"

He laid the Bible open on his lap and bowed his head. He held his hands palms up and began to pray aloud in a conversational tone like a person would use with a best friend. "Father, You ain't never let me down in the love department. No matter what has befall me, You have pull me through. Now I lift up this boy here. You say You give any man wisdom who aks You, and I aks You to give William Dove wisdom concernin' the love he feel for Miss Maggie. You the one invented love, and You made the male and the female for each other, so I aks You to guide this man in his thoughts, his words, and his actions. Mmhmm, just bless him and give him what he need. Above all, we aks that Yo' will be done and You glorify Yo' holy name. Amen." Mr. Byrd closed his Bible and set it back on the nightstand.

William's soul was soaring. *"Bless him and give him what he needs."* What he needed was Maggie, and with every heartbeat he was even more convinced that asking her to marry him tomorrow was the thing to do. He felt lighter than he had in months as he stood up tall and drew a deep breath to face Mr. Byrd. "Thanks for the coffee and the prayer, sir. I better be heading on home."

"You welcome." Mr. Byrd stood, too, placing a warm hand on William's shoulder. "You let me know how it go, hear?"

CHAPTER FOUR

Maggie sat at the long mahogany table in the dining room at home, her eyes fastened on the centerpiece of a crystal vase holding a spray of dried pussy willow, as she tried in vain to gather her thoughts. This conversation she was planning with her dear childhood friend was too important to leave to impromptu words, and she was attempting to craft her reasons for joining the Navy before she talked to him. She tapped the cap of her pen on a piece of ivory writing paper, which after forty-five minutes still held only the Roman numeral I at the top.

"Lots of people marry the boy-next-door and they're perfectly happy," Eugenia had said. But what did she know? Sure, Genie may have kissed a half dozen boys, she may have read a hundred romance stories, so she knew about fluttering hearts and pulsing lips. But Genie was inexperienced when it came to real, honest-to-goodness love.

However, there were a couple of comments that spilled from Genie's lips that stopped Maggie stone-cold every time she tried to list her reasons for leaving. *"This kind of love doesn't happen twice in one lifetime,"* and, *"I think you'll regret this."*

Maggie took a deep breath. "Oh, Genie," she said softly, "without a doubt, you've helped me through so much, and I know you're only thinking of my heart, only going by all those silly stories I told you about me and William, but how could a couple of nineteen-year-olds know who they want to spend the rest of their lives with?"

Like waves crashing on a beach, Maggie felt a memory moving in. It was that night at the Varsity when she kissed William for the first time. The images moving over her were so tender, so beautiful and *strong*, she feared they might be enough to pull her out into deep waters, to make her lose her resolve enough to run next door right now and throw herself into William's arms. "Stop it this instant, Maggie!" she hissed, finally managing to pull herself to the surface for a cleansing breath.

She stared at her paper until her eyes crossed. *Am I taking what I had—have—for granted?* Maggie tried to shrug out of her anxious thoughts.

Chewing on the tip of her pen, she glanced at a picture of her father that sat on top of the sideboard. She remembered something he often said when he advised her about an issue; *"Wisdom comes with age, sweetheart."*

He's right, she decided. *My father's a smart man. I need to find some older, experienced woman to talk to.* She could ask her things like: What's the difference between affection and love? Can a person work herself into feeling love for someone who just happens to be convenient, or is love something providence hands to you? And, how do you actually know when you're in the kind of love that's meant to last forever?

But most of all, and what scared Maggie so she could hardly

swallow when she thought about it, was another question: What if you loved someone, and you married him, and then he died before you did? How could you possibly put one foot in front of the other after that?

Maggie's mind ran through the women she knew who'd had long, committed relationships with men. The only one she knew well enough to talk to, and who had lost her husband, was dotty Mrs. Webster. She often boasted to Maggie that she'd been married for over fifty years. If the old woman were still in her right mind, she might have a bit of wisdom to offer.

Maggie set her pen down and gazed intently at her father to see if he could offer a solution. It was his high school graduation portrait, and his hair was mashed down by a mortarboard. There was none of the despair in his face he wore now. He was young and untroubled, looking so pleased with himself, his world. Even his eyes were smiling. And why wouldn't he be happy? He'd been class valedictorian and was going steady with the girl of his dreams.

The many times over the years her father had told Maggie about his senior year, about asking for her mother's hand that following summer, came to her like petals drifting in the wind. They fluttered over her, bright spots of color. She could clearly see her parents standing at the altar in their wedding clothes, laughing together during their honeymoon at Niagara Falls, then living in the tiny house on Second Street. Even though these were her father's memories, they were a pleasant place to rest awhile, and Maggie closed her eyes, smiling.

The sound of someone in the kitchen just off the dining room pulled Maggie from her daydream. Josephine Harmon, the Culpeppers' housekeeper, was clattering around preparing dinner. Maggie could hear her humming bits and pieces of "Oh! Susannah" as she chopped, stirred, and opened and shut the refrigerator.

Miss Jo, as she had instructed Maggie to call her, wouldn't know any answers. A stout woman in her late fifties, she'd never married. She had moved into the small apartment over the carriage house behind the Culpeppers' house for good now, having been hired part-time last November as Maggie's mother's strength waned.

For the most part, Miss Jo kept out of Maggie's business, and she was certainly a one-woman wonder when it came to cooking and cleaning. Right now the air was swirling with the scent of sautéed onions and bell peppers mixed with orange rind, which probably meant she was preparing a recipe called Spam L'Orange.

Meat was a rarity these days thanks to the war. The war had changed a lot more than food, and Maggie longed with every fiber of her being for her mother to sit with her in the evenings, on the cozy sofa in the den, listening to war reports on the radio, saying, "Don't you fret, darling. I promise you, everything's going to be okay." Nothing felt too difficult or too frightening when Mother was still here.

The house was empty now. Maggie was constantly aware, with actual physical pangs, of the deserted rooms above and below in the enormous Georgian home. There was this very echoing formal dining room, full of memories but now scarcely used because Miss Jo preferred to serve all their meals, even on Sunday, in the kitchen.

Words could not begin to say how much Maggie missed her mother's touch, her voice, the way she filled their home. The way she filled their lives. When her mother died, the bottom dropped right out of Maggie's life.

Maggie sighed, pushing away from the dining table to tiptoe across the foyer and up the staircase to her parents' bedroom. From her mother's dresser she selected a cut-glass bottle before sitting down on the edge of their canopy bed. Squeezing the atomizer bulb, Maggie released a cloud of lilac water, her mother's favorite scent, into the air. Her eyes closed as she inhaled like a drowning girl clutching at a life preserver, as if she might find some remnant of her mother there in the little droplets, might breathe in some of her strength and wisdom.

"I am doing the right thing, aren't I, Mother?" she asked through her tears. "Genie says she's never thought of me as the military type, but I remember how you told me to always follow my heart. You always said I was strong and smart, and you knew I could do anything."

Maggie folded her hands in her lap and focused her gaze on her mother's silver brush and comb set on the dresser. She waited for a sense of her mother's presence, her blessing. As the minutes ticked by and the lilac scent faded away to noth-ingness, Maggie pressed her teeth together so hard her jaws ached. Finally, an image of her mother's body, shrunken with pain in this very bed, her beautiful, gaunt face barely registering the arrival of Christmas those last days of her life, was all that materialized.

It felt like someone punched Maggie so hard her breath flew out. How totally unfair for a person so good and generous to die. Sobbing, she began slapping the bedspread. "Why, God?" she cried. "My beautiful mother dead and gone? She was a saint! She was too young to die! Reverend Peterson is wrong. I'll never believe You love me!"

Exhausted, Maggie fell back on the bed and closed her eyes. It was at this moment she realized it would never be possible for her to accept her mother's absence. She could never have those mother-daughter talks to get advice from such a wise soul on matters of the heart. She would have to choose her own path from now on, and luckily she'd found the perfect solution— to lose herself in service to her country.

"Margaret? Are you okay?" Miss Jo's concerned voice startled Maggie. "I thought I heard some kind of tirade going on up here."

Maggie blinked at the woman's stout body, standing not five feet away from her. Feeling a bit disoriented, the way she did when she woke from a daytime nap, she rubbed her eyes. At last she smiled. "Uh, yes ma'am. I was—I was praying. Just having a little talk with the Lord."

CHAPTER FIVE

Time was not passing fast enough for William. Each minute since leaving the tree farm this afternoon seemed more like an hour. It was now dusk and supper was done, the dishes cleared away, and the rest of his family in the middle of their various nighttime routines. His brothers reluctantly finishing up their school lessons, Father reading the newspaper in his study, and Mother on the phone in the kitchen, talking with her sister.

The deviled eggs and pimiento cheese for tomorrow's picnic were covered in waxed paper in the refrigerator, and lined up on the counter were the oil, the canister of flour, the salt, and the pepper and spices, ready for frying chicken in the morning.

William occupied himself by pacing the house. First, he'd walked the hallway and the bedrooms upstairs. Now he was downstairs walking the length of the front of the house—the stretch of parlor, foyer, and dining room, then the adjoining kitchen, laundry room, and the walk-in pantry.

Finally he heard his mother say, "Just a minute, Bess," into the phone. She called out to him, "Will, darlin', you're going to wear out the floor or your shoes if you don't stop walking back and forth that way."

William forced himself to stop. He lay down on the camelback sofa in the front parlor, lacing his fingers behind his head. He watched the fabric over his chest rise and fall with each breath. Was it really going to happen? Had Maggie actually agreed to a date tomorrow? That beautiful, confusing woman who had become his whole world and then pulled away— Had she really told him, "Sure, Will. I'd love to," last Wednesday night out on her back porch?

Yes, she had. He was happy, knowing he had someone who loved him, knowing he had his Maggie back.

He closed his eyes, the tension draining from his neck as he welcomed a daydream. Maggie's slender, muscular frame leaning back against a warm stone at Harris Shoals, sunlight falling through the oak leaves, glinting in her electric green eyes and lighting up her thick auburn curls. She was beckoning him with a playful smile. "My beloved," she whispered, just before he drew her close to feel her heart beating against him.

This seemed to William the perfect bridge into sleep, and it didn't take long before he was gone.

* * * * *

At ten o'clock, William flinched as an unfamiliar noise pulled him from his slumber. It was like a swish followed by a skidding. Something hitting the wood floor just inside the front door. He lay there for a minute before opening his eyes.

He rolled to his side a bit, rubbing a sore place in his neck and twisting his head around to blink at a white envelope.

Another minute passed before he could pull himself together enough to rise to a sitting position on the edge of the sofa.

Hadn't the mail already come today? It always came before noon and it was pitch dark outside. In fact, everyone seemed to be in their beds. The house was shut up for the night, the only thing burning a small table lamp in the foyer.

Maybe it's an invitation to a neighborhood war bond party, William thought to himself. He stretched, stood, walked over, and bent to pick up the envelope, surprised to see his name written in Maggie's unmistakable hand.

He smiled. She hadn't tucked the envelope's flap in; instead she'd licked it shut. William reached for his pocketknife, enjoying the anticipation of her letter. *Maggie, Maggie, Maggie, you're always surprising me.* He slit the envelope open, pulling a folded sheet of stationery out, smoothing the creases between his fingers.

There was only one hastily scrawled paragraph in the center of the paper:

Dear William,

I really need to talk to you about something important. Can we please cancel our picnic tomorrow? I'm happy to talk tonight or it can be tomorrow morning if you're in bed and don't find this till later. Come on over. I promise I won't be sleeping tonight.

Maggie

William shook his head like a dog shaking off water following a dip in the lake. He read it again, his eyes darting left to right in rapid succession. It felt like all the air had been sucked from the room.

Somehow he willed himself to walk into the dark kitchen. Reaching into the refrigerator, he took out a pitcher of tea. Tilting his head back, he guzzled a good quarter of its contents, the sugar setting his teeth on edge as he sat down heavily in a pine chair at the breakfast table.

William considered driving out to the tree farm to talk with Mr. Byrd, but just as quickly he decided against it as he figured the old gentleman was probably in bed for the night. He was still sitting there when the lights in the kitchen came on.

His father was standing in the doorway in his robe and slippers, a water glass in hand.

"Son, what's wrong?"

Caught off guard, William blinked. He could feel the ball of anxiety in his chest. Taking a deep breath, he said, "Maggie's backing out of our date."

"Hate to hear that," his father said, setting his glass in the sink and walking over to open the refrigerator. "I know you were looking forward to that little shindig. Your mother said you've been turning the house over getting ready for it." He stood at the refrigerator, rustling around, and finally pulled out a deviled egg. William watched him pop it into his mouth. He swallowed, burped softly, and ran a hand through his thick gray hair. He turned and looked hard at his son. "You know why she changed her mind?"

William shook his head.

His father's brow wrinkled. He shoved his hands into the pockets of his robe and strode up and down the length of the counter for several minutes. "Well, I'd say just give her some space," he said at last. "Your mother reminds me all the time— it's a woman's prerogative to change her mind. A week or so from now, William, I expect she'll be singing a different tune. If you know what I mean."

William looked hard at his father, at the sure set of his jaw. "A different tune?" he prompted.

His father nodded. "Looks like you've been at a disadvantage with no sisters, hmm? I grew up with two sisters who were crying and screaming constantly, and now with your mother's mood swings, it can feel like a roller coaster around here sometimes." He sighed deep and long. "Just about wear a man out."

William stared at his father. He'd never heard this much distress mixed with powerlessness coming from him. "What do I do?"

"My advice, son," he said, giving a firm pat to William's shoulder, "is remember, women are the weaker sex. Just give Maggie some space. Things will work out."

When he was gone, William sat up straight in his chair. Maggie wasn't the weaker sex by a long shot, but with her tightly wound temperament, her passionate approach to life, of course she was going to have mood swings. William couldn't fathom what poor Maggie must be going through to have clouded her thoughts enough to cancel their date.

Even though his father had said to give Maggie some space, William decided he would go to her now. After all, she'd said she wouldn't be sleeping tonight. He would hold her, talk to her, and change her mind with a kiss. Someday they'd look back at this night, at her note, and laugh.

It was almost midnight when William stepped outside. The early springtime air had that nighttime chill to it, and he spied a full, luminous moon hanging directly overhead. He closed the door behind him then leapt down the steps and sprinted across the stretch of grass to the Culpeppers' property.

William paused to eye the imposing old home, get a read on it. The entire house was dark except for a faint glow coming from Maggie's bedroom window on the top floor. He decided it was her bedside lamp, and breathing hard, he bent to pick up a pebble from the flower bed below her window. He aimed it perfectly and it bounced off the screen.

Several moments elapsed, and William wondered if she was even up there. Then, finally, the sheers at her window moved to one side and he saw Maggie's face peer down.

"Maggie!" he whispered and shouted at the same time.

She stood, frozen, for what seemed an eternity, before disappearing from view. Finally William heard a faint creaking noise as the front door opened.

"Hi, beautiful," he ventured, as Maggie stepped out into the night barefoot, wearing a housecoat tightly cinched at her narrow waist. "I got your letter."

She nodded as she began to slowly descend the steps.

There was definitely something different about Maggie tonight, William decided. He wanted nothing more than to enfold her in his arms, but he knew this would not be a good thing at the moment.

"Want to talk in your mother's garden?" he asked when she was in the grass about ten feet in front of him. Mrs. Culpepper's rose garden was legendary in Watkinsville. A member of the garden club, the woman had loved flowers, roses especially. She had her shrine to the genus at the right side of the stately home. There, a C-shaped wide brick wall, so worn down by the elements it was a burnished red, held huge planters spilling over with pink, red, yellow, and white blooms in season. A trellis stretched up tall at one end of this, literally covered with a tangle of thorny vines.

"Okay," she said at last, without meeting his eyes.

William held out a hand, beckoning her to come to him so they could walk together, but she kept her hands clasped in front of her and he let his hand drop to his side, stepping through liriope in a lush patch at the side of the house. He could feel Maggie following him, past a swathe of monkey grass, an ornate birdbath, and a weeping willow, until they came to the rose garden.

The garden glittered in the night, and droplets of water suspended on rose leaves and reflecting moonlight made William think of tiny diamonds. It smelled of rain and earth. Maggie stood quietly in the center. He marveled at her beauty, ethereal yet solid, her hair and her eyes gleaming. He removed Ernie's letter jacket, using it to dry the moisture from a wrought-iron bench.

She sat down, with her hands pressed together between her legs, her chin jutting forward, and her slim body so rigid she looked like she'd shatter if he touched her.

William sat down about a foot away and cleared his throat. Finally she turned her head to look at him, and for a fraction of a second, William wondered, *What is going on in that head of hers?* He thought about the two different approaches he'd been considering. The first was laughing her note off like it was just some crazy joke, and the second, getting right down to business and kissing Maggie until she felt the power of their love, until she told him their date was still on. Which was the right one?

"Are you feeling okay?" he asked finally.

Maggie nodded.

"You didn't mean it about canceling our picnic at Harris Shoals tomorrow, did you?"

The silence between them grew heavy. A dog howled in the distance.

William looked at the sky beyond a pair of towering pecan trees at the edge of the Culpeppers' property.

"I've enlisted in the Navy, Will," she said at last. "I'm leaving Watkinsville."

"What?" It felt like the ground was dropping out from underneath him, like he was suspended weightless over some cavernous black pit.

"What?" he managed again, reaching out to clasp her hand. She didn't draw it away.

"I wanna help beat the Germans. And the Japs."

He held her hand a little more tightly. "But what about us?" His plaintive words hung in the air for a long minute.

"Oh, William, I'm sorry," Maggie said finally, pulling her hand away. "I'm only sure of one thing right now. My future is up north, in the service of our country."

It was William who broke the long silence that followed. "But, Maggie, this war's not for girls."

"Don't you dare say such a thing!" Maggie cried, the little-girl expression on her face carrying him back to the countless altercations they'd had together over their years as playmates, and then best friends—spats they'd had in this life they'd lived together. Their story, a story he didn't want to end here.

"Don't get mad, please." He was begging. "This war's ugly. Ernie sends me letters, and he says it's awful in the foxholes, just plain awful."

Ernie. William's stomach knotted. His good pal had been away for close to a year now, and still the pain of seeing him leave to fight overseas was fresh. Now Maggie was leaving too? He'd have no real friends his age left to talk to if Maggie left.

"He sees two or three casualties every single day. He says it's like those newsreels we saw of Guadalcanal, Maggie—utter carnage!"

"William," she said calmly, "please keep it down out here. It's not like I'm going to be in the middle of the fighting. I'm going to be in the WAVES."

William paused. "The WAVES?"

"Women Accepted for Voluntary Emergency Service." She

stood up and faced him, taking both his hands. "Will, women aren't in combat. We work on military bases, behind the scenes."

He was relieved to some extent, yet still so unnerved at the news he couldn't collect his thoughts. "It's usually the other way around, you know," he countered. "The man goes off to fight in the war, leaving his beloved behind. I'm sure you can change your mind if you want to."

"I don't want to change my mind. This is our war too! President Roosevelt *wants* women to enlist. He says the war has reached a new critical phase, and I want to help fight Hitler! If the U.S. doesn't have enough men to operate the ships and fly the planes, we aren't going to win this war."

William could see the determined set of Maggie's jaw. "Fiery" was a good word for this girl sitting here, her red hair lifted off her face and neck by a slight breeze.

He thought about President Roosevelt. He respected the man, watched him intently during every bit of newsreel footage that featured him. He wasn't sure of the extent of FDR's polio, but one thing he noticed was that the president was never shown walking. He was always riding or sitting. And they never showed him in his wheelchair either.

A lump formed in William's throat as he contemplated the president's battle with polio, and then his own. Was he crazy? Maybe he was, thinking a girl like Maggie, so full of life and energy, would settle for a disfigured man like him. "I was planning to ask you to marry me when we were at Harris Shoals," he said, hoping Maggie couldn't hear the nervous beating of his heart that sounded like a big bass drum in his own ears. "I don't have money for a diamond, but I figured we could go into Athens and pick out a pretty ring, you know, maybe an aquamarine, just until I can afford something better."

Maggie closed her eyes and lowered her head. She didn't say anything for the longest time and William decided she was praying.

"Maggie Jane?" he said at last.

She raised her head, stood, and walked to the edge of the bricks. William could see she was fighting tears when she turned to face him. "William," she said softly, "you're better off without me. It wouldn't be fair to say yes to you when I'm so unsure of things. I promise, you're definitely better off without me."

William rose to his feet, moving himself on numb legs to stand facing Maggie. "No, I'm not. You're not thinking clearly."

"What I'm thinking is this, Will—I need to serve my country and I don't need any divided loyalties. I need to pour myself out for the good of our troops. I want to be able to give to my job one hundred percent."

William took a step back. Gradually it was all sinking in. "You're breaking up with me?"

She nodded, her eyes sparkling with unshed tears. "Let's just see what time and distance bring to our relationship, William. You may forget about me. We don't need to make any lifetime commitments right now."

"Maggie, don't say that. I'll never, till my dying day, forget about you. I'm in love with you."

"Well, if you're truly in love with me now, then you'll still be in love with me when I return. Right? But you might find that absence does not, as they say, make the heart grow fonder. When I'm gone, some other girl may come along, and then I'd hate for you to bear the guilt of breaking up with me."

"That would never happen! Believe me, Maggie, I've been praying about this a lot, about asking you to marry me, and I think God's saying a great big yes."

Maggie spun around. Her eyes shot sparks. "Save yourself the trouble, Will. I don't think God exactly has me and my concerns on His heavenly radar." She folded her arms across her chest. "Do you know how long and hard I prayed for Mother to get better?"

William blinked.

"Do you have any idea what it was like watching her linger at death's door the way she did? She cried and moaned, curled up in this little ball, while I sat out in the hall, listening, so I could be there to get her things she needed. I prayed my heart out, Will, but Mother wasted away right before my eyes. I cannot understand how a God who loves me, who loved Mother, would let her endure such pain. If anybody was a saint, it was my mother."

Maggie's words were so full of anger William was shocked into silence. He finally released a long, slow breath and rocked back on his heels. "Maggie, please, don't talk like that. God still loves—"

"Don't preach at me, William Dove," Maggie warned. "I've heard all the preaching I ever want to hear from Reverend

Peterson. Try to understand. I need to go serve my country. When Mother died, I promised myself I—" The words seemed to clot in her throat.

William felt Maggie's pain go straight to his soul. He stepped in front of her and gently put his arms around her, willing calmness into her trembling body. She let him hold her for a moment, but when, at last, he felt her taking in a huge gulp of air, she pushed him away. Tears had left silver trails down her freckled cheeks. He pulled a folded handkerchief from his pocket, dabbing at the wetness on her face.

After a bit, Maggie lifted her head. "Night, sweet William," she said softly, firmly, turning to walk toward the house.

He followed every move with his eyes, waiting till she'd had time to climb the staircase and get back into her bedroom. The outline of her body appeared at the window, the shape of her hand waving good-bye before he gathered the presence of mind to concentrate on putting one foot in front of the other.

* * * * *

"I know you upset, son. But you can trust the Lord. He ain't never gonna let you down. No matter what has befall me, He always pull me through." Mr. Byrd sat on the steps of the cabin, his sleeves rolled up to his elbows and his hat at a jaunty angle to allow the afternoon sun on his dark face. Beside him lay a half-eaten sleeve of Fig Newtons along with a chipped coffee mug, which held water.

Sunday was his day off, and William noted to himself how the man had always observed this literally. No labor at all, not even brewing coffee.

Having unburdened himself, having heard Mr. Byrd's assurance that things would work out all right in the end, William stood perfectly still, staring out beyond the cabin at rows and rows of stalwart cedars. Stretching above the trees was a sky of milky blue filled with the scattered songs of birds. He swallowed the lump in his throat.

"Thanks, Mr. Byrd," he replied at last. "Yesterday was pure torture."

Mr. Byrd nodded. "I been prayin' for you. Been prayin' for Miss Magpie, too."

Suddenly William felt like someone had punched him. "She's furious with God because her mother died."

Mr. Byrd didn't look surprised. "She be hurtin' a good while yet. I been mad with God."

"You have?" This admission surprised William.

"Mmhmm." Mr. Byrd looked out into the distance like he was gathering his thoughts. "Trustin' God ain't somethin' comes easy to most folks. I been walkin' with the Lord a long time now, and I know I don't understand everythin'. But one thing I do know is a body got to trust Him. Been times I felt jus' like them Isra'lites," he continued, his hands clasped in the denim crease of overalls between his skinny thighs. "Cast into exile and walkin' many a mile in a country seem to be fill with nothin' but empty places. Tears be rainin' outta me, and I ain't able to wrap my mind 'round no lovin' Creator who would do me that way."

Mr. Byrd didn't say anything more for a long time, and when he did start up again, the words were like singing a beautiful melody. "But by and by, the Lord done pick me up and show me the way back to my faith and my peace and my joy. Now if my tears flow, they like gentle rivers what carry a story."

William swallowed hard. Mr. Byrd's words were awe-inspiring, and he wished he had a pen and paper so he could record them. Curiosity mingled with compassion. There had been something in the man's life that was unspeakable. Mr. Byrd had never divulged his full life story, only bits and pieces woven into their everyday conversations, but William always figured that what the man wanted him to know, he would tell him. There was only silence between them for several minutes.

"I know I must sound like a baby, Mr. Byrd," William ventured at last. "I have to admit I do feel a little guilty, whining about this with a war going on, but I just can't help myself."

Mr. Byrd chuckled. "Sit down, son."

William sat down and the old man put an arm around his shoulders. This gesture touched William deeply. In fact, it brought him the first bit of real calm he'd felt since receiving Maggie's note. He thought it was funny that Mr. Byrd's skinny arm could steady his soul as much as it did.

"Don't ever think God too busy with all the fightin' goin' on overseas to care about the details of yo' life. We ain't able to comprehend God. He ain't limited the way we is. He able to listen to a million prayers at one time, and He know how many hairs on your head right this minute. If somethin' be important to you, it be important to Him."

"Okay," William said. "I just—I just wish I could *make* her love me."

"You ain't really want that."

Looking over at Mr. Byrd, William nodded. "I know. I didn't mean it the way it sounded. I know she loves me. What I meant was I just wish she would admit it to herself and not be so stubborn. She claims she doesn't want to divide her loyalties while she serves our country." He clenched his jaw so hard his teeth could have cracked. "I cannot believe she enlisted. Of all the crazy things."

"Margaret Culpepper a spunky woman, Will. It be hard for any man to hold her down."

"Yeah, I know it. Sometimes it's the things I love about her that I also hate."

Mr. Byrd threw back his head and laughed. He picked up his water, took a long swallow, wiped his mouth, and said, "Things worth havin' don't come easy, you know. They did, you wouldn't 'preciate 'em."

"I appreciate Maggie Jane," William said, shaking his head at the thought of her.

"What I be saying is you ain't been through the fire with her, son. Somethin' call 'for better or for worse,' and what you gettin' now is just a little taste of that. Real honest-to-goodness love ain't Clark Gable droolin' when he look at Miss Vivien Leigh."

William smiled for the first time since Friday night. "I know women are hard work, Mr. Byrd, but I don't care. I'll take Maggie Jane Culpepper for better or for worse. I promise you, I'll never stop loving her. I'll just keep on until somehow, someday, she comes to her senses and sees this thing we've got together is the real thing."

Mr. Byrd studied his shoes. Finally he turned to William. "Now, don't you go stickin' your head up in the clouds," he admonished. "Whatever happen, God will use it in His perfect plan. He know best about everythin'."

William turned his head away at this. He believed in the providence of God and in Mr. Byrd's heartfelt testimony. He believed in keeping the faith at all costs. But what he really wanted was Maggie Jane Culpepper to be his. He refused to believe there could be any other outcome.

CHAPTER SIX

It was late afternoon on Monday, May 15, the sun mellowing the landscape with tones of warm honey. Inside the Silver Comet, dozens of perfumes mingled with the excited chatter of a boxcar full of women.

Maggie pulled her eyes from the scenery and focused her attention on a solemn-faced girl walking down the center aisle with a cardboard suitcase in her hand. The two of them exchanged a brief nod, and for a fraction of a second, Maggie wondered, *What compelled her to enlist? Is she in it purely to help our country, or is she running away from something, or maybe running to a new adventure? Which is it for me?*

The train had been stopping all along the Seaboard Airline, a route that ran from Birmingham, Alabama, to New York City to pick up passengers. There was a collection of girls on board as varied as the flowers in springtime, and Maggie decided there were probably as many stories as there were girls, each with her own reasons for enlisting.

Maggie shifted in her seat and fingered the smooth cardboard box of stationery and pre-stamped envelopes Eugenia had pressed into her hand that morning back at the station in Athens. "There's still time to change your mind, Maggie girl," she had said, "but if you're so intent on leaving, here's a little going-away gift. You know, just in case the Navy doesn't give you stationery." Eugenia was still looking pleadingly into Maggie's eyes as the train pulled out. Now Maggie tried to shake off the ache she was feeling at leaving the security of this dear friendship.

Eugenia, perhaps more than anybody, knew Maggie's "story." There were many nights since she'd enlisted, since she'd told William about enlisting, that Maggie slept over at Genie's house. The girls sat cross-legged on Eugenia's bed in their pajamas, sipping Cokes and eating Baby Ruth candy bars, as Maggie pulled bits and pieces from the tangle of emotions inside her. Eugenia was a good listener, and every so often, she wrapped Maggie in a big hug. Maggie could tell Genie was trying not to cry, and her heart broke for her friend, whose empathy was so deep and painful. More often than not, Maggie would have to dry her own tears and cheer Genie up. She stopped telling Genie things she would just as soon forget herself.

In fact, Maggie had determined she would forget everything that lay behind her and just live in each moment while looking forward. But before they were even out of South Carolina, a thought came to her. She steeled herself against it for a good thirty miles or so, but it was an insistent knock on the door of her mind, and at last it managed to slip by her mental barriers. *How is William holding up?*

A twinge of guilt followed by a pinch of anxiety made her throat constrict. Her heart began to race, and struggling to draw in a breath, she gripped the armrests, whispering, "Stop it this instant, Margaret Jane Culpepper!"

"Hey, you scared?" Helen LaMotte reached out to deliver a flutter of little pats on Maggie's knee. Maggie glanced up at Helen, a buxom blond with penciled eyebrows, from Florence, South Carolina.

"Pardon?" Maggie managed.

"About riding a train, I mean. It's my first time too. I saw you talking to yourself, and your face is white as a sheet. Relax, hon. I think it's exciting. We're fastened onto the railroad tracks, and if we hit a cow or something, I don't think it would slow us down a lick." Helen shook her head. "Isn't it something, the way they've got a whole car just for dining?"

"Yeah, it's something all right," Maggie mumbled, concentrating on breathing in and out as her pulse began to slow. She slouched down in her seat and turned her focus outside the window at a wide expanse of purple-blue sky with puffy clouds.

The day had been long and exhausting for many reasons, but one reason, a major one, sat right there. Helen was assigned one of the seats facing Maggie, and she had not stopped her breathless chatter for more than a ten-minute stretch since she boarded. Nothing Maggie did or didn't do seemed to discourage her.

Evidently, feigned sleep didn't deter Helen, because now she leaned in, tapped Maggie on her other knee, and asked, "I've been wanting to ask you, who do you think's the dreamiest Hollywood actor? I vote for Gregory Peck."

"He's okay," was all Maggie said.

"Well, I think he's fabulous." Helen's face lit up. "He's making a new war picture called *The Keys of the Kingdom*, you know. Speaking of which, I went to see *Casablanca*, because honey, everyone was talking about Humphrey Bogart this, and Humphrey Bogart that, like he'd hung the moon or something. But I guess Humphrey Bogart's just not my type, because I went to see him, and all I felt was a big fat nothing. I mean, I can take him or leave him. But did you happen to see *Edge of Darkness*?" She raised her eyebrows and leaned in closer.

Maggie shook her head.

"Oh, you have got to see it! With that handsome Helmut Dantine? He was in *Mrs. Miniver*, too, and I have to confess, I'm not going to lie, he really melts my butter!" Helen released a cascade of high-pitched giggles that set Maggie's teeth on edge.

"But now I'll be honest with you," Helen continued. "As far as Hollywood stars go, I think Clark Gable as Rhett Butler in *Gone With the Wind* has to be the cat's meow. I must dream about him at least once a week." She paused for a very necessary breath, and Maggie noticed her face had an almost ethereal glow. "While I'm sleeping, I mean," Helen continued. "I can promise you I daydream about him a lot more than that! But now that was a whole 'nother war, wasn't it, Margaret?"

Maggie didn't answer.

"Hey, you got a fella back home?"

"Nope," Maggie replied.

"Me neither," Helen said, fingering her pearl earbob. "And

I'm getting so tired of playing the field at my age. I'm twenty-two years old, you know, a little bit old for all the seventeen-year-old boys left in Florence. Let me tell you, girl, first dates with inexperienced kissers are just no fun! But I bet you know how that is. With all the men off fighting, there isn't a lot to pick from anywhere. Not much chance to have an exciting love life. Right?" She trained her long-lashed eyes on Maggie and added in a heartfelt voice, "I just didn't think I could stand it for one more minute back home in Florence."

Maggie looked hard at Helen. Clearly her reasons for enlisting didn't include a selfless act of patriotism. She was looking for a sea of *men* to choose from, and Maggie couldn't imagine what Helen was going to think when she actually arrived at boot camp. It seemed all her ideas about war were based on Hollywood films.

A good number of male Hollywood stars *had* put on a uniform—on screen, that is. But the majority of war films Maggie had seen or heard about avoided the realities of it all. They were made to transport a nation, especially the fighting men, away from the grim battle scenes. Soldiers wanted movies with lots of laughs and pretty girls.

Unlike Helen, Maggie wanted truth. She scoured every newspaper article about the war she could get her hands on. She knew it was of utmost importance to liberate the rest of Europe from Germany.

Recently she'd read that there were nearly a million and a half American soldiers encamped in southern England, so many that citizens were calling it "occupied England." She was amazed at the hundreds of thousands of different supply items reporters said were being used in this war. Tons of everyday things like dental fillings and socks, as well as necessities for fighting, such as ammunition and vehicles. But what disturbed her most was the report of the innumerable coffins needed.

Sometimes Maggie felt a fleeting urge to pray for the men fighting, dying for her freedom. Today when the notion to pray hit her, she scowled, folded her arms across her chest, and stopped that thought in its tracks.

"So, Helen," she said after a bit, "what do you think about amphibious invasions?"

"Huh?" Helen's mouth went slack.

"You know, military maneuvers?"

Helen cocked her head to one side. "I thought amphibians were some type of water creature."

"Amphibious. When you're talking in military terms, it means things like aircraft that can take off and land on either ground or water."

Helen looked hard at her, confused. "Why ever would we need something like *that*?"

Maggie sighed. "Because they're important in our fight against Hitler and his Nazis."

Helen's shoulders drooped. "Oh, yeah. Hitler. I hate that evil man. But that's no fun to talk about. Let's talk about our uniforms. I certainly hope our uniforms are flattering. Don't you?"

Maggie sucked in a breath and fell forward, laughing so

hard tears sprang to her eyes: "I certainly do, Helen," she said when she could finally talk again, feeling a release, a definite lift in her spirit.

There was a pure innocence about Helen that let Maggie know she'd encountered virtually no heartache or real issues in her life beyond not having a current boyfriend who could kiss properly. It was an innocence that let Maggie tolerate Helen's cascade of inane conversation as they passed through the state of Virginia.

Toward late afternoon, a bubbly girl carrying a pink train case boarded the Silver Comet and settled into a seat close enough for Helen to engage her in conversation. The two hit it off, and Maggie was grateful for the time to think.

She eased down into her seat, stretching her legs and uncrossing her arms as she gazed out the window, following the rear view of an old farmhouse as they passed it. A stout woman was pinning laundry to a clothesline, with bright spots of flowers growing all over the homeplace and some type of hound lying devotedly at her feet.

For an instant Maggie imagined herself living in that idyllic pastoral setting, then she redirected her view toward the hazy horizon off in the distance. The future looked soft and inviting. "I'm on my way to New York," she whispered, "to the Navy, where I can lose myself and my past." This powerful Silver Comet was taking her away; every second she was traveling farther from painful memories, uncomfortable yearnings.

* * * * *

By the time darkness began to fall, they were riding through open, flat countryside, empty of all but the occasional farmhouse and silo. Maggie felt weary down to her very core. Even her brain felt sore, from the chatter of hundreds of girls. She figured she'd fall asleep instantly to the rhythmic chugging of the train.

The Silver Comet had pull-down berths, and she crawled eagerly into hers when it was time, wrapping herself up in a little cocoon of cotton sheets, waiting for the escape of heavy slumber.

But before Maggie could lose herself, strains of "Boogie Woogie Bugle Boy," a song made popular by the Andrews Sisters, floated in from one of the other berths. It sounded like two girls singing together, maybe even three, and Maggie realized that wherever you have a group of girls, seldom will you have quiet. Sighing, she pushed aside the curtains in her cozy little compartment and with heavy-lidded eyes watched more pastures passing by, stars twinkling above them.

After a noisy hour, ending with a rousing round of "Chattanooga Choo Choo" and interspersed with much giggling as the girls changed the words to "the cat who chewed your new shoes," the singing finally stopped. The words of her fellow passengers' conversations were not discernible any longer, just a droning backdrop, and Maggie closed the curtain once again, snuggled down a bit deeper into the bed clothes, and closed her eyes.

At first she thought she was dreaming, the scene playing

inside her eyelids had that kind of faraway, hazy feel to it. But a ways into it, she realized she was floating in and out of a memory of her last encounter with William. Too tired to fight, she had no choice but to let it come.

She saw William's shadow before she saw him. The day was sunny and she was kneeling on the bottom step of Mrs. Webster's house, facing the front porch, with an American flag draped over her thighs as she re-fastened a dangling cord from the flag back onto the flagpole. Somehow one corner had come loose during a storm in the night.

The unmistakable outline of the shadow falling over Maggie made her suck in her breath. Heartbeat pulsing in her ears, she turned around slowly. When she saw William, sunshine glinting on his golden brown curls, her heart did more than pound. It gave a sudden lurch. She felt vulnerable down on her knees like that, so she rocked her weight back onto her feet and, cradling the flag, stood up hesitantly, pressing one hand to her chest to quiet the pounding of her heart.

"Jeepers!" she said under her breath, irritated at herself for reacting to William like this. It wasn't really a new sensation. This kind of thing happened all the time when she was near him, and for that very reason, she'd been carefully avoiding him, making sure she would not see him even from a distance. And she'd been successful, managing to keep space between them for the three weeks since their talk in the rose garden. Now she could only stare at William for a moment, paralyzed, afraid of her own yearnings.

"Hey, Maggie Jane," he said, the gorgeous dimple in his left cheek nearly blinding her. "Need some help with that?"

Before Maggie could answer, William was bent over her slightly, reaching down to steady the long, unwieldy flagpole before re-tying the flag's corner. She could see his magnificent biceps and triceps contracting, could smell that scent of his sweat mixed with cedar like he'd just come from the tree farm, and she was flooded with a longing to reach for his hand, to twine her fingers in his and hold on for dear life.

"I'm assuming it goes here?" William nodded his head at the holder affixed to one of the posts on Mrs. Webster's porch.

"Yep," Maggie replied, clasping her hands together tightly behind her back and working hard to sound offhand.

She followed his every move as he carefully inserted the flagpole, twisting it to force it down completely, and giving it a firm shake to be sure it was steady. This done, he turned to face her again, giving her another of his smiles. "That ought to fly proudly now."

"Thanks for helping," she mumbled, looking off in the distance, hoping he'd take the hint and leave.

"You're absolutely welcome," he said. "Guess that's the least I can do in service to my country, hmm?"

The very sound of his voice stirred her, and she nodded, sucking in a breath to try and keep her mental distance. The moment felt almost surreal—William wasn't acting like a thing out of the ordinary had happened between them, like they hadn't seen each other in three weeks. For two people who used to see each other every day, several times a day, this was an eternity.

"I'm proud of what you're doing, Maggie Jane," he said after a bit. "I'm proud of the fact that you're going to serve our country. I really, truly am."

"Thanks," she replied in a near whisper.

"Don't thank me. You're the one who deserves my thanks. Going off like this to work for our freedom." William still kept his distance. "I'm planning to write you every single day. I'm going to write you letters about what's going on here at home in Watkinsville. So you can stay connected."

Maggie raised her eyebrows in response.

William looked at Maggie for a long time. "Hey, how would you feel about taking a drive out to the farm with me? I know Mr. Byrd will want to see you before you leave for New York."

"Uh, I can't," Maggie said. "I've—I've got some things I need to take care of." Even as she said this, her heart felt like a heavy stone as she pictured Mr. Byrd's face.

"Well, okay. Guess I'll tell him you were too busy." William bent down and plucked a clover, twirling it between two fingers as he stared at it.

She could feel her heart beating as she stared at the playful cowlick on the crown of his curly head—that swirl she'd spun her fingers in a million times. If she let it, just that cowlick could drain her of all willpower.

Please just go! A thousand sensations swirled inside Maggie. Fear over her own yearnings, sadness about refusing to see Mr. Byrd, and fury at William for knowing just how to get to her.

"Hey, guess what?" William looked up and spoke again, his words laced with a bit of awe. "Mr. Byrd says he's been through some long, dark valleys. Don't know the details, but he said he used to be furious with God. Can you *imagine*, Maggie, someone like Mr. Byrd mad at God?"

Maggie ground her teeth, staring into space.

"He says if God doesn't answer our prayers the way we want, it's because He can see what we can't. The way Mr. Byrd talked about the dark places he's been, how God's brought him through them, it's powerful. I asked him to pray that you'll find peace about your mother's passing."

From out of all Maggie's tangled emotions, anger surged up and demanded an exit, tasting as bitter and dry as a mouthful of dirt. "Don't waste your time," she spat. "I believe I made myself clear when I said 'no God talk.' In fact, no talk at all, William Dove. Don't you dare write me any letters from home because I'm not going to read them!" She spun on her heel and headed for home.

* * * * *

The high, lonesome sound of the train's whistle pierced the darkness along with Maggie's half-dream. Reaching out a hand to pat her forehead, she found she was drenched in sweat. She drew a long, deep breath and held it in to get a hold of herself.

No longer near sleep, she pushed the curtain aside once more and focused on the wide expanse of sky.

The moon was full—big, heavy, and intensely orange—the kind of moon that set all the dogs in downtown Watkinsville to howling, and the kind William used to call "the eye of God."

Much as Maggie hated to admit it, the connection between them that day at Mrs. Webster's house had been more intense than she liked, at least on her part. The feelings his presence released in her were more than she could deny. It was almost like there was an invisible cord pulling them toward each other, making everything else disappear whenever their eyes met.

Well, that sure proved she couldn't hang around Watkinsville, trying to hide from William.

Maggie curled herself into the smallest shape possible, hugging her knees to her chest, tucking her head in as well. *I am making my way in this world. I'm a Navy woman.* These were her last thoughts as she finally drifted toward sleep.

* * * * *

Dawn was just breaking when the Silver Comet pulled into the New York depot. Maggie wrestled her luggage down the steps and found herself in the middle of the huge station, following a stream of girls to some long wooden benches where they were to wait for the subway that would take them to Hunter College.

The subway baptized Margaret Jane Culpepper. It took her under, then lifted her up and released her smack-dab in the middle of the bright lights and energy of a bustling city. She blinked her eyes, clutching her duffel bag filled with loafers and sweater sets. She looked at milling crowds of strangers with her mouth hanging open, feeling the excitement spread through her.

This was her chance for freedom. This was the wide world. She knew she would never be the same. This venture was like a zipper that opened up her insular, small-town world. New York was definitely a place where she could *lose* herself.

* * * * *

July 21, 1944

Dear Genie,

Forgive me for not answering any of your sweet letters. Believe me, I read them over and over. This is the first time I've had time since I've been gone to sit down and write.

You'd be miserable here, Genie. No frilly curtains on the windows, no china cups for morning coffee. In fact, this mattress I'm lying on is as lumpy as oatmeal, and the spread is like sandpaper. But I couldn't care less, and nobody here really complains about stuff like that, even the prissy girls. Not with our servicemen out there in foxholes.

Sometimes it feels like a dream to be a part of 30,000 WAVES keeping the homefront affairs of the United

States Navy going while the men are serving all around the globe. I remember the first moment I arrived and saw our American flag flying over Hunter College. Talk about a wide-eyed recruit. I can still hardly believe I survived basic training. I'll describe a little bit of what I had to do to "earn the right to wear the Blue."

We had classes on Navy rules and regulations, along with some on ship and aircraft classification. That was hard enough, but physical training is a huge part of boot camp. The worst were marching drills, which lasted for hours. I thought I was one tough cookie, but when we were out there lifting our knees in unison, up and down that field, I thought my legs were literally going to drop off.

Every Saturday we had a full-dress review. They'd blow a bugle and we had to jump out of bed (hit the deck) immediately, pull on our uniform, and march straight to inspection with a drill sergeant so tense I thought she was a mannequin. Some days I wondered if I'd be able to stand at attention, eyes straight ahead, while they inspected me.

But I did it. I finished, and now I'm a Seaman, First Class, assigned to Mercer Field in Trenton, New Jersey, which is a naval air station. You're not going to believe this, but I'm an aircraft mechanic. I passed the examination with flying colors, even though when I first got here I didn't know a screwdriver from a wrench.

Our everyday uniform is exactly what the men wear: bell-bottom dungarees, a dungaree shirt, a little square white cap, and these big, clunky shoes. Our dress uniform does have a skirt, but it's not exactly flattering.

You asked if I pine away for William. I swannee, Genie, I stay too busy to think about men or love. My work hours are 6 a.m. until 4 p.m., ten days on, followed by a day and a half off. I work on planes called TBF Avenger Torpedo bombers. Everything about them has to be absolutely perfect. It's a lot of pressure, but I feel like what I'm doing is important, so that really helps. I'm planning to make this my career—a lifer. Can't you just picture me as a salty old sailor?

Some of the men resent females being in the Navy because they have to clean up their act. They have to quit using bad language and telling filthy jokes and just generally cutting up the way guys do when they get together. They fuss about having to wear shirts in the crew's room.

The "chow" they serve in the mess hall is nothing like Miss Jo's gourmet cooking. I've lost weight and when I lie down, I can feel my ribs sticking up like piano keys. I dream of homemade peach ice cream and peanut brittle. But I'm not here for the cuisine.

As far as this war goes, I know you've heard all about D-Day and how General Eisenhower landed Allied armies on the northern coast of France. FDR was asking everybody to pray for the invasion of Normandy and the "chapel" in the rec hall had continual services—Protestant, Catholic, and Jewish. Everywhere I looked folks were down on their knees. Turned out that D-Day was one of the bloodiest days in U.S. military history, but on a happy note, it spelled doom for evil old Hitler's dream of a Nazi-controlled "Fortress Europe."

Here's something that'll make you smile. A friend of mine named Helen LaMotte, whom I met on the train to New York, got her duty assignment at Mercer Field here in New Jersey, too. In fact, we're roommates. Helen's job is secretarial, but I believe the biggest job she's working on is finding a man here. She can really crack me up sometimes.

Last Tuesday when I went to get some papers from the office, Helen said she was feeling kind of savage. I wondered what this odd comment was leading to, and then she told me she wanted to form a beauty, sewing, and cooking club on base because her grandmother, a pillar of the church in Florence, South Carolina, wrote her about how the trend of women joining the military is dangerous for our society. She said we need to keep our feminine selves alive, that if we are off somewhere without a good beauty parlor or dress shop, wearing men's clothes, forsaking our rightful duties of hearth and home, it would be the end of our civilized culture. We'd turn into savages.

Well, I started laughing so hard my eyes watered. I told Helen we had bigger issues to worry about than our nails and hair (like the Nazis and the Japs)!

I miss you so much, Genie. Miss staying up half the night talking. However, I don't doubt my decision to join the Navy. I must close now as five o'clock comes mighty early.

Love,

Maggie

CHAPTER SEVEN

For a solid week after Maggie's departure, William slept past noon every day. When his Big Ben sounded its alarm at the customary six thirty, William snaked his hand out from the covers and shoved the lever to the OFF position. Then he pulled the covers tighter over his head, hugged his pillow, and willed himself back into the soft, insular womb of sleep.

William's mother seemed to understand that he needed this numbing-time the way a sick person needed medicine, and she didn't utter a word against it. William figured her mama-bear instincts had come out in a big way, because his father didn't ride his back either. He didn't insist on a nine-hour workday as he normally did. William's younger brothers didn't make their usual ruckus in the mornings as they got ready for school, which was totally against their natures. Everyone in the Dove household, even the cat, seemed to realize instinctively that this was a fragile time for William.

Finally, on day eight, which fell on a Saturday, the old saying that "seven days make one weak" zipped through William's brain before he was able to silence the Big Ben, and he told himself he could not continue this schedule. Forcing himself to sit up, he placed his bare feet on the cool floor. Blinking and taking deep breaths, he gathered his faculties together. Shafts of early morning light streamed from the window by his bed and let him see to stumble to the bathroom, where he splashed cold water on his face.

Downstairs, William ate a toasted English muffin with homemade blackberry jam and drank a glass of tea. The kitchen was quiet, as his brothers were still asleep and his mother was outside in her garden. He recalled that his father was off working at the town council's drive for scrap metal and old tires. After the Office of Civilian Defense had issued a plea earlier in the week calling on each American family to be "a fighting unit on the home front," his father had decided to get more involved.

He told William that running the tree farm would be on William's shoulders entirely, at least until the war was over. His father had been busy collecting scrap metal from which armaments could be made, and there were half a dozen plywood signs leaning against the house reading, SAVE YOUR SCRAPS TO BEAT THE JAPS. He'd also signed up for the thankless position of ration-board clerk and was contemplating becoming an auxiliary fireman.

William had to admit he was proud of his father, and it would be good to be back in his old routine, steady and sure among the trees, working side-by-side with Mr. Byrd to get everything ready for the coming holiday season.

He'd promised Maggie he was going to write her daily, and now that he'd pulled himself out of the mire of self-pity, he planned to keep that promise. No matter that she'd told him not to write, no matter how drained or exhausted he might be from his duties at the tree farm, William determined he would schedule his after-work hours with letter writing in mind.

* * * * *

A couple months into his routine, William settled in at his desk and picked up his pen to stare down at yesterday's offering. He shook his head at the collection of words that had poured out of him like a summer thunderstorm. There they were—fits and starts, scratch-throughs, little puddles of ink, splotches, and additional thoughts scribbled in the margins.

What he'd been doing was writing five days' worth of letters before he tucked the sheets into an envelope and mailed them to Maggie. One problem was that there was always so much he wanted to share with her, and he tended to write fast and furiously. Often it seemed he got to rambling, so that in his letters there would be a bit of his heart, followed by a bit of what was going on in Watkinsville, then perhaps some stories of his work on the tree farm or how he felt about the war.

Taking great pains to make today's portion legible, he dove in.

August 1, 1944

My Dearest Maggie Jane,

It's a quarter till nine at night, and I'm staring at your picture on my desk, the one of you taken last fall. You know the one I'm talking about. You're standing on a bale of hay beside that silly scarecrow on Jackson Street, wearing his straw hat, with his corn cob pipe between your teeth.

I spent today at the farm. It was one of those legendary steamy Southern afternoons. You know—the kind where it's been blazing hot and sunny all morning, and then, about one o'clock, along comes a thunder shower so fierce you have to literally take cover. Well, it came and went fairly quickly, but afterward the air felt like a wet towel as I walked over the squishy earth between two rows of Leyland Cypress. While I was looking at how the sun shone on wet branches, kind of sparkling, I sure had a hard time remembering there's a war going on.

But I listen to war news on the radio a lot, and I keep hearing that Hitler's chain of fortifications around Europe—from the Channel to the Aegean Islands to the Vistula—is formidable. I'm sure you know how often the announcers say, "Another one of our bombers is missing."

When I hear things like that, and I know Ernie was supposedly flying where they're talking about, I can't rest until I get word he's okay. I'm proud of him, of course, and of the fact that he's already flown on over 25 missions, but I live in fear that his folks might get one of those "we regret to inform you" telegrams.

I want this war to be over. I believe in fighting for peace, and I'm all for preserving our republic, but two of my biggest reasons are selfish. I want Ernie safe and

I want you to come home. Knowing you're not in combat is small consolation.

When you left home I felt like part of me left with you. Mr. Byrd always says stuff like, "William, let patience have its perfect work." I'm not feeling patient.

Yours forever,

William Henry Dove

* * * * *

September came, and though William had yet to receive a letter from Maggie, it never ceased to amaze him how excited he got when it came time for the mail to arrive. One day, toward the middle of the month, he was eating lunch when he heard the distinct rumble of the postal carrier's engine coming up the slight slope of Harden Hill, followed by its idling hum, then the *slap-slap* of Fred Ward's feet down the walk and up onto the porch.

William had spent a long, arduous morning hauling scrap metal to a collection site, and he just knew there was going to be some kind of providential reward for his selflessness in the form of a letter from Maggie. The magnitude of this expectancy made him feel like a breathless child waiting to open birthday presents. The excitement had stolen his appetite away and all he could do was sip sweet tea.

He swung the door open even before Fred could lift the brass flap, catching his arm in midair. "Afternoon, Fred!" William said, looking out to see Fred's tall, lanky figure duck down. Fred's blue, close-set eyes did not quite meet William's, and William felt his heart sink, literally.

"Anything else?" he ventured, surveying the single advertisement Fred handed him.

"I'm afraid that's it."

William shook his head. What he wanted to do more than anything was to grab the mail satchel slung across Fred's shoulder, dump it out, and see for himself. "You sure?"

"Positive," Fred said in a muffled voice, turning quickly on his heel. "Well, have a good day now."

William tossed the flier onto the dining table. He sank down on the seat of the hall tree, resting his elbows on his thighs, putting his head in his hands, and letting out a long whoosh of air. He felt divided inside. Mad, let down, and disgusted with himself. He didn't like feeling sorry for himself this way, not when he heard constant reports about American soldiers shot down while fighting the Germans.

Suddenly William shot to his feet. He ran out the door, across the porch, down the steps, and up the walk, calling, "Wait, Fred!"

Fred, almost to his vehicle, spun around, wide-eyed.

"I just don't understand it," William said, breathing hard from his exertion. "Even if a woman is devoting herself to the military, even if she is unsure about a romantic relationship, don't you think it's common decency for her to respond to a man's letters when he writes her day after day after day?"

"You're talking about Maggie?" Fred said, looking down at his shoes.

"Yes. Listen, you've been delivering the mail for as long as I can remember. You're an expert. Don't you think she at least *owes* me a response on account of our long history?"

Fred's prominent Adam's apple rose and fell dramatically as he swallowed. "Uh, yeah," he said after a bit, "I'd say she does. 'Specially after all the letters she writes to Eugenia."

William felt like someone punched him in the gut. He stood, staring without seeing, as the realization hit him. Maggie had simply erased him. He'd been telling himself she was just too busy to write.

"Hey, buddy, you okay?" Fred looked at William quizzically, before shrugging one shoulder and saying, "Reckon I better be getting back at it."

When Fred's vehicle was out of sight, William turned on his heel and trudged back down the walk and up the steps to slump into a rocker on the porch. Okay? He didn't know if he'd ever be okay again.

* * * * *

After knocking on the Petersons' door, William stepped back to study the impressive piece of architecture. Behind an apron of perfectly manicured lawn sat two stories of weathered bricks, the bottom level with a covered wraparound porch and the top with a terrace stretching between two dormer windows.

"William?" The door opened, and Eugenia's round, porcelain face, framed by soft wheat-colored waves, was smiling at him.

"Hope I'm not interrupting anything."

"No, I just finished lunch. Won't you please come in?" She opened the door wider and stood to one side. "Let's go sit in the sunroom. I'll fix us some lemonade."

William wiped his boots on a mat inside the door. His heels were loud on the highly polished floor as he passed piece after piece of perfectly polished antique furniture, bookcases lined with leather volumes, and fancy clocks. The walls were decorated with gilded mirrors. As he walked through the ornate dining room to a central hall, he felt roughhewn and coarse, like a peasant among nobility.

"Make yourself at home and I'll get our drinks," Eugenia said, pausing at the entrance to the sunroom. Feeling more relaxed, William plopped down at one end of a little settee, leaning back against a purple pillow.

"It's really great to see you," Eugenia caroled, setting two lemonades on a coffee table and perching at the other end of the settee. "So tell me, what's going on in the world of Christmas trees?"

"We're thinking of what to order for the Yule-Tide Shoppe. November will be here before we know it."

"You're right. Time flies and all that."

He nodded. There was an awkward moment filled by the squawking of some loud blue jays right outside the window.

"Heard from Maggie?" William asked.

"Well, no phone calls, if that's what you mean."

"Any letters?"

"A few."

"Is she okay?" He was nervous, in a funny way.

"She's fine," Eugenia said quickly.

William's pulse ran a mile a minute. He picked up his lemonade, tracing cold circles in the condensation. "Would you mind if I read her letters?"

"*My* letters?"

William's voice was steady. "Yes."

"I absolutely would mind. No, you can't see them."

It felt like Eugenia had slapped him. "Why not?"

"I'd feel like I was, I don't know, betraying her, telling secrets or something, if I were to let you read one. You know what I mean?"

There was an awkward silence while William sat, processing this. Was Eugenia hiding something? He glanced out the window at a tall magnolia tree to try and calm himself. "Okay," he said at last, turning his gaze back inside the room. "I can understand that." He willed himself to keep a straight face. "Believe what I need to do is just send her a pin-up of me."

"A pin-up?"

"Yep. Something's telling me that's the ticket. That'll inspire the girl to write me a letter. Maybe you'd help me shoot the photograph?"

Eugenia's eyes were huge, unblinking. "What?"

"You know," William continued. "Kind of like the male

version of one of those Betty Grable or Rita Hayworth pictures? Ernie says the soldiers love to have a pin-up. Some of their girlfriends even send pin-ups of themselves in a swimsuit. So, I don't see why it should be any different for me and Maggie, with her serving and me back home."

Eugenia twirled her thumbs around each other. "I guess I could," she said after a long pause. The horrified look on her face made William finally break his concentration and laugh.

"Relax. I don't really think I'm pin-up material."

She stuck her tongue out at him. "You're so funny I almost forgot to laugh!"

"Actually, Genie, I'm confused. I feel like Maggie's writing me off cold-turkey."

Eugenia took a dainty sip of her lemonade and set it down again, reaching out a tentative hand to pat William's shoulder.

"I write her every single night, and every day I'm certain I'll get a letter. But I haven't." He stood and began to pace the length of the porch, his feet pounding the boards, his insides feeling like a volatile mix of chemicals swirling around inside a tightly corked container. "Guess it'll be Thanksgiving when she's home on leave before I get to talk to her."

"Oh, Will." Eugenia sighed. "Maggie's not coming home for Thanksgiving."

William's heart lurched. "What?"

"You know how she said her destiny is to help our boys in uniform during this war. Now she says she's going to be a lifer, and she's not putting in for a leave at Thanksgiving."

William sank back down on the settee and stared at the floor.

"It's not like I get a letter a day. I've only gotten three letters in almost four months." Eugenia shook her head with a small smile.

"That's three more than I've gotten."

"You poor baby." Eugenia's eyes were warm and sympathetic. "I'm sure she's *planning* to write you at some point."

"You really think so?"

"Sure," Eugenia said, but there was something in her tone that was slightly off, as though she didn't quite believe what she was saying.

William picked up his lemonade for a quick swallow. "Are you serious about her staying in even after the war's over?"

"Yes. Our little patriot wants to be a salty old Navy person forever." Eugenia spoke more softly now. "She says she's staying up north for Christmas, too. To see real snow."

William was speechless. *To see real snow.* This simple phrase was salt rubbed into his wound. Could Maggie have said anything that would hurt him more? After all the times the two of them shared this dream out at the tree farm? His heart sank like a rock in a pond. He forgot to breathe, shaking his head as his thoughts raced. Some part of him was aware of Eugenia's concerned blue eyes on him as he began punching the cushions of the settee.

"I'm sorry, Eugenia," he said when he'd exhausted himself. "Seeing snow together was one of our big dreams. We promised each other that one day we'd go up north and we'd step in real fluffy white snow together. I guess I'm just so—so mad, or something."

"You know, William," Eugenia said in a careful tone, "I think what you need is some sort of strategy here."

He merely looked at her.

"Maybe, you know, like some type of military strategy? My father told me something interesting he heard in a report about the D-Day invasion of Europe." Eugenia sipped her lemonade. "Okay, on D-Day, an armada of Allied ships assaulted the beaches of Normandy, France. Right?"

"Mmhmm."

"Well, simultaneously, thousands of airplanes dropped paratroopers into the action. Got that?"

William nodded.

"Along with the paratroopers, the Allies also dropped hundreds of rubber dummies behind the enemy lines. The dummies were intended to simulate an attack to confuse the enemy."

"Okay," William said, wondering how this applied to him and Maggie.

"They called them 'Ruperts,' and as the Ruperts landed, some German outposts were tricked into fighting these 'paradummies.'"

"Interesting."

"I thought so. My father said that, apparently, this deception created a vital crack in the walls of Fortress Europe. So I'm thinking maybe you need to simulate some kind of love 'paradummy.' Tell Maggie you're seeing someone." Eugenia folded her hands in her lap and looked hard at him.

He scowled.

"Women are jealous creatures, William. The day Maggie came by here to tell me she'd enlisted, I told her you were gonna be in hot demand back home when she was gone, and I could tell she didn't like that one bit. She turned kind of pale and got really argumentative. You need to make her believe someone else is interested in you, and she'll come running home and throw herself into your arms."

William didn't say anything.

"Don't you think that's a wonderful idea?" Eugenia urged. "Make Maggie so jealous she'll throw herself into your arms?"

"Well, I do want her to say she'll marry me once this war's over. I sure wouldn't mind if she got leave to come home for a bit and let me put a ring on her finger," he said carefully. "But *lie* to her?"

"Come on, William. How much clearer can 'all's fair in love and war' be? We accept that kind of deception I just told you about all the time. In the words of my brilliant father, 'It's part of a legitimate military operation designed to thwart oppressive forces.'" She drained her lemonade, the clink of ice against an empty glass filling the small porch.

"But this isn't oppressive forces. This is my Maggie!"

"If you're that worried about it, then maybe you really should ask someone out and you wouldn't be telling a lie." Eugenia gave him a satisfied smile.

Everything in William recoiled at this. He had no desire to actually go anywhere with another girl, other than as just friends. "Like who?" he asked, running his fingers through his hair.

"Oh, let's see…," Eugenia said, her eyes searching his face. "Like Betty Hall?"

"Ha! Betty'd never look my way."

"Wanna bet?"

"I'm not a betting man," he said, "and even if I were, I know where the odds would lie on that one."

"Well, you'd lose if you bet Betty'd say no. She thinks you're a cutie."

William felt his cheeks grow warm. No other name Eugenia could have mentioned would have shocked him this much. He pictured Betty Hall—president of their senior class at OCHS, head cheerleader, a girl with a gorgeous, movie-star face framed by jet black hair in a stylish cut. Betty with her easy confidence, that laugh of hers.

"Men *are* mighty scarce in these parts." Eugenia raised her eyebrows playfully, and this defused the moment.

"But," William reflected, "I still feel like I'd be cheating on Maggie."

"William, look at me." Eugenia's voice was firm. "Maggie *released* you to play the field. Remember? It's okay to make her jealous if it's for a reason. You've got to trust me. Do you really think you're the one for her?"

"With all my heart."

"If that's the case, then what's the problem?" Eugenia tucked a blond sheaf of hair behind her ear. "When Maggie sees how desirable you are, she'll realize she loves you and she'll want to marry you and she'll quit saying all that silly stuff about being a career Navy person."

"There's one problem," William said.

"What?"

"I don't even know if Maggie reads my letters..."

"Then I'll write her about it," Eugenia promised. "She says she reads my letters over and over again."

CHAPTER EIGHT

September 1944

Maggie had a few minutes to spare between duties, so she stopped by the office on base to visit with Helen. Helen was rifling through a file folder with a rapturous smile on her face, and she didn't even look up when Maggie came in.

"Hey, girl," Maggie said. "You look like the cat that swallowed a mouse."

Helen lifted her eyes for a split second to nod hello.

"What are you reading that's so wonderful you can't even pause and talk to your roomie?" Maggie teased. "Doesn't look like the latest issue of *Modern Screen* to me."

"It's even better."

Maggie walked around the counter to peer over Helen's shoulder. She saw that the file folder was chock full of women's pages torn from the Sunday paper. Laid out on the desk top in front of Helen were articles on flower arrangements, wedding cakes, and wedding dresses.

"Well, well. Looks like you're planning some complex military maneuver here."

"Oh, silly, have a seat." Helen reluctantly closed the folder and laid it down. She looked at Maggie, almost a little shy.

"You getting married?"

Maggie said it in jest, but Helen nodded.

"You're not serious!"

"I am, girl. Jasper proposed to me." Helen's voice was laced with awe. "Out behind the mess hall at lunch."

Maggie blinked, shock waves rendering her mute. She'd listened for maybe a week as she and Helen were in their bunks before falling asleep, while Helen gushed about this big, strapping, college-football-player type named Jasper from somewhere in Connecticut. Jasper was training to be a medic, and Helen had said to Maggie numerous times, "Jasper's the one, I just know it." But Maggie had dismissed this all as Helen's wishful thinking.

"Helen, the two of you hardly know each other," she managed at last.

"Margaret," Helen said, hands on her hips now, "we love each other, heart and soul. It's like God made us just for each other. Why in the world would I need any more time? He upped and asked me to marry him, and when we kissed, I didn't have a single, solitary doubt in my mind it was the thing to do to say yes."

Maggie couldn't think of a response. Helen looked absolutely sure of herself and happier than any time since they'd met on the train to Hunter College for boot camp. Finally, she stood and hugged Helen and said, "Well, congratulations."

"Thank you, dear," said Helen. "Now, I do want you to be one of my bridesmaids. And you can help me pick out the dresses. Okay?"

Maggie took a deep breath and let it out. "Sure," she said, checking her wristwatch. "Looks like I better head back to the hangar." She turned and walked out, past the dispensary, the exchange, and the barracks, where the marines who guarded the base lived. Her eyes were on the hems of her bell-bottom dungarees and her clunky shoes as she told herself that Helen's engagement proved her theory that there was no one true love for each person. It was all a matter of timing. It was time for Helen, and so she had just latched on to whoever was convenient.

What troubled Maggie more was the huge sense of foreboding she felt on behalf of her friend and roommate. An awful scene that happened on base quite a bit, and was unspeakably crushing to witness, was when a girl received a telegram from the War Department informing her that her man was gone. Maggie did not think she could bear it if something like this were to crush Helen and all her dreams.

* * * * *

"Oh! I just adore that song!" Helen closed her eyes and hugged herself. "I promise you, girl, there's nothing like a Glenn Miller tune to get me in a fun mood." Her blond tresses were teased and sprayed up into an artistic bubble on top of her head, with the ends turned under like scrolls. She wore a daisy-print dress with a coordinating cardigan thrown over her shoulders and a red shade of lipstick that couldn't be missed from a mile away.

It's good to be sitting here, Maggie thought, eating tomato pie in downtown Trenton, listening to "Fools Rush In."

A cheerful buzz of conversation surrounded Maggie and Helen along with the pungent aroma of garlic. The smooth, swingy tune seemed to have a positive effect on many of the patrons.

On her days off from her military duties, Maggie felt a small sense of panic, of loose ends, and Helen was easily convinced to go with her to Rocky's Tomato Pie, where the easy joking, the dancing, and the relaxed jubilance of the place proved to be good distractions.

Candles flickered on each table, adding to the ambiance of the classic Italian décor, with red-checked tablecloths, shakers full of parmesan cheese and red pepper flakes, brick walls, and café curtains on the windows. Maggie noted the highly polished wooden floor with a central dance area where the sheen had been worn away by revelers and the soldiers sitting on barstools at a long bar quaffing ten-cent beers.

"Thank you for agreeing to join the Feminine Club, Maggie," Helen said, holding up her mug of Coca-Cola in a toast. "I'm appointing you the secretary."

"No, that's okay," Maggie said, lifting her own glass to lightly graze Helen's. "I don't need to hold an office. I'll just be a regular member." She was still in a state of mild shock that she'd even agreed to this on their walk through downtown Trenton. Her acquiescence had more to do with wanting to make Helen happy than anything else.

It had been five weeks since Helen's engagement day, and now Maggie's worst fear was realized. Jasper was officially missing in action, and Maggie knew Helen walked a thin line between elation over his proposal and anxiety over his safety.

"I just believe there are some things we females shouldn't abandon," Helen was saying. "I wrote my grandmother that I was starting the club, and the sweetie wrote me back and sent all kinds of articles we can use for our meetings."

Maggie looked at Helen. "What kind of articles?"

"Oh, there's a recipe she cut out of the paper for buttermilk biscuits, and then there's the instructions on knitting a swaddling blanket, and then this wonderful article from her church's annual letter, all about how women are supposed to act."

"How women are supposed to *act*?" Maggie's voice came out almost shrill.

"Yeah, silly. It's from Paul's letter to Titus, where he wrote about how older women are supposed to be sound in faith, reverent, and all that stuff. Plus, they're supposed to teach the younger women"—she smiled as she paused—"and that's *us*, to love our husbands and children. You know, all that stuff about being chaste, domestic, and submissive to our husbands."

Maggie almost choked on a bite of pizza. "Umm, I may have to withdraw from the Feminine Club. I'm not sure if I exactly agree with all that stuff."

"You are so funny, Mags," Helen said, laughing and shaking her head. "I love you to death. Don't worry. We'll have some lighter type meetings about things like… Well, let me think how to put it. Like how to be more alluring to men." She took a breath and leaned back. "So, how does that sound? You know, kind of an antidote for how we're forced to wear manly uniforms, and how some girls, ahem,"—she stared pointedly at Maggie—"some girls just let their looks go. I mean, go natural. It's like they're not even a bit concerned about attracting a fellow."

Maggie stared at the candle's flame. "Helen," she said slowly, "I've found myself here in the Navy. I'm a good aircraft mechanic, and like I said, I'm making it my career. I won't be settling down and getting married and having babies."

Helen covered her mouth with her hand. "You're just teasing me, aren't you?"

Maggie watched her friend staring off into space, absentmindedly scraping a red fingernail in the dripping candle wax, obviously beyond being just confused. This news Maggie delivered was probably akin to telling the girl that the moon was made of cheese.

Ever since her engagement to Jasper, all Helen's idle moments were devoted to planning their wedding ceremony. She was certainly a loyal fiancée, Maggie mused. Even though many of the cute marines who guarded the base made eyes at Helen whenever they were in Rocky's, she didn't let her eyes, or her devotion, stray one smidgen.

Helen LaMotte was amazing. To look at her one would

assume she'd be the flighty type, easily led astray, but the girl had an intensely loyal heart. She knew how to focus in on her desires, and her determination could be inspiring if Maggie let it.

Maggie's desire, she was certain, was pouring herself exclusively into her Navy career. Proof of this was that she stayed so focused, so busy, that often she would forget to eat. Who cared about missing a meal? She preferred to exhaust herself, to wear herself to that point of beautiful oblivion, where her brain was so tired she couldn't dwell on anything else but her devotion to the U.S. Navy.

There was only one problem. Genie's most recent letter was making that part of Maggie's plan a little harder.

"Mags," Helen prompted, her voice yanking Maggie from her thoughts. "I just don't see how a person can squish that part of them down. That romantic part that needs to love someone and be loved. And anyway, I think Brent Lawton over there has his eye on you." She smiled mischievously, nodding her head in the direction of a tall man standing at the end of the bar.

Maggie shrugged, took a sip of her Coke, and purposely stared toward the kitchen where a man tossed a circle of floppy dough up into the air and caught it. What did Helen know? The two of them were obviously wired differently. Of course Maggie could squelch any kind of carnal desires, any need for physical passion.

"Moonlight Serenade" was playing now, and Maggie let the soothing rhythm shoot through her, allowed it to carry her away until, at last, her body relaxed a bit. "You know what I love about Glenn Miller?" she asked finally.

"His dreamy eyes?" Helen smiled.

"What I love about Glenn Miller, besides his music, is that he got an officer's commission in the army air force, organized a service band, and he's been playing and performing at military camps and war-bond rallies." Maggie ran a hand through her tangled hair. "Isn't he great? So patriotic."

"Yeah, sure," Helen said in a distracted voice. "Say, back to our earlier topic. Who are all those piles and piles of letters you get from?"

"Letters?" Maggie felt her face grow warm.

"Yeah. Some of those things look like pillows they're so fat." Helen pursed her red lips and took a long drink from her straw. "I see you writing letters too. You're a regular correspondent, aren't you, girl?"

"Uh, not really. I write my father once a week, and I write to my best girlfriend back home every now and then." Thoughts of Genie's latest letter made Maggie squirm...again.

"Your father writes you those long letters?"

"Actually, his are fairly short and sweet. Usually just a couple paragraphs, with some money tucked inside."

"Then who are all those fat ones from?"

Maggie tensed. She refused to say William's name out loud. Just as she refused to read his letters. She did acknowledge to herself, on some level, that she was afraid to open them, lest they stir up feelings she was not ready to deal with. Most of the time she told herself she didn't read them as a matter of self-discipline, that she was losing herself in service to the Navy.

Maggie searched for something interesting and distracting to say. "Hey, know what I heard?" she said with a forced laugh. "Now this is a real classic line. General Patton said, 'My men can eat their belts, but my tanks gotta have gas.'"

"He said his men are going to eat belts?" Helen giggled.

"Well, he was being facetious. Or maybe he wasn't, actually," Maggie reflected. "He was talking about the fact that nothing's more important to the Allies than getting fuel and supplies from the Normandy beaches to the armies trying to advance across France."

"Hmm, okay," Helen responded. "If it's your girlfriend who sends you all those big, fat letters, she must sit around and write all day."

Maggie didn't want to think of Eugenia. She was still trying to shake away the thoughts of William and Betty Hall that haunted her after Eugenia's latest letter. Betty was movie-star beautiful and had that same confidence and charisma as well. Shiny black hair, big dark pools of eyes, a smile that would mesmerize any male. She could just imagine William and Betty, holding hands and running through the tree farm together, falling down in the grass, laughing, loving. She ground her teeth to banish the image.

"She must not have herself a fella if she's got that kind of time," Helen mused.

"Huh?"

"This friend of yours. Maggie! Are you even paying attention to me? I said she must not have a fella if she can sit around writing you letters all the time."

"Uh, no. Genie's not dating anyone special. The boy she was dating left for Germany, but they weren't serious."

"Oh, okay…," Helen said, a faraway look coming into her eyes.

Maggie saw the scared little girl inside the woman. "Have you heard anything?" she asked, leaning forward to pat Helen's wrist.

Helen shook her head. "But I bet Jasper's just fine. Probably got a little inconsequential wound and he's in some hospital somewhere and they don't have a record of it. Happens all the time in combat, don't you know? Before long, here will come Jasper, and I'll say, 'Oh, I knew I didn't need to worry. Why was I so silly?'" Helen was talking much too fast. She got to her feet, straightened her shoulders, and gathered her handbag off the back of her chair. "I believe I need to go to the ladies' room to freshen up a bit."

When Helen was gone, Maggie summoned the waiter. Pulling a pocket-sized spiral notebook from the waistband of his apron, the balding man with one gold front tooth looked at Maggie's face hard. "Madame?" he said, with a smile, "do I perceive two ladies who need some dessert and coffee?"

"Yes, please," Maggie said, returning his smile. "Are you a mind reader? A psychiatrist?" She liked the presence of this man who had a twinkle in his eye, this look like he didn't take life too seriously.

"Neither," he said, giving a small bow. "I am merely an expert at reading women's facial expressions. I've seen chocolate pie and strong coffee cure many ills."

Maggie laughed. "Cure our ills, please."

Ten minutes later, sitting across from Helen, both above steaming cups of espresso, she was amazed at the shift in moods. Another Glenn Miller melody, "Don't Sit Under the Apple Tree," filled the air, while rich wafts of coffee heightened her senses. Helen had freshened her face—the smudges of teary mascara were gone and her red lips were perfect again.

"Anyway, Mags," Helen said, after a long gulp of her coffee, "if anything *had* happened to Jasper, somebody would have found his dog tags by now. That right there proves he's okay."

Maggie took a deep breath. "Of course it does." She hated to lie.

The waiter arrived with a tray holding two saucers of chocolate pie. He made a great fanfare of presenting their desserts. "More coffee, madame?" he asked, looking into Helen's cup, already almost empty.

"Yes, please," Helen responded. "Maybe you ought to just bring us a whole pot since it's almost nine o'clock."

He bowed and left.

Maggie was shocked at how quickly time had flown since they'd left the base at five. She reached for her fork, settling a creamy, sweet bite of chocolate on her tongue. Once it had dissolved a bit, she chased it with a gulp of hot espresso. It was a perfect encore to their cheese and tomato pie. "Mmm, delicious," she murmured to Helen.

"Good," Helen answered distractedly. She was aiming fork-fuls of pie into her mouth, her eyes on a couple one table over from them.

Maggie turned her attention there also. They were indeed an amusing pair—both fiddling nervously with their salads, taking great gulps of birch beer to cover uncomfortable pauses in the conversation.

"So, uh, where'd you say you were born?" She overheard the quavering question of the boy. Obviously it was a first date.

Maggie had a quick flash of William and Betty, saying things to each other like, "So, what's your favorite dessert?" or "Do you like math or science better?" Those little bits of trivia she imagined a couple might exchange on a first date. It had to be a tricky prospect, getting to know all the quirks and secrets of someone.

She wouldn't know because she'd grown up with William. She knew so many of the details of his life. Somehow, though, Maggie didn't imagine there would be many awkward, uncom-fortable pauses in conversation with someone like Betty Hall. She wondered if Betty and William were to that place where they had opened up yet, telling each other things they didn't share with just anyone.

Maggie turned away from the couple. She took a drink of her water, biting down hard on a piece of ice.

"Talking about places where a person was born," Helen said with a dreamy smile, "I was born and bred in Florence, South Carolina. God's own country." She paused for a moment then continued. "Florence has to be the prettiest place in the world. Maybe even the universe. I promise you, Maggie, I adore that place. I miss it so bad. I miss playing cards with Daddy, and I miss Mama's home cooking.

"We live in a big old house up on a hill, with a back porch where we listen to the radio and dance." Her eyes were shining. "And there's this tire swing hanging in our backyard, from the limb of a gigantic tree, and if you swing up high enough, you can see Johnson's Creek winding along through the pasture just like a snake." She shook her head, smiling. "I warned Jasper. I told him he's gonna have to agree to move back home with me. Mama would have a fit if her baby girl ended up somewhere like Connecticut."

Home. The very word stung. Maggie wouldn't be surprised if she was literally green. *Why do I resent Helen her beautiful memories?* Maggie felt ashamed of her jealousy. She longed to feel the glow she saw in Helen's eyes when Helen talked of home. But home would never be the same.... She tried to focus on the coming morning's task of pulling oil strainers out of the bombers, to check them for metal particles that might indicate possible engine trouble.

"Were you born in Watkinsville, Mags?" Helen's question hit hard.

Maggie blinked. She hated, despised not being in total control of her thoughts and feelings. "Yes. Born and bred," she admitted at last, hating her tearful sounding voice.

"Oh, poor baby," Helen crooned. "Sounds like you're

homesick, too." She reached across and touched Maggie's wrist lightly.

Their waiter returned, bringing more cream and refilling their water glasses. He was subdued this time, seeming to realize that a very private and somber conversation was under way.

Maggie slugged down the last of her espresso and set the cup onto the table with a loud noise. "I think we should call it a night."

Helen shook her head in such a discreet way, Maggie wasn't even sure that's what she was doing. She set her fork on the saucer, bent in closer, and whispered through her teeth in an excited tone. "Maggie, don't look now, but I think I see a certain somebody heading our way."

Maggie kept her eyes on Helen's face until a man's figure loomed beside their table.

"Excuse me, ladies." A deep voice poured down on them. "Mind if I join you?"

The breath left Maggie's lungs when she looked up to see Brent Lawton, a tall, polished lieutenant commander, backlit by the faint light from the bar. The candle on their table gave his face an almost unearthly glow. Even before he uttered another word, Maggie felt the power of his presence.

This feeling surprised her. If she were to describe Brent Lawton in one word, it would be *commanding*. Muscular and tall, he was every inch the officer in his crisp uniform complete with collar insignias and sleeve stripes.

"Sure, have a seat," Helen said, waving to the empty chair between herself and Maggie.

Officer Lawton sat down. "How are Helen LaMotte, professional secretary, and Margaret Jane Culpepper, mechanic extraordinaire, this evening?" His voice held a note of amusement, but what startled Maggie was that he knew her name. Her full name.

"Just fine," Helen said, but Maggie merely blinked at him, open-mouthed, until Helen gently kicked her underneath the table.

"Umm," she said, "I'm fine."

"Oh, I'm sorry," he said, gazing directly into Maggie's eyes. "I'm such an idiot. I've forgotten my manners, haven't I? Allow me to introduce myself. I'm Lieutenant Commander Brent Lawton, but please, just call me Brent."

"Pleased to meet you, Brent," Helen said in the perfect hostess tone.

Maggie only clutched the napkin in her lap. She didn't want to admit she liked the way this man said her name in his long, tall, Texan drawl.

She recalled the first time she'd laid eyes on Brent Lawton. It was her second day on base, a crisp sunny afternoon, and he was standing outside the crew's room talking to a couple of marines. Maggie had been impressed by his military presence, his precision, and the way he carried himself. She found herself in awe of him and, at the same time, annoyed that he caught her attention. She wasn't given to flights of fancy. She didn't allow herself this.

Brent lit a cigarette. "Care for a smoke?" he offered politely, tipping the package of Lucky Strike cigarettes toward Maggie and Helen.

Both girls shook their heads.

"Looks like this is the spot to be tonight, hmm?" he asked.

"Sure is." Helen took a sip of her espresso. "Good music, good friends, and good food. Good soldiers, too." She giggled. "That reminds me of something funny Maggie said."

Maggie looked hard at Helen. She couldn't recall anything funny she'd said.

"What was that?" Brent said, raising his eyebrows.

"She said that General Patton said he was going to feed his men belts."

"I did not!" Maggie protested. "What I said was that he said, 'My men can eat their belts.' He meant nothing was more important to the Allies than getting supplies and fuel from Normandy to the armies trying to advance across France."

Brent looked at Maggie, nodding. "Patton's Third Army needs between 350,000 and 400,000 gallons of fuel a day to keep going. Without that, they can go nowhere. The Germans still hold the mouth of the Scheldt River and that sixty-mile piece of water between the North Sea and the Antwerp docks. Not a drop of gas can get through until they're cleared out."

"Hitler," Maggie growled. "Too bad that assassination attempt failed." She was on the edge of her seat now.

"In a way it backfired," Brent observed. "Now Hitler's convinced he's surrounded by traitors, and he's clinging even harder to the belief that victory can still be his. The man's working feverishly."

Maggie listened intently as Brent leaned back in his chair, stretched his long legs out underneath the table, and filled them in with details about Hitler's latest strategies and field equipment.

"Also, you're not going to believe this," he added, "but Hitler's ordering every man from sixteen to sixty to serve in the armed forces."

"Sixteen!" Maggie gasped.

He nodded. "Rumor has it there are even some fifteen-year-olds. Mere children! And, I heard there are some cripples and some soldiers who are half-healed. It's a makeshift army, all right."

Maggie could see Brent's military mind working, and it impressed her. She was amazed at how comfortable she suddenly felt.

"Do we have to talk about such unpleasant things?" Helen pouted.

"Fair enough," came Brent's playful voice. "I don't suppose you'd want to dance?"

Maggie stared into her empty coffee cup, waiting for Helen to politely decline his request. Time ticked by and she began to feel like she had as a child during those moments in the classroom when the teacher's eyes scoured the students, waiting for a reply from someone. *What in the world's taking Helen so long?* Maggie wondered.

When she looked up, she found Brent's gaze firmly fixed on her.

Maggie bit her lower lip. *He's asking me! What in the world do I do?* She could feel herself blushing. In her mind's eye she pictured the way her freckles always darkened and splotches infused her cheeks.

His request, his nearness, was just a little too threatening, and Maggie made herself sit still as a statue. But just then Glenn Miller's "Stairway to the Stars" began, and the words, the melody shot into her feet, through her knees, straight into her torso. Plus, the intense caffeine was rushing the blood through her brain fast, making the sight of all those couples whirling, spinning, and laughing very appealing.

Watch it, Maggie! she forced her brain to yell at her temptation. *Remember your promise to yourself. Don't you dare say yes to this man.*

* * * * *

Dear Genie,

I'm exhausted. All day I was sitting out in the crew's room, watching airplanes, with my heart in my throat. The reason I was scared half to death is because whenever one of "my" planes is up there in the air, I feel so responsible. I try to make sure every single little thing, every detail I'm in charge of, is flawless—from pulling oil strainers out, to putting the wing rockets on, to making sure the brakes are absolutely perfect. It's one thing to ace the mechanic exam and quite another to actually be sitting in the crew's room with the pilot's life in your hands!

I get so scared I might have messed something up that it's almost enough to make me want to pray sometimes. Not that I think my prayers would do a lick of good. It just seems like praying would be a nice kind of mental relief. A release, I guess.

My heart breaks every single time I hear about a soldier being killed. Believe me, Genie, some of them are just boys! But I try to be real reassuring to Helen, even though, from my point of view, things don't look good as far as her fiancée Jasper's fate is concerned.

She hasn't heard from him in way over a month, but I always agree with her when she tells me he's probably wounded and in a hospital and they just don't have a record of it.

I know he's dead, and I'm dreading the moment that girl gets the telegram. I've been thinking up what I can say to her then, because I used to hate it when people said things like, "Time will heal all wounds," or, "God needed your mother up in heaven with Him more than we need her down here." Those kinds of comments really stink if you're the person left behind.

You asked me in your last letter if I miss the balmy air of Watkinsville. I do not! I love this wonderful, crisp New Jersey air. The only things I miss are you, my dad, and Mr. Byrd. Well, naturally I miss my old friend, William, too.

Speaking of William, I'm happy for him that he's seeing Betty Hall. But I am curious about something— you'd think he wouldn't have the time to write me those tomes he still does! Tell him I'm trying hard to give my full attention to my career, and he'd be better off just to totally forget about me. Really, Genie, the WAVES are enough for me. This war going on consumes me more than any kind of physical passion or emotion.

That reminds me—I guess I should tell you something. Now, please bear in mind I'm NOT seeing anyone romantically. As I mentioned, I have absolutely no need for that.

But, I have struck up a friendship (PURE innocent friendship) with a Navy officer named Brent Lawton. We hang out together, but the thing is, it's totally platonic. Like me, Brent's looking for a career in the Navy, and we discuss military strategies. The first time we went out for coffee I looked the man straight in the eye and told him I didn't want to get romantically involved with anyone. He said he doesn't want any romantic entanglements either. What I like about Brent is I can trust him. He's perfectly in control of himself.

Since William's seeing Betty Hall, I give you my permission to tell him I'm seeing someone—if you want. In fact, please DO tell him.

Love,

Maggie

CHAPTER NINE

William stepped outside the back door of his house and stood on the bottom step, studying the sky. The sun was already out in full force, but the day was cool for the end of September, at least by Georgia standards. He let his weary eyes glance over the trees. What his mother called "beautiful fall color" was on early display; a palette of reds burnished the maple trees and the gingkos were a yellow so bright it made him blink.

"Here's Betty's number, Will. I'm writing Maggie tonight that you're dating Betty, so now all you have to do is pick up the phone and dial and our Maggie will be back in your arms before you can even blink."

Eugenia's words from several weeks back seemed ridiculous now. Time, along with a new letter from Maggie to Eugenia, had given William a new, crystal-clear perspective.

Speaking of clear, the odd expression on Eugenia's face when she showed up at the house yesterday evening still haunted him. He'd been out on the back porch at twilight, sitting in the swing and watching the stars slowly appear.

"Will?" Eugenia'd said after climbing the stairs to stand beside the swing. She was out of breath from the quarter-mile walk, and her face looked startled and sad and excited all at once. "I got another letter from our Maggie."

"You did?" he'd said, stopping the swing immediately.

"Yeah. It's funny, you know, but I guess when she got my letter saying you were dating Betty, she decided to tell me she's seeing someone too."

"But I *haven't* asked Betty out!" He'd jumped to his feet, shaking his head at the injustice.

"I know, William. I talked to Betty yesterday."

He tried to keep breathing. "Then why? Seeing someone? I thought Maggie was devoting herself to the Navy! Undivided loyalties and all that!"

"Oh, William," Eugenia soothed, sitting down beside him. "I'm so sorry. Stuff happens. Folks can't help it when they fall for someone. It's out of their hands. Please don't be mad at me. You did tell me you were gonna ask Betty out."

William could not say a word. Fury was spinning his thoughts around and around. He wanted Eugenia to leave.

"Why not keep your mind open? Give Betty an honest chance?" Eugenia asked him after a bit. "You've got to think about yourself, William. Do you want to end up a lonely old bachelor?"

"I really, really didn't expect this," was all he could say.

* * * * *

William spent a sleepless night wrestling with the knowledge Maggie was seeing someone else. The love and life and future he wanted with her seemed like a schoolboy's dream. Maybe she'd been right about things when she said he was better off without her. What if their love couldn't survive what time and distance brought?

Didn't Mr. Byrd say he didn't want William sticking his head up in the clouds? William determined that he would come back down to earth and play the field as Maggie had suggested that night in the rose garden. Maybe he'd fall for Betty Hall. After all, she had been the most popular girl at Oconee County High, with swarms of males at her beck and call.

William sprinted up the back steps, sat down at the desk in the kitchen, and lifted the heavy black handset of the phone.

"Hall residence. This is Luvenia. Who you wanting to speak to?"

"Uh, hello," William heard himself saying. "Is Betty available?"

"You mean Miss Betty?" The voice on the other end sounded amused.

"Yes, please."

"May I ask who is calling?"

"William Dove."

"Let me go see if she here."

William heard Luvenia's poor attempt to cover the mouthpiece as she yell-whispered, "Miss Betty, there's a man called William Dove on the line. You available?" This was followed by some yell-whispering in return that William could not make out.

Finally, Betty's high-pitched, breathless voice said, "Will? Is that you?"

"Yes, it's me. Hi, Betty. How are you?"

"I'm just fine, thanks. How are you?"

"Doing all right," he lied.

There was a long pause. Then William drew another, deeper breath and jumped in. "I was wondering if you might like to grab a Budwine soda at Dawson's Grocery with me later on this afternoon. Say, four-ish? Then head out to the tree farm for a walk."

"Oh, how sweet! Hold on a minute and I'll check my social calendar."

William could feel Betty hovering in the background, tapping her foot while holding the receiver, waiting the appropriate amount of time. His jaw started aching from clenching his teeth together, but at last Betty came back on the line. "Why, yes," she said, "it looks like that'll work."

* * * * *

Not two seconds after William knocked on the Halls' door, Luvenia appeared in the doorway. She was a fierce-looking, stick-thin woman with pecan-colored skin. She looked directly into William's eyes and said, "May I help you?"

"Yes, ma'am. I'm William Dove, here for Miss Betty." He held out a hand.

Luvenia ignored it and turned her head to call over her shoulder, "Woo-hoo! Miss Betty! William Dove is here!" When there was no answer, she left William standing at the door and walked up the wide, curving staircase.

From upstairs, a door slammed and Betty called out,

"Coming!" She came down the stairs wearing a shell-pink sweater set over a crisp dark skirt, her tiny feet in burgundy loafers.

William was surprised to feel a little jolt of gladness at seeing her.

"Hope it's not too cold outside," Betty said, smiling at Will as if they had a secret together. "I'm not really in the mood for a coat."

"Oh, the weather's nice enough," he replied.

Luvenia cleared her throat and directed her words at William. "Miss Betty eat her supper at seven o'clock sharp." Her arms were crossed on her chest.

"Yes, ma'am," William answered. "I'll keep that in mind."

Betty put her hand on the woman's shoulder before they left. "Now, Lulu, you go fix yourself a nice cup of coffee, put your feet up, and don't you worry one second about me."

"Come on, Will," she said, turning to pull him by the arm and out the door. "Let's go get our sodas."

William felt Luvenia's stern eyes on him as he put his hand under Betty's elbow to guide her toward the pickup truck parked at the curb. He opened the door and settled her into the passenger seat then got himself up into the driver's seat.

Before he'd even cranked the engine, she'd scooted over on the pickup's bench seat until her thigh was nearly touching his. With every small movement she made settling herself in, a waft of her perfume, which was something to do with roses, billowed up to William's nostrils.

She sure smells good, he thought. Where Maggie was all angles and sinew, Betty was softness and curves. Where Maggie's hair was fiery and full, Betty's hair, as well as her eyes, put him in mind of shiny black obsidian.

When they were on the main road, Betty turned her face to him, nudged him with her elbow, grinned, and said, "Hey, Will, you sure you don't want to turn around, go back, and get Luvenia to go with us?" Then she slapped her knee, leaned forward, and laughed so hard little tears appeared in the corners of her eyes. When she straightened back up and gathered herself together, she added, "We could stick her back there in the truck bed."

William laughed. He had forgotten how high-spirited this girl could be. After all, she had been a cheerleader and captain of the tennis team. He noted that Betty had painted on some stockings, a new trend as real stockings were in short supply because of the war. He nearly missed the turn to Dawson's Grocery on account of being transfixed by the precise line Betty had drawn on the back of her leg. *She is one pretty girl*, William thought as he pulled into a parking spot. *Real pretty.*

A few minutes later he returned to the truck and put an ice-cold Budwine soda in her hand. "Here you go," he said.

"Thank you, Will. I've been looking forward to this." Betty sounded as if she meant it, and William let out the breath he'd been holding as they pulled out of the Dawson's Grocery lot to head down Highway 15. He wished he could think of something interesting to say. He cleared his throat.

"What a fabulous day!" Betty exclaimed in the next moment. "Would you just look at that blue sky? It hardly seems like there's a war going on, does it, William?"

"Hardly," William replied, though thoughts of Ernie's most recent letter lay coiled in his brain, and it didn't take much to make them strike. To squeeze out the images of Ernie's wounded and dead fellow soldiers, William tried to focus on the empty road.

"Know what my daddy said?" Betty asked, crossing her legs so that her top leg bobbed up and down. "He said the Japanese have these pilots called kamikazes, and they make surprise attacks on American troops."

"Is that right?" William felt his jaw tightening.

"Mmhmm. Daddy says the Japs have this thing about suicide, that's what kamikaze means. They just intend to *die*! Can you believe that?"

"Hardly." William clenched his teeth even harder.

"Also, my daddy says the Japs are masters of surprise warfare. They dig foxholes in the ground and then they leap out and scare the living daylights out of our men. Want to know what else I heard?" She didn't pause for a breath. "I heard that there are Nazi submarines spying on the Florida coast. I think the Nazis are even more evil than the Japs."

William cleared his throat again.

Betty looked at him, her eyes imploring. "I just don't understand all this fighting. The world feels like this insane place now. How come people have to kill each other?"

"I don't know," Will said in a quiet voice, though he did have an idea of why people killed each other. Because they were greedy, power-hungry, and self-centered, lusting for control, prejudiced, or full of evil desires like Hitler. Or maybe they were simply afraid.

"Want to know what really amazes me, William? I can hardly believe *women* are in the military now! That our very own Maggie Culpepper's gone off to fight!"

William froze. Hearing Maggie's name spoken aloud stole his breath away for an instant, as if he'd heard some startling bit of news or had seen some possibility that had never crossed his consciousness before. "Well," he said carefully after a moment, "technically, she's not fighting."

From the corner of his eye, William saw Betty turn her face toward him. Her pink tongue flickered out quickly and licked her shapely upper lip. "So," she said in a demure voice, "I take it you and Maggie aren't going together anymore."

William sat so erect his spine didn't touch the seat's back. He knew this would be coming and he concentrated on the road as he chose his words carefully. "No," he said, "Maggie is pouring herself out for the good of our troops. She wants to be able to give to her job one hundred percent."

"Ah well," Betty said, sighing happily. "I suppose we can't all be so noble. I guess being in the military is like being a nun, huh? Got to be focused. Anyway, some of us have to stay here and hold down the home fort. Some of us have to be homemakers and raise babies."

* * * * *

Despite his limp, William's stride remained fairly agile. As he and Betty made their way down between the first and second rows of Leyland Cypress, he reached for her slim, cool hand, marveling over how many guys would *pay* for this chance.

The feel of her hand was not unpleasant, but he realized he wasn't feeling anything like desire. Maybe it was something in the air or maybe it was that it was too cold outside, or he realized it might take a kiss to get things stirred up.

They walked this way for a good hour, breathing in the scent of cedar and pine and chatting about nothing of consequence, William having worked hard to steer the conversation away from the war. William almost felt like an actor in some play. It was the first time he'd ever had a date with anybody but Maggie, and how to act, to relate, was more or less a mystery. But, like a lot of things in life, he supposed, this was something that he had to learn.

As they walked along, he began to offer little witticisms and comments about everything from local politics to the missionary who'd recently visited his church, not just the friendly or polite kind of interaction, but the let's-connect-on-a-deeper-level kind.

During a lull in the conversation, he squeezed Betty's hand in a meaningful way, stopped, and pulled her close enough to him that he smelled the soft fragrance of roses. The sinking sun glittered in her dark eyes.

A quick glance at his watch told him it was nearly six and an image of Luvenia's stern face saying Miss Betty eats her supper at seven was all the catalyst William needed to shake off the stage fright. "Would you mind if I kiss you?"

Betty smiled up at him. "I was wondering when you'd ask. How about we go somewhere we can warm up?" She dipped her head at the Yule-Tide Shoppe.

Taken aback, all Will could think to do was nod.

"Come on," Betty said, tugging him along.

From a distance, William couldn't tell if anyone was inside the cabin. The curtains were drawn and the door was shut. As they drew nearer, he found that his palms were sweating.

But Betty didn't seem to notice as she led him up the three cinder block steps.

William made three sharp raps on the door that brought no answer, and he turned the handle, easing it open and stepping carefully over the threshold with Betty.

The dimness inside made him momentarily blind, and the familiar smell of Vick's VapoRub mixed with coffee met his nostrils. Squinting into the corner, he called softly, "Mr. Byrd? You home, sir?"

No answer, and William decided Mr. Byrd was off fishing or on one of his nature walks. Taking a deep breath, he shut the door gently, took a step closer to Betty to put his arms around her, and pulled her close. "Ready?" he asked.

"Yes," she whispered.

With his heart beating a mile a minute, William leaned in

until he felt her lips beneath his. He stroked her silky hair as she returned his kiss.

He was afraid he was doing it all wrong when he didn't feel anything after a moment or so of determined kissing. But clearly, Betty was enjoying herself, if he judged by the little noises she was making in her throat and her tightening grip on his back. He pressed in more, but he may as well have been kissing his pillow.

The emptiness between them seemed cavernous and finally he pulled away, cleared his throat, and fumbled for words. "How about we go back outside and—"

He was cut off by a voice, smooth as molten honey, coming from the corner of the cabin. "William, my man."

"Eek!" Betty squealed at the same time William felt her flinch.

He saw Mr. Byrd's shadowy form rise up from his cot in the corner. "Oh me, oh my. I ain't expectin' no comp'ny," he said. "Just let me get myself up from here and offer y'all some refreshment."

"It's okay. It's just our caretaker," William said to Betty, at the same time letting out a long breath of relief. "Mr. Byrd, I'd like you to meet Betty Hall. Betty, this is Mr. Tyronious Byrd."

She gave a quick smile and said, "Pleased to meet you. I— I wasn't expecting to see anyone."

"Me neither." Mr. Byrd's amused smile was directed at William. "How do, ma'am," he said, turning to Betty. "Sorry to scare you. Reckon I was deep in my afternoon nap." Mr. Byrd waved his hand amiably toward the makeshift kitchen. "How 'bout some coffee?"

"Uh, sure," Will said, looking at Betty, whose eyes were wide as she inspected the tiny hot plate with two burners and the dented percolator.

William led her to the wooden bench, and she sat on one end while William eased down onto the other, spinning the lazy Susan. "Mr. Byrd's a tree expert," he mentioned at last. "You can ask him anything about any kind of tree, and he knows the answer."

"Well, I know 'bout Christmas trees," Mr. Byrd said. "Don't know much 'bout those redwoods I hear grow out West."

"My favorite are the cypress," Betty said. "The firs have that awful prickly stuff that breaks my skin out. But my mama prefers the firs because they smell so good, and that's why my daddy gets a fir every single, solitary year. I don't even help hang the ornaments because my arms would be miserable!" She looked over at William with a little smile. "But I may, just may decide to come with my daddy to get our tree this year."

William focused his attention on Mr. Byrd. "Speaking of Christmas, it'll soon be time to get the Yule-Tide Shoppe up and running."

"Sho' will," the old man said, pulling a can of coffee down from the cabinet. "Gonna be runnin' over in here with snow and Santas and Rudolphs." Mr. Byrd chuckled. "William, yo' daddy tell me some story go along with the Rudophs." He poured two cups of steaming black liquid and set them on the table with a Mason jar and two spoons.

William noted the scant bit of sugar in the jar and was touched anew by the old man's generosity.

"Want some cream, ma'am?" Mr. Byrd hovered at Betty's side.

"No, thank you. This is just fine. But you *can* put me down for one of those Rudolphs." Her voice turned high-pitched with excitement. "Those guys are so cute! My niece got one of the Rudolph coloring books from Montgomery Ward last December and she about wore that thing out, reading it and coloring in it over and over. It's the sweetest story, I do have to say, about this poor little reindeer who's teased because he's different, on account of his red nose." She poked out her lower lip. "But, in the end, Rudolph's a hero. He saves the day with that bright nose of his!"

William smiled. He liked this story—a creature with a difference, a handicap, somehow using it to shine. A victor.

"Hey, I've got an idea!" Betty's exclamation interrupted his thoughts. She sat on the edge of her chair now, bouncing up and down with excitement. "Put me down for a whole *bunch* of Rudolphs. You know that toy drive the city has every year for underprivileged children? I help with it, and you should see their faces when it's time to open presents. It would be so much fun to see them opening Rudolphs."

"Sound like you got the real spirit of Christmas inside you." Mr. Byrd's rich chuckle warmed the air. "Will? What you wantin' this Christmas?"

"Peace, love, and joy," he said in a flippant tone, just to get the question over with, because what he really wanted was Maggie to come home. To decorate the tree with him like she had every year. To want him.

"Peace sho' be a good thing" Mr. Byrd smiled. "Make this war be over."

"Amen to that," Betty said, glancing around the cabin furtively. "Excuse me, Mr. Byrd. Is there a bathroom around here?"

"Yes, ma'am." Mr. Byrd hopped up and led Betty to the back door of the cabin. Opening it, he motioned with his hand, saying, "Just follow the path yonder and there be a outhouse beyond the pines. Brand-new Sears catalog in there."

Betty smiled. "Please excuse me."

William couldn't believe the good timing. As soon as Betty was out of earshot, he turned to Mr. Byrd and said, "Looks like I answered one of my questions."

The old man raised his eyebrows.

"Betty doesn't light any sparks in me, Mr. Byrd."

"Look like you was makin' quite an impression on her when I woke up." A wide smile revealed several gaps in Mr. Byrd's teeth. "Betty put me in mind o' one o' them movie stars."

"Yeah. Everyone's crazy about Betty. I know guys who'd fight to the death for her. But I don't feel a thing for her. Beyond friendship, I mean."

Mr. Byrd looked hard at William. "You tellin' me I be dreamin' when I woke up and saw you kissin' her?"

"No, you weren't dreaming. Remember when you prayed I'd have wisdom?"

"Mmhmm."

"Well, I pulled my head out of the clouds like you said, and I'm playing the field like Maggie said, and I'm using a military strategy like Eugenia said."

"Military strategy?"

William nodded. "Eugenia told me if I went with somebody, she'd tell Maggie in a letter, and then Maggie would get jealous and want me again. It's like a tricky fighting tactic."

Mr. Byrd was scowling, rubbing his chin, and William could see the question on his dark face.

"Eugenia said all's fair in love and war. Anyway, Maggie got that letter and then she wrote Eugenia that she was seeing someone on base, and so I decided I may as well go on and actually play the field." William got to his feet, his hands clenched. "But I'll tell you something, this date today with Betty proved something. Here's the most desirable girl Oconee County has to offer, and I wasn't even tempted." He could hear the desperation woven throughout his words. "I'm even more certain I can't live without my Maggie Jane!"

Even after all these months, the anger, the sharp corners of his pain over missing Maggie still shocked William. "We're meant for each other, Mr. Byrd," he said, stomping the floor. "I promise you."

"Take it easy now. Take it easy," Mr. Byrd crooned. "War and love two different things, son. The path to true love ain't that simple. Ain't that crooked neither."

"Okay," Will managed.

"Only military strategy you need here be surrender."

"Surrender? I'm supposed to give up? That's crazy! Remember when I told you I'd *never* stop loving her? That I'd keep on until somehow, someday, Maggie comes to her senses and sees what we've got together is the real thing?" Anger rippled through William like an earthquake. "Mr. Byrd, there was a night she promised me we'd spend every Christmas together."

The old man set his coffee cup down. "I done told you, son, I be prayin' for you. Been aksin' the Lord to do what best. But you got you a job to do here too. Yo' job be to put it in the Lord's hands and leave it there. Surrender it."

William felt heat rush to his face. He got on his feet, arms akimbo. "How in the world am I supposed to—"

"Whoa, now. Surrender ain't mean you gettin' beat or givin' up. It just mean you leavin' it in the hands of Yo' Creator. Because His hands be capable hands. Believe me when I say it be safe to give Him control o' your future."

William felt his brow furrow into a scowl. "You make it sound so easy."

"Naw. It ain't easy, that for sho'. But then ain't nothin' worth havin' ever easy." Mr. Byrd cleared his throat. "You recall me tellin' you God ain't never goin' let you down? That whatever happen, He goin' use it in His perfect plan?"

William nodded.

"Believin' that be the secret of surrender, of yieldin' to the Lord. When you able to do that, *He* fight for you. You goin' at it wrong, son, lookin' for some strategy. Some trick."

All the fury drained out of William, leaving him with an

exhaustion so deep he slumped in his seat. "Look, I don't know how to put this into His hands and leave it there. I only know I can't go on like this. It hurts too much. I mean it. Nothing makes me happy these days. Not fishing, not reading. Even being out here with the trees doesn't make me happy. Seems like all the zest in my life is gone. I was living for the evenings, for when I was writing letters to my Maggie Jane, and then for Fred to bring the mail."

"She ever write you back?"

"No," William said, his heart sinking even lower. "But you're telling me if I put this into God's hands, He'll change her heart and she'll love me?"

"I ain't sayin' that. I ain't no prophet. All I be is a pilgrim who done travel a road what had some beautiful mountaintop experiences and some pitch-dark valleys."

William felt like the road he was traveling on, the road of his faith, or lack thereof, was currently hitting a dead end with a tall, thick, curving wall so that he could go neither left nor right. He shook his head, releasing a long, tired sigh.

"Don't you be losin' hope, son." Mr. Byrd spoke in a gentle tone. "In time you gonna find what you long for. A love that be written in God's plan."

"I'll never be happy without Maggie, Mr. Byrd!" William came up off the bench.

Mr. Byrd's silence spoke volumes.

William thought about a certain conversation when Mr. Byrd had told him there'd been things in his life he'd wanted badly—things denied him. He also remembered Mr. Byrd giving thanks for gifts in his life that he claimed had come to him painfully wrapped *because* of this denial. All this chilled William to the bone, especially when more of the old man's words came to his memory, echoing like they were spilling out of a bullhorn. "I be sayin', 'Lord, You just gotta help me. Please, Lord!' But ain't till I got down the road a piece I seen He had a better way, that He be an artist who use the dark and the light to take a ugly lump of clay and mold Hisself a masterpiece."

The silence stretched between them in a slow-moving arc, much like the sun going down outside the cabin. William wondered what would happen if he were to lean forward and say, "Tell me, Mr. Byrd. Please tell me your story."

But he was too afraid. Whether it had been for divine purposes or not, something inside him, his soul, perhaps, trembled and broke out in a cold sweat at the thought of no Maggie in his life.

CHAPTER TEN

The corners of Maggie's sheets were absolutely perfect. Her clean, pressed uniforms were hung in the closet like soldiers at attention. She leaned back against the wall in the room she shared with Helen, satisfied, smiling as she watched her roommate move around like a nervous little bird, fluttering, fussing, and fixing.

The whoosh of the wind outside made the windows of the barracks rattle with its force. It was the end of October and it was growing cold, mercilessly cold, in Trenton, New Jersey. The word on base was that there would be no quick end to the war in Europe. Allied commanders continued to battle the German defenses. General Patton was frustrated because supplies like fuel and ammunition were still inadequate. The makeshift army of mere youth and disabled men the Germans had cobbled together, those Hitler had rushed into service, put up an unexpectedly fierce resistance.

"I can't even put into words how excited I am to be getting out of here in less than a month!" Helen gushed, looking up to Maggie as she made another feeble attempt to produce a regulation corner on the sheets of her bunk bed, the lower of the double-decker. "I'm already giving thanks for Thanksgiving. I bet it's still nice and balmy in Florence. Probably in the seventies, with loads of sunshine!"

Maggie shrugged.

"Don't you hate this cold weather, Mags? A Southern gal like you?"

Maggie stifled a wistful thought of Watkinsville's mild temperatures then felt a tender place inside her as she recalled the wool socks her father had sent several days back, along with a letter describing what Miss Jo was planning for the Thanksgiving menu. She swallowed the truth. "Nope. I love the cold weather here."

Helen shook her head in disbelief. After a few more tries with her bed sheets, she huffed in defeat and sank down on the mattress. "Humph! Well, I can't believe you're staying here for Thanksgiving, and I can't believe you love this freezing cold weather! Only thing I hate worse is bunk inspections. I absolutely *detest* bunk inspections! Who gives a flying fig if the blanket overlaps the sheet by exactly six inches!" She crossed her arms. "Besides not having cold weather like this back home in Florence, we also have a maid. I never in all my days had to worry about the corners of my bed! Don't y'all have maids in Watkinsville?"

Maggie ground her teeth together and looked at the spotless floor. "Well, we have Miss Jo. She's a cook and a maid." She tried not to think of her father opening her letter saying she wasn't coming home for Thanksgiving.

Inevitably, thoughts of him led to thoughts of her mother, and she wanted to keep her thoughts away from her mother at all costs. When fellow WAVES in the mess hall spoke of their mothers and fathers and asked about hers, she would simply say, "My father lives in Georgia and my mother passed away." She would never offer details. She always worked hard to change the conversation to more pleasant subjects.

"Hop up, Helen," Maggie said, tucking a stray strand of hair behind one ear. "I'll do your bed for you."

"Gee, Maggie, thank you from the bottom of my messy heart. I don't think I could have asked for a better roomie."

Maggie folded the corners of Helen's sheets with great precision. Her cheeks still felt a bit warm with the mention of back home. "I like cleaning barracks," she said. "I like bunk inspections, too." This was not a lie. Maggie did love the tidiness, the disciplined nature of the Navy. She had great respect for the standards of behavior, the decorum, and other elements of service life. Whenever it was time for the WAVES Masters at Arms to come around and inspect each room, Maggie took great care cleaning her portion of their room so that it was immaculate. Then she watched Helen like a hawk until she managed to get her side somewhat presentable.

"I know one place in here that's not tidy," Helen said in a teasing voice. "Your foot locker's going to explode if you stick one more letter into it!"

Waves of indignation and irritation filtered through Maggie. "That's none of your business, Miss Smarty Pants!"

"Sorr-ee." Helen threw up her hands. "Didn't mean to upset you."

Maggie did her best to let it go, but the truth was, the unopened letters from William weighed on her mind more than she liked to admit. She could literally feel their presence in her foot locker against the wall, pulsing like a live heart. Time did seem to be easing the tender memory of their breakup, but now and then pangs of longing, of missing William, came in such powerful waves that she was *almost* inspired to read his letters. She had managed to resist so far. She had considered many times just throwing them away, but something inside her couldn't bear to let go of William completely. "You know what, Helen?" she blurted. "I'm getting to where I almost hate mail-call!"

"Oh, hon," Helen said, draping her arm around Maggie's slumped shoulders, "you and I have the exact opposite problem. You're tired of getting all those fat letters, and I'm tired of getting *no* letters. The other thing I hate about this place besides bunk inspections is that mail from our men overseas is slower than molasses on a winter's day." Her wistful sigh said everything.

Maggie leaned her head on Helen's shoulder. She could feel her own heart squeezing up in pity as she searched in vain for something comforting to say.

Helen broke the silence between them. "I'm just going to laugh like a hyena when I see Jasper coming, aren't I, Mags? I'm going to laugh at all my silly fretting."

"Yep," Maggie said, "that's right," all the while thinking, *You phony baloney, Maggie! What kind of a friend are you?*

It was getting harder and harder to believe in Jasper's safe return. Telegrams from the War Department were making appearances all too frequently. Just three days ago, Maggie had almost prayed—for ear plugs. She was sitting on her bunk, sewing a rip in her uniform, when she heard Mary, the girl who lived two doors down, screaming, "I wish I were dead! I wish I were dead!" over and over. Mary's roommate tiptoed down the hall, telling everyone Mary had gotten a telegram from the War Department saying her fiancé had been killed in Germany. The whole floor heard Mary wailing until the doctor on base came and gave her something to help her sleep. Mercifully, Helen happened to be away at the time, and though she'd heard about it through the grapevine, she'd not had to bear the weight of hearing the girl's grief.

Maggie knew that Helen went off by herself and had a little cry of her own after hearing the news. Her eyes were pink and puffy when she returned to their room that evening at curfew. But, like every other night, Helen got down on her knees on the cold hard floor, her head bowed and her hands folded together, as she said her bedtime prayers aloud, ending with a fervent request for Jasper's safe return. Then she climbed into her bunk and said, "G'night, Mags. Sweet dreams."

Maggie had lain awake listening to Helen's instantaneous soft snore. It never ceased to amaze her how full of hope and faith and peace this girl was. Almost made her ashamed of her own nauseous foreboding in regard to Jasper's safety.

But not quite. She knew happy endings were as scarce as the fuel General Patton needed for his tanks. She dreaded the day when Helen would know it too.

* * * * *

The radio in the corner of the lounge was playing "In the Blue of the Evening" by Tommy Dorsey. A group of WAVES invited Maggie to join their bridge game, but she declined. She leaned into the arms of the sofa and chugged back a Red Rock ginger ale, letting the fizzy liquid burn a trail down to her empty stomach. She was exhausted from a long day in the hangar.

At one time, she'd scoffed at obsessively busy people who poured themselves, body and soul, into their jobs. But now— now she was so very glad to be at a naval air station in New Jersey. Right in the crux of things, of a nation at war. Busy. Needed.

Helen's voice interrupted her reverie. "Hey girl, what time's your hot date tonight?"

The question appalled Maggie. "It's not a date! Brent and I have a very professional relationship!" This was true. Maggie knew exactly where things stood between her and Brent Lawton. Completely platonic.

"Sorry, Mags," Helen said, "but you gotta admit, the man's handsome."

"So?"

"Oh, come on now. He's gorgeous. How can you not notice? He works fast too. It wasn't a month ago you told me you were giving up men. But then Brent asks you to have coffee and you can't say yes fast enough. Just goes to show you, our Feminine Club's working its magic." Helen gave a smug little smile.

"You're silly, Helen," Maggie said, dismissing her with a laugh.

* * * * *

Rocky's Tomato Pie was packed. Maggie's hand went up to her freshly washed hair and then to the silky powder on her cheeks as she stood with Brent, waiting to be seated. She almost wished she could run back to the barracks and put on her uniform instead of the emerald green sweater and skirt set Helen said brought out her eyes.

Brent was in uniform, and it seemed everyone there knew him, from the hostess to the waiters. He was a well-respected man, if Maggie judged by the way they all straightened up, practically stood at attention whenever he was near.

"I asked for the best table," he told her. "That one near the fireplace."

Maggie looked across the restaurant in the direction Brent was nodding, at the small table for two, tucked into the shadowy far corner. Her pulse accelerated. She couldn't exactly put into words why this made her feel nervous. Maybe it was just that the table she was used to, the one where she and Brent generally sat, was right smack-dab in the center of the dining room, in the middle of the hubbub.

Louis Armstrong's raspy voice was crooning "Jeepers Creepers" as Brent pulled out a chair for Maggie to sit down then settled himself across from her with his back to the wall.

"Good evening." Their waiter was there immediately with menus under his arm and ice water on a tray. "What to drink, sir?"

Brent ordered a beer, which made Maggie feel even more nervous. None of the men in her life back home were drinkers, and Reverend Peterson had often preached on the evils of drink. On their previous visits, they both had only had coffee. The waiter turned to her. She fumbled with the menu he placed in her hands. "Oh, no thank you. I—umm—sweet tea, please."

When the waiter left, Brent leaned in and smiled. "I bet y'all drink sweet *Southern* tea back home, hmm?" He winked at Maggie, and she felt a warm flush beginning in her cheeks.

Thank goodness for the low lighting in here, Maggie thought, tongue-tied.

"Isn't that what they put in your baby bottles?" Brent leaned back and lit a Lucky Strike. "Satchmo and sweet tea. You ought to feel right at home."

Maggie tucked a strand of hair behind her ear. She was puzzled for a minute until she remembered that Satchmo was Louis Armstrong's nickname.

Maggie found it a little disconcerting the way Brent looked straight into her eyes, and she could feel her palms beginning to sweat. She blotted them discreetly on the cloth napkin in her lap. "Yeah, that's right. Sweet tea in our bottles."

She reached for a warm breadstick, looked up to find Brent's eyes still on her, and said the first thing to pop into her mind, in a voice much too bright for the subject. "Helen and I passed our bunk inspection once again."

"Did you now? That's commendable." Brent narrowed his eyes as he glanced at the menu open on the table in front of him. "What's your pleasure this evening, ma'am?" he asked in that long, lazy, easy-listening Texas drawl of his.

Maggie couldn't think. She sat mesmerized by the play of firelight on every nook and cranny of Brent Lawton's face—those intense dark eyes; that long, straight nose; and that wide, full mouth. Actually, he was handsome, she decided, *if* a girl cared about that kind of thing.

"Ready to order?" Maggie jumped as their waiter set down a tall glass of iced tea with a jaunty lemon slice wedged on the rim. He held a pencil poised above his pad.

Quickly she glanced at the table next to them where a man was gesturing and talking loudly. On his plate was a wedge of steaming tomato pie with the cheese melting off in puddles.

"I'll have what he's having, please," she decided. It really did look good, if a little messy.

"I'll have the same. And another beer," Brent said, nodding at his empty mug.

Maggie cleared her throat. "So," she began cautiously, "you have any updates on Peleliu Island?"

Brent scowled and shook his head in exasperation. "Those sneaky Japs," he said finally.

Maggie froze for a moment. Peleliu Island was where Jasper had gone. After a bit she leaned in and put her elbows on the table, though she knew this was bad manners. This wasn't a date. She didn't have to watch her etiquette. "What are you talk-ing about? We did win, didn't we?"

"Yeah"—Brent took a long slug of his beer—"we won. But when we were fighting there, actually I should say when we were fighting outside of the island and the Japs were fighting inside the island, we ended up losing ten thousand marines. I mean, it was a seventy-day battle and all, but that's an extremely high casualty rate."

"But we won," she repeated, her heart hammering. "At least we won."

"That we did, but you've got to understand, Maggie, when you're up against an enemy as dangerous and unpredictable as the Japanese, your defenses are going to suffer terribly. The Japs are very tricky. I heard our boys were having to stick bayonets into them to make sure they weren't just playing dead. Makes me sick to think of the number of our casualties."

The waiter returned with their tomato pies, and Brent wasted no time polishing off a quarter of his.

Maggie looked down at her steaming food as though it were made of sawdust. She felt no hunger. Actually, she felt rather unwell at the moment, but she forced herself to fork up a small bite and aim it into her mouth. Warm cheese, tomato sauce, and Italian herbs filled her senses. Chewing, swallowing, gulping down tea, she decided to take the plunge. "You know Helen," she began softly.

He nodded.

"Her fiancé, Jasper McCartney, was on Peleliu."

"Really? What's he got to say about the whole awful mess now that it's behind us?"

It was hard to say the next words. "He doesn't say anything. He's been missing in action since sometime in September."

Brent studied Maggie for a long time, a serious expression on his face. "She's heard nothing from the man since September?"

Maggie shook her head. "The ten thousand men who didn't make it—" She continued, her throat constricting a bit. "Did they get every one of their names?"

"They can't. The military tries to positively identify every man when they're evacuating casualties, but it's just not possible. Some are blown to bits and there's no way to know who they are, were. Most of the ones termed 'Missing in Action' generally turn up to be dead when it's all said and done. I hate to say it, but more than likely, if she hasn't heard from him at this point, he's gone."

Shock filtered through Maggie. She couldn't breathe.

"But they haven't found anything," she said after a bit, sounding just like Helen. "They haven't found Jasper's dog tags. They haven't found *any* kind of identification. You'd think if he were dead, if there was a body, they'd have found *something*."

Brent set his beer down. Maggie could see his mind working hard to come up with an answer that would soothe her. "Well, there have been some instances of a soldier showing up months down the road," he said at last. "Somebody who was wounded in action. It's possible he'll turn up. It's rare, but it's possible."

This was something for Maggie to cling to—a military man saying it was possible.

The fire behind her made her too warm now, though she didn't say so. She glanced at a large clock on the wall behind the bar. It was almost eight o'clock. Cigarette smoke wafted in clouds, and the smell of beer overpowered her. Maggie closed her eyes a moment and was thankful when, like a miracle, "Tuxedo Junction," a swingy, fun tune by Glenn Miller, began to play. The carefree sound of the piece lightened the mood almost immediately, and her insides began to uncoil a bit.

She took another nibble of her tomato pie as she watched Brent scraping his plate clean with the side of his fork, slugging down the last of his beer, and leaning back, stretching lazily, then lacing his fingers behind his head. "So, you still having fun in the hangar?" he asked, his dark eyebrows raised.

"I am."

"Nice." He smiled. "You women are an absolute vital part of the war effort. I've met city WAVES, farm WAVES, women who literally *amaze* me with their devotion and their expertise. Doing a man's job, some of them! No way the Navy could defeat Hitler and Mussolini in Europe or the Japanese in the Pacific without you gals. You're heroes."

Maggie basked in his praise. Coming from Brent Lawton, in that Texas drawl and with such sincerity, it took on an almost spiritual quality. With the light from the flickering fire pouring over his face, he seemed almost like some Greek god.

Brent lit another cigarette. "Care for some dessert?"

Maggie looked down at her partially eaten meal and shook her head. "No, thank you." She sipped her tea.

"What's the matter?" he asked, dipping his head toward her plate. "You getting homesick for home-cooking?"

Maggie blinked. His question threatened to take her back to a time and a place she wasn't willing to go. She dug desperately down into her reservoir of safe topics. "Did you know Bob Hope's coming? To put on a USO show?"

"Believe I did hear something about that. I also heard Gypsy Rose Lee's coming to make a bond commercial with a group of singing WAVES." Brent held up his empty glass.

Their waiter scurried over with a fresh, foaming beer. He collected the plates, utensils, and empty glasses. "If I can bring coffee or dessert, just ask," he said, bowing slightly toward Brent before making his way back to the kitchen.

Maggie heard yet another Glenn Miller tune flowing through the air, "Sunrise Serenade," a beautiful slow number that prompted several new couples to move out onto the dance floor. From the corner of her eye she watched them leaning into each other, smiling as they moved. She was glad Brent showed no signs of wanting to dance.

"Tell me, Margaret Jane Culpepper," he said after a bit, leaning forward and arching his brow, "how did you come to join the United States Navy?"

Maggie looked down at her lap. The question seemed a little too personal, and she wasn't sure how to answer it. "Well," she ventured, "I've always been a little bit of a tomboy."

"I can see that. You're a real spitfire, aren't you?"

"It's been said." Maggie smoothed back a lock of her hair.

"I like knowing I'm helping people. You know—fighting for peace."

He laughed. "Isn't that a contradiction in terms? But I know what you mean. I like helping people, too."

"I'm thinking of volunteering at the Navy hospital on my off-days. They've got a huge number of convalescents." Her throat felt tight as she thought of a flier posted on a stall door of the ladies' room outside the mess hall.

Brent looked impressed. "That's mighty noble of you."

Maggie didn't know how to answer. She didn't know if her motives were that noble or not. At least some of her intent to volunteer at the Navy hospital was to keep busy. Escape. Keep running in order to keep one step ahead of things she didn't want to confront.

"So, what do your folks think of all this?" he inquired. "Do they like having their little girl doing a man's job?"

Maggie winced. "My father's fine with it."

"And your mother's crying into her kerchief every night," he teased.

Here it came—the rapid heartbeat, followed by the panicky sensation of falling. Maggie clutched at the table's edge, trying to steady herself. "My mother passed away," she whispered, her eyes closed.

"Oh, hey, Mags, I'm sorry to hear that," Brent offered at last.

Maggie could only dip her head in response. She mentally willed him to change the subject.

"She must have been a special person, to have raised a daughter like you."

Rats! Maggie's heart was pounding so hard she heard it in her ears. *Breathe, breathe, breathe,* she commanded herself. She had to get it together and respond to Brent's statement about her mother, because if she didn't, it would be like saying she wasn't special. She couldn't desecrate her mother's memory.

"My mother," Maggie began in a trembling voice, "was a saint. A pillar of the church. Dedicated, selfless, faithful, loving, patient, pure. She was the kind of person who, if she said she was going to do something, she did it. No person was too lowly for her to help, no cause too humble for her." She paused to gulp, swallowing the taste of memories and death and a past she could not alter by ignoring. "I can't hold a candle to her."

Here came those annoying tears. This was what letting her guard down did. Maggie worked to quell the hot rivers pouring down her cheeks by pressing her napkin to her eyelids, and at last she managed to compose herself somewhat. She sighed, wiping her damp jaw line.

"Are you okay?" Brent asked, leaning forward, his voice filled with concern.

She nodded. The vice grip of grief was gradually releasing her. Had anyone else noticed? She glanced around furtively. No, all seemed to be involved in their own conversations. Weak from the experience, she just sat there a moment, staring at the dancing couples, music spinning carelessly around her.

"I'm fine," she answered finally. "I must have swallowed my drink down the wrong way. Sorry if I alarmed you."

"You sure? Do I need to take you home?"

"No, thanks." Something in Maggie knew that going back to her room right now would not be the thing to do. "It's nothing, honestly," she added, also realizing she wasn't ready to confide in this man. "Guess I'm just a little stressed out about the way this war's dragging on."

"I know. The way I see it the whole darn world has gone crazy." Brent gulped down the last of his beer then shook his head. "I've only been shore-based for three months, and looking at it from here gives me a whole different perspective."

"I bet."

"I hear you're pretty good at your job," he said, a twinkle in his eyes.

"Thanks," she smiled, faking a confidence she didn't feel. "I love my job."

"Yeah," he said. "I've been aiming, living for this, as long as I can remember."

"Really?"

"Mmhmm. Discovered my purpose in life early. I never wanted anything else but to be a Navy man. From elementary school on, all I could think about was getting into the United States Naval Academy."

"And you did," Maggie replied. "I think that's wonderful. You pursued your passion with razor-sharp focus. You should be proud of all you've accomplished."

"Can't really see myself doing anything else." He shrugged. "I'm fascinated with Sewer Pipes."

"What?"

"That's a nickname for submarines," he explained with a grin. "We've got some even funnier names for specific subs. Pigboats are what we call the old type, and Hellcats is our nickname for a group of subs equipped with FM sonar. We use them when we're conducting mine detection missions, when we penetrate the Sea of Japan." Brent's eyes narrowed. "Want to hear what the Germans call their submarine fleet?"

"Sure."

"Ubootwaffe. A single one is called a U-Boat."

"I've heard that one," she said. "There's lots of talk around here about U-boats, and to be honest, I'm terrified of them. Do you believe those stories about Nazi submarines landing spies on Florida's shores? Or the ones that say U-boats are lurking in the Gulf of Mexico?"

"I believe them," he said, shrugging. "But, to be honest, I'm not scared. I think our fleet is superior. I know our men are."

Maggie searched his eyes. He seemed sincerely calm and confident. She marveled at this self-control, this possession of his emotions, wondering if she hung around Brent some more, whether it might rub off on her. Because if she had the kind of attitude that he possessed, everything she was now struggling with could become a thing of the past. Every surge of fear when she thought of her mother's passing, every sweating palm as she sat in the crew's room watching one of her planes in the air, every nervous palpitation of her heart when she thought of Jasper missing in action...

At this moment, Glenn Miller's infectious dance number, "In the Mood," came on. The music shot up through Maggie's feet and she sat a little straighter, turning her head to see the flicker of candles burning on each table. Couples were flocking toward the dance floor, smiling couples who looked like they didn't have a care in this world.

"Want to dance?" Brent looked at Maggie with an amused smile.

"Uh, no thanks," she said, reaching for a gulp of her ice water then just as quickly saying, "actually, maybe. Well, wait a minute. I don't know."

Just as she said this, a log tumbled down from the andirons in the fireplace behind her and bounced against the fire screen, shooting out a spray of sparks like fireworks.

"There's your answer," laughed Brent. "It's telling you to let go and live a little, Maggie. Let's dance." He was already on his feet, a playful look on his face as he held his hand out to her.

Maggie rose, her heart in her throat as Brent led her to the dance floor. He faced her, gathered her into his arms, and she drew a deep breath, holding it in, while at the same time holding herself back a bit and waiting several beats. To see.

Relief flooded her when she realized there was no tingle in her fingertips, no buzzing in her brain at being this near to the man. There was no chemistry between them like there had been with her and William.

Brent moved well with the rhythm of the song, and Maggie allowed herself to be drawn closer to him as she completely gave herself over to the music. They spun across the dance floor, catching admiring glances from the other dancers, and Maggie knew it was all to do with Brent, with his finesse as a dancer and his self-confidence. But still, she let herself get caught up in the admiration, feeling every cell in her body buzzing with energy.

Twirling, spinning in Brent's arms, Maggie realized she'd let go and released all her worries, just for a bit. It felt wonderful, allowing the music, the beat, to drown them out until she was totally lost.

"You know," Brent said, as he spun her around expertly, "last couple of times we've been in here, I've asked you to dance with me and you wouldn't."

She only smiled. *Of course I didn't let myself dance with you. I hadn't learned to trust you yet.*

"Bet you're a pro at jitterbugging," he remarked after a minute.

"Not hardly," she said, smiling up at him even more. "In fact, I've never tried it."

"Well, we ought to enter one of those jitterbug contests they have on base," he said, and her ear was so close she heard the echo of his words within his chest.

"Maybe," she said, feeling light inside.

"Hey, want to spend Thanksgiving together?" he asked when they were back at their table. "I heard you were staying here, and I'm not able to get leave either."

Thanksgiving? Maggie couldn't believe the excitement inside as visions of turkey and cornbread dressing, of green bean casserole, pumpkin pie, and cranberry sauce danced through her mind. "Sure," she said. It seemed that dancing with Brent Lawton had, for a shining moment, set her back into life.

"And speaking of holidays, don't know if you plan to spend Christmas on base or not, but if you do, we could hang out together then as well." He watched her with the question on his face. "May even find us a tree to decorate."

Maggie's heart kicked into high gear. She felt as if she were standing on the edge of a cliff. *Christmas trees.* "Well," she said carefully. "I—I might…"

"I know it's a little early for making Christmas plans," he said. "You just think about it."

Later, as they stepped into the icy air outside of Rocky's, Maggie had the sensation there was a tug-of-war going on inside her. One side said here was her answer to filling those off-days, that free time that scared her to death. The other side was making her feel tender and vulnerable. This was the side that pictured William walking beside her in her mind's eye, that gorgeous dimple in his left cheek when he smiled and the way his right shoulder dipped slightly each time he drew his right leg forward. She wasn't completely sure, but it felt like William's side was tugging a bit harder than the Navy's.

* * * * *

Maggie lay in bed that night and could not sleep. The foot locker full of William's letters seemed more of a live presence than ever. Like they could jump up and say, "Maggie, how could you even think of hanging out with that man for Thanksgiving! Run from this Brent Lawton! I have a feeling he's bad news."

But of course Brent wasn't bad news! He hadn't kissed her, hadn't even touched her except during the dancing. Anyway, as good-looking as the man was, she had absolutely no feelings like that for him. She hardly thought of him unless they were together.

On the contrary, the memories of and feelings she had for William had a mind of their own. They beat right along with her heart, surfacing sometimes at totally unexpected, inconvenient times. Even after such a long time of not seeing him, after working so hard her body ached, she still felt vulnerable to these, well, she guessed *longings* was a good word for them.

Surely she was keeping busy enough, wasn't she? She'd become a WAVE, she'd left the entire state of Georgia, and she was pouring herself into her job as an aviation mechanic.

This must be a night for apparitions, she decided, when she saw Eugenia's face hovering above her cot, saying, "I told you so, Maggie. I told you that you couldn't forget William."

* * * * *

The next evening, Maggie waited until Helen was gone, volunteering at the Navy hospital. With the room quiet, she sat cross-legged on her bed and took out her box of stationery. She doodled in the margins of a sheet of paper for a good fifteen minutes, deliberating over how to begin. It had been a long time since she'd written Eugenia, and there was so much to tell. Or *not* to tell, as the case may be.

November 14, 1944

Dear Genie,

Hope you're well. I miss you so much! I know I told you I'm not coming home for Thanksgiving, but now I've decided I won't be home for Christmas either. My buddy Brent says he likes to cook and that he'll be glad to fix both these holiday feasts for us. I'm really looking forward to some home-cooked turkey and dressing and pumpkin pie for Thanksgiving. It'll sure beat "penny soup," which we have way too often here in the mess hall. It's not literal pennies, just all the vegetables cut into penny shapes with no meat, only broth.

I hope you don't mind if I get something off my chest, but I'm really irritated with my roommate, Helen. I know she just can't help herself, and if I didn't know she was walking such a thin line over her fiancé's continued absence, I'd resign from her silly Feminine Club. Helen keeps on insisting I'm dating Brent.

Genie, as my best friend, I'm telling you, it's totally platonic. Brent and I dance occasionally these days, but we're not romantic at all. I mean, he's kissed my cheek a time or two when we've gone out for coffee or a meal, but it's like you'd kiss a great aunt. I get no swoony feelings, and my knees don't turn to jelly. I mean it, girl, I feel no "carnal desire," as our lit teacher would've called it.

I tried to convince Helen that Brent and I are just friends during the Feminine Club's last Sharing and Victory Time. Picture us, seven girls total, gathered in a circle around a table in the lounge. Tons of giggling before Helen calls the meeting to order. Then we all say our creed together. Here's our creed: "I promise to remain a civilized lady at all costs, to aspire to the ideal of a Christian woman who is virtuous in character, feminine in action, and reverent in worship. To maintain my femininity in a world of combat and aggression. I promise to be modest, sensible, chaste, domestic, kind, and submissive to my husband when I get one."

Believe me, Genie, I leave off some of the words— just move my mouth. After that, it's fairly regimented. Helen should have been an officer instead of a secretary. She has everybody hold hands and she leads a prayer. Group members say aloud specific soldiers they're concerned about. Helen says Jasper's name, of course, with this voice that's trembly around the edges as she asks God to protect him and bring him home to her.

After that we have a sewing lesson and a beauty lesson, then Helen passes out a recipe for us to put in our hope chests. Next is a "Scripture Meditation." This last time it was a verse about fleeing youthful lust.

Finally, and this is when I lost my patience with Helen, we have a Sharing and Victory Time. Helen always asks, "Does anybody have a love hook-up or romantic rendez-vous to report?" This time no one said anything, and I thought we were done and free to go, but Helen stopped everyone and said she had a very big victory to share. She called it "monumental," and I thought maybe she'd heard from Jasper, but she looked straight at me and I knew exactly what she was fixing to say.

My teeth were clenched together so hard, Genie, my jaw ached, and I wanted to grab Helen and clamp my hand across her mouth. But I don't think that would've stopped her. She told the group that Maggie Culpepper, the member who had given up on men, was dating some-one. She said "See, ladies? Our club is working, because Maggie and Brent are one hot item!"

I stood up and told them that Brent and I are just friends, but then Helen said I was sticking my head in the sand. Every single girl in the Feminine Club was nod-ding her head, agreeing with Helen like she was some brilliant psychiatrist! It made me so MAD. But after I had a chance to get out of there, had some time to think things through, it just made me laugh. I know, absolutely know, that Brent's only interested in me for the military talk. I am absolutely safe with him in that department!

Believe me, we're going to have fun spending Thanksgiving together.

Well, I hope you have a nice Thanksgiving. I'm planning to write my father after I finish your letter.

If you see William, maybe you should please tell him, again, that I still haven't been able to read all those fat letters he writes. Maybe you could suggest that he'd be better off to stop sending them? Anyway, I keep wondering how in heaven's name he finds the time if he's going with Betty Hall?!

Hugs,

Maggie

* * * * *

As November continued, the air grew colder, and Maggie was dismayed to find that Brent's steeliness had still not rubbed off on her. When a test pilot came in to take one of the planes up over the bay, to check everything Maggie had worked on before it was added to the fleet, she sat in the crew's room, biting her nails, her mantra still a trembly, "Please, don't let anything I did or didn't do cause somebody to lose his life."

Not that she was praying, because she still couldn't understand how someone who loved people like God was supposed to would allow the pain war produced. Seeing the look on a girl's face when she got word that her boyfriend or fiancé or husband or brother or cousin or other loved one had died in service to his country was all the convincing evidence she needed to believe God didn't care.

Whenever something tugged at her heart as she walked by the chapel, whenever something gave her a wistful sort of feeling, like there was something missing in her life, Maggie would turn her head and look in the opposite direction, at the furling banner of the American flag.

The chapel was always well attended, but Maggie told herself the women only went because they were afraid, and the men went because the women were there.

CHAPTER ELEVEN

Right now, there were only a couple of things in life William Dove knew for sure. One, he'd done a really stupid thing taking Eugenia Peterson's advice, and another, that he was confused about this surrendering stuff Mr. Byrd talked about.

Impatience clawed at him like a mother bear defending her cub as he and Betty were saying their good-byes to Mr. Byrd. He helped Betty up into the truck's seat, shut the door, strode around the tailgate, and hopped in the driver's seat.

He turned the ignition key while Betty was scooching over close to him again, batting her eyelashes, her sultry smile telling him more than any words ever could.

He frowned and gunned the engine, hearing gravel flying out from the back tires as they took off for home. He felt like a pouty child acting like this, but his deep impatience mixed with his confusion weighed heavily on him.

"I had a wonderful time, Will," Betty said as soon as they hit the highway. She turned her great dark eyes to him and licked her upper lip. "I'd love to see more of you."

"Is that right?" He kept his eyes fixed on the road.

"Mmhmm. As a matter of fact, Luvenia's making chicken and dumplings for supper tonight, and I know she wouldn't mind if you stayed to eat with us."

William didn't say anything.

"Will?"

"I believe I'll have to decline," he said in his smoothest voice.

"What?" The way Betty was looking at him let him know she wasn't used to being turned down. "Why?"

"Maggie broke up with me when she left to join the Navy, but I can't stop loving her, and I've decided to surrender everything to God." He paused for a breath. "So He'll bring her home to me. It's like a military strategy, but in a spiritual battle."

Betty looked over at William with wide eyes. She scooted over to the window on the passenger's side and sat there, silent and still, the deepening shadows of dusk covering her as they neared Watkinsville.

"You wouldn't want me anyway," William said with a feeble laugh, slapping a palm on the steering wheel when they reached Betty's house. "With this gimp leg, stuck here tending prickly Christmas trees."

He pulled to a stop and before he could get out, Betty had shoved the door open, jumped out, and was gone, leaving William to stare after her.

* * * * *

Over a week later, on a Sunday afternoon, when he should be having a calm day, surrendering and walking in faith, William hated that his mind betrayed him. Instead of filling his heart with peace about his future, the impatience had not relented. Instead of leading him to green pastures of rest, his thoughts led him straight to the notion that he must call Eugenia Peterson.

A big part of Will knew this was not what putting it into the Lord's hands and leaving it there meant. But a bigger part of him was desperate. He strode to the desk, picked up the black receiver to the phone, and dialed the Petersons' number. He walked with the cord as long as it could possibly stretch and threw open the back door, breathing in the brisk morning air of November as he waited.

"Hello?" a voice answered after seven rings, out of breath.

"Eugenia?"

"Is that you, William Dove?"

"It's me."

A giggle came, followed by, "Well, well, lover boy. How's it going?"

"You need to write Maggie another letter." William's voice was direct. "Tell her that I'm not seeing Betty Hall anymore. This very instant."

"William," Eugenia said, "calm down. It's Sunday. Even if I did write her today, it wouldn't go out till tomorrow. Why don't you tell me what's going on."

"It was an awful date," William said in a voice so fast the words fell all over themselves. "I felt absolutely nothing for Betty, and I hate thinking Maggie's thinking I'm dating Betty. Now I know there's absolutely no other girl for me, and I don't care if all is fair in love and war, I'm surrendering to God so He'll bring my Maggie home."

"You still need to calm down, William, and get a breath." Eugenia's voice was one you'd use with a child.

"Listen to me!" William said before inhaling heavily then fumbling for his next words. "So far I've written one hundred and fourteen letters to Maggie, and I haven't received a single one in return. Something's got to change here."

"William, you're too impatient. Rome wasn't built in a day. I sent the letter. I'm sure Maggie's read it by now, and soon the green-eyed monster will get his clutches into her, and she'll realize just how much she loves you."

"You're not even listening, Eugenia!" William squeezed the phone in his hand so hard it was shaking. He closed his eyes. "I don't *want* her to think I'm dating anyone. Because I'm not, and I'm not going to. Do you understand what I'm getting at?" A wave of despair threatened. "Eugenia," he was begging now, "in your letters from Maggie, does she ever mention me? Does she mention I send her letters? Does she say if she reads them? Is she still seeing that guy you mentioned? You've got to tell me, Eugenia. I need to know."

A stretch of quiet fell between them.

William drew a deep breath. "I'm not stupid. I know girls talk. Maggie doesn't want me because of the polio. Right? She doesn't want a man who's unfit. Crippled." As these words spilled out of William's mouth, everything became suddenly clear. His heart sank inside his chest. "It's not that she's pouring herself into service for our country and doesn't want her attention divided. It's not that she wants time and distance to make sure our love is true. It's because I'm broken." William sagged down to a seat on the bricks. "I'm gimp-legged and pathetic and broken."

He heard Eugenia exhale heavily. "William," she said, "get a hold of yourself."

"I just—I need to know what's going on in Maggie's brain."

"Look, William, you're talking silliness now. Nobody can know, really know, all that goes on in another person's head." Her voice became gentler. "I don't think it has a thing to do with your leg, your handicap, or whatever it is. You know Maggie's not that shallow of a person. If it really means that much to you, I'll write her again, and I'll tell her you're not seeing Betty Hall."

"Thank you, Genie." William released a long breath. "Promise?"

"Yes, I promise. I'll write it today and I'll mail it tomorrow."

William breathed a silent prayer of thanksgiving. A few seconds ticked by as his mind spun forward. It didn't take many moments of contemplation to come up with his next idea for wooing Maggie home. "Eugenia?" he ventured.

"Yes? What is it now?"

"Do you think you might do me another favor?"

"Maybe."

"Well, I've got this letter I wrote to Maggie last night. I was going to mail it tomorrow, but anyway, it's all about this nine-foot-tall Virginia Pine I've picked out for the two of us this year. The most beautiful, perfect tree on our whole farm. Even Mr. Byrd thinks so. The trunk is straight as an arrow, full limbs, shaped beautifully, not a single insect..." His heart was beating fast and furious now. "Anyway, I was thinking, that if you wrapped your letter around mine, the one you're going to write Maggie about me not seeing Betty, if you put it in the envelope with your return address, she'd at least open it." He swallowed. "I don't want to spend a Christmas Eve apart from my Maggie."

"Umm—well, actually, Will..." Eugenia hesitated.

"Please, Genie?" he breathed in his sweetest voice. "It's an invitation to spend Christmas Eve with me."

"All right," Eugenia answered finally, her voice still a bit hesitant. "You can bring it over sometime in the morning, after seven."

* * * * *

After hanging up the phone, William guzzled a quart of tea straight from the pitcher in the refrigerator. He began to pace the front length of the house, his mind whirling like a fan on high speed. He couldn't seem to focus on much besides getting the letter over to Eugenia in the morning.

What can I do until then? He paused to glance out the window at the spindly branches of a dogwood tree. When the thought of heading out to the farm came into his mind, an uneasy feeling formed in his gut, and he tried to talk himself out of it. *It's Sunday, Mr. Byrd's day of rest, and plus, it would be too extravagant since gasoline is so hard to come by.*

William shook these thoughts away. He needed to go. Whenever he felt like a small child who needed consoling, it was walking amongst the rows of beautiful green trees that calmed him. He was having such a hard time with this surrender thing Mr. Byrd had advised, and it felt almost impossible to pray and leave it with God. He could visit the tree he'd picked for himself and Maggie. That always lifted his spirits.

Why am I still feeling so reluctant to go? He paused at the long mahogany dining table to pick up his mother's crystal salt shaker. As he stared at the facets of glass, a startling insight struck him over the head like a two-by-four: *You're scared you'll hear about all that stuff Mr. Byrd calls his "soul travail."*

His mind played over all the teasers he'd heard through the years. Things like, *"God use the dark and the light,"* and, *"He the divine artist workin' to create Hisself a masterpiece fit for heaven."*

But he managed to remind himself, even if it was some shocking event, a staggering horror, lurking back there in Mr. Byrd's past, hadn't God lifted Mr. Byrd up above whatever it was? Mr. Byrd was a happy man. Surely, if it came down to hearing about his soul travail today, it would only bolster William's faith. He set the salt shaker down and plucked the pickup truck keys from their peg on the wall beside the door.

The sun was still high in the sky as William turned off Highway 15 onto the long dirt drive of the farm. He parked, stepped out of the truck, and immediately drew a deep breath of crisp air that smelled like Virginia pine. He held it in his lungs for a long moment, savoring it.

After a bit, he began to walk up and down a row of six-foot-tall Leyland Cypress, their needles a beautiful bluish green, their boughs wrapping around him like heavenly arms. He released a long, contented sigh as his soul filled with the pure, natural wonder of God's creation.

He walked along the strip of grass Mr. Byrd had left to prevent soil erosion between two rows of cedars. It didn't seem that long ago that this part of the farm had been only a wild tangle of woods iced with a lush coating of kudzu. In fact, William was certain he and Maggie had once played a game of Statue right where that cedar on the corner stood.

For an instant, William could feel his younger self, his spindly limbs flailing wildly as Maggie spun him around in circles before releasing him, his body careening to its crazy resting spot. He closed his eyes and saw them sitting beside one another, catching their breath and laughing. He saw her beautiful green eyes, the freckles sprinkled playfully across her cheeks. But then his gaze traveled to himself in this memory. It had been summertime and the deformed muscles in his ankle were as obvious as the blazing sun.

The air flew out of William's sails and he opened his eyes and shook his head, trying to comprehend how one little virus, a *microscopic* virus he should add, could change so much about a person's life. Here he stood, still in Watkinsville, Georgia, while most of the boys from his high school class were overseas fighting—while his Maggie was all the way in New Jersey, serving her country.

Why? Because this unseen virus had somehow found its way in and attacked his nerve cells. He guessed things could have been a whole lot worse than this partial paralysis he'd been left with. Some victims were left in wheelchairs. He should be glad no one he knew of had caught the polio virus from him. That he hadn't died.

This pep talk wasn't exactly doing the trick right now. Not when his consolation for having to stay home, for shouldering the disgrace of being 4-F, should be that he would have his Maggie still here with him. Had she really gone off and joined the Navy for good? That delightful girl—now the woman who had become his very life over the years and who he thought would be his forever—had she actually left him?

She wasn't even going to be here for Thanksgiving. What would he have to give thanks for? This surrender thing was incredibly hard. He wanted Maggie, and he wanted her now, but he'd have to wait for Christmas. He was grateful, at least, that Eugenia was sending his letter, and Maggie would definitely read it.

Stuffing his hands into his trousers pockets, William decided to go look at the tree he'd picked for their Christmas Eve. This particular Virginia pine was the star pupil of its class, and every time he came to the farm it received his special attention. Standing a good two feet taller and at least half again as full as the other trees planted alongside it, it was a stunning masterpiece.

Gently, reverently, William swept his palms down the side of the pine. The limbs felt warm from the sun, and they seemed to glow. He breathed in deeply, smiling. What people said they loved about this particular variety of tree was the *smell*. And indeed, the aroma was indescribable in its rich pungency.

Many customers would accept no other kind of tree, and that was why William's father kept Virginia pines, though the variety was sensitive and required much more work than the others. They needed more shaping and more help fighting off insects.

William stepped back to gaze at the stalwart tree. He willed himself to imagine the trunk in a bucket inside the parlor of his home, wrapped in a festive cloth to hide the container, he and Maggie adorning the boughs with ornaments and tinsel.

In this daydream, a log was burning in the fireplace and there were two mugs of spiced cider on a small card table that also held a box of Christmas decorations. Firelight flickered on Maggie's hair, and when she turned to smile at him, he could see the reflection of the flames like tiny diamonds in her green eyes.

"William, my man!"

The voice startled William from his daydream. He turned, blinking, to see Mr. Byrd shuffling toward him, his face beaming like a light.

"How you doin', son? You okay? Look like you seen a ghost."

William managed a nod. "I'm okay, Mr. Byrd," he said at last. "Sorry I didn't let you know I was here. I was just—"

"You ain't surprise me. I know yo' truck." Mr. Byrd laughed and shook his head. "Fact, I seen you wanderin' along that row of little cedars up close to the cabin, but you so deep in your musin's I ain't want to bother you."

"Yeah, uh, I was thinking about… They're looking good, your baby cedars."

"Thank you kindly, but the Lord get most o' the glory!" He laughed. "I see you ain't got yo' lady friend out here with you today."

Now William laughed. "Nope. I think I scared poor Betty. Hey, I almost forgot to tell you, please don't let anyone cut this Virginia pine."

"No worries. I seen the tag and figgered it was fo' yo' fam'ly."

"Thanks. I've been coddling it, and I finally tagged it last Tuesday, right before you put up the sign for folks to come choose and cut."

"Beautiful tree," said Mr. Byrd, nodding his head. "I been doin' a little extra shapin' on it myself."

"Thanks, sir."

"You welcome. Know what?" He shook his head. "What amaze me is how most folks be surprise to learn trees don't grow into no Christmas tree shape naturally. When I explain it take lots of shapin' and shearin' to get that nice, postcard look to 'em, folks look at me like I be pullin' they leg. I tell 'em, I say, 'Only a rare few can do it without help from peoples.'" He chuckled.

"That sure is the truth, Mr. Byrd. You do a major shearing twice a year, don't you?"

"Mmhmm. May and September." Mr. Byrd looked out

across the farm. "Leyland Cypress the easiest far as the shearin' go, but they can't hold a candle to no Virginia pine far as a nice Christmas smell. No sirree."

They stood in silence for a while as peace from the natural beauty and the smell of the trees washed over William like a gentle rainfall. The farm had certainly been the cure he needed today. Feeling much more relaxed, he decided he could handle heading on home.

"Been nice visiting, Mr. Byrd," he said. "Guess I'll take off and let you get your Sunday rest."

"You ain't got to skedaddle off right away, do you?"

William hesitated. "Uh, no, not really, I guess."

"Well then, come on back to the cabin and let me get you some water and we can visit a spell longer."

The pair headed toward the cabin. After they'd gone about twenty feet, Mr. Byrd stopped dead in his tracks to look hard at William. "You all right?" he asked, his eyes narrowed.

William stopped too. "Why?"

"I ain't never seen you limp that much."

William shrugged. He hated to worry the old man. "Oh, maybe I just didn't sleep too well last night or something. Got lots on my mind, you know. I still haven't heard anything from Ernie."

Mr. Byrd nodded. "You been listenin' to them war reports on the radio too? Can sure weigh a body down. See that flag yonder?" He nodded his head toward the American flag fluttering atop a pole beside the Yule-Tide Shoppe.

William looked that direction. "Yep."

"Well, ever mornin', I go out there and I raise that up in honor o' yo' buddy, Ernie, and every time I see it I raise up a prayer for him."

"Thanks, Mr. Byrd. I pray for Ernie to come home safe too."

"You welcome. I pray for all the fightin' mens. Even pray for the Japanese and the Germans."

William looked hard at Mr. Byrd.

"We s'pose to love our enemies. S'pose to pray for them that despitefully use us." Mr. Byrd narrowed his dark eyes on William. "Our Lord Jesus say that in His Sermon on the Mount."

William prayed daily for Ernie and all the other Army Air Corps fighter pilots. What put his stomach in knots and made it hard to sleep, besides the steady stream of radio reports telling of American pilots who'd lost their lives, was the fact he hadn't heard from Ernie in way too long. He understood what Mr. Byrd was saying about loving enemies, but he knew he could never bring himself to pray for Nazi or Japanese soldiers. However, he managed to hold his tongue as they walked along.

As they passed the shed covering a row of shovels, post-hole diggers, and a small tractor, William noticed that Mr. Byrd was not as spry as usual either. In fact, he was creeping along, wincing with each step.

"How are *you* feeling, Mr. Byrd? Talk about somebody limping."

Mr. Byrd didn't respond for a moment, and William

wondered if he'd even heard him. But after a bit, the old man said, "I 'magine we look like the blind leadin' the blind out here…or should that be the lame leadin' the lame?" He gave a small snort of laughter.

William looked at him and saw that Mr. Byrd's laugh didn't quite reach his eyes. "So, how are you feeling?"

"Be honest, my arthritis been actin' up pretty fierce. I be so stiff this mornin' took me till nine to get myself up out of the bed." He shook his head in exasperation. "Listen at me!" he said, rebuking himself just as quickly. "Complainin' be foolish when you a child of the King."

William knew that getting out of bed "late" probably hurt Mr. Byrd more than the achy swollen joints and the tender inflammation. The man prided himself on being up by six at the very latest every day, including Sundays.

"I'm sorry," William said at last. "That must be hard. Do you have enough of your pain medicine?"

Mr. Byrd nodded. "Mmhmm. Got my tablets, but some-time, sometime all I can do is just wait it out."

They walked along in silence for a while, finally broken by the sound of a hoot owl off in the distance. "Dad says our sales haven't fallen too far this year," William said as they got closer to the cabin, his steps in sync with Mr. Byrd's. "He says we're holding our own. The Yule-Tide Shoppe's doing all right too."

Mr. Byrd nodded. "Praise God."

As they reached the back steps of the Yule-Tide Shoppe, a hawk rose up from a nearby pine and flapped to the pinnacle of the flag pole, perching to look down at them. William's mind flashed to thoughts of some prophetic meaning, but he couldn't imagine what it might be.

"Home again, home again, jiggety-jig," Mr. Byrd said in a playful voice as he led William up the steps. "I know you be thirsty."

"Sure am," William replied as Mr. Byrd closed the door firmly to shut out the November wind, which seemed to be picking up.

Inside the cabin, William noted that a tall wooden folding screen had been added—a nice fence of privacy separating Mr. Byrd's living quarters from the shelves overflowing with Christmas decorations. Mr. Byrd gently compressed this and slid it over to the wall, beckoning William to have a seat at his table. "You just relax. Make yo'self at home," he said, rustling around in the cabinet.

William took a seat.

"Here we go." Mr. Byrd smiled as he set two jars down on the scarred table top then turned to the tiny icebox for a pitcher of crystal clear water he poured into the jars.

"Thank you, sir," William said, lifting his jar to swallow half in one gulp. It was so cold it gave him a sudden shooting pain in his head, but he smiled and swiped the back of his hand across his lips as his eyes wandered around the shop, taking in a shelf full of fuzzy brown reindeer. There were probably a dozen, standing shoulder-to-shoulder, complete with plastic antlers and what looked like red bulbs for noses.

"They light up?" he asked, nodding at them.

"Sho' do. Come with a storybook, too. Imagine we be sold out 'fore December even get here."

William shook his head in wonder. "Those marketing people for Montgomery Ward are brilliant, aren't they?"

"Mmhmm. The chirren love anythin' to do with old Santy Claus, and the mamas lose they heads over Ugly Ducklin' type stories." He lifted his water to take a swallow. "Reckon I got to admit I like hearin' stories 'bout critters who able to overcome when life hand them a hard blow." He looked meaningfully at William.

A little ping of anxiety hit William right along with Mr. Byrd's words about life and hard blows. What was he leading up to? From the corner of his eye, William studied the serene-looking old black gentleman in denim overalls so faded they were milky-blue.

Mr. Byrd scratched a sprinkling of white whiskers on his stubbly chin, looking off into the distance at something unseen. The long ensuing silence settled on William like a ton of bricks.

Finally Mr. Byrd cleared his throat. "You know hows we been talkin' 'bout surrenderin'?"

William nodded.

"Well, first thing I got to say is, sometime when life give a person a hard blow, the Lord don't reach down and deliver 'em out of they troubles. Sometime He give 'em the strength to endure and overcome."

William frowned. More of this riddle talk was not what he wanted to hear.

His silence was all the encouragement Mr. Byrd seemed to need. "Mmhmm. I know I done told you this forty-leven times, but if God ain't answer our prayer the way we want, in the time we want, it may be on account He can see things we ain't able to."

For a moment, William had the urge to get up and leave. But at last he murmured, "Yes, you've told me that."

"When our situation get desp'rate, we think we know what we need from God. We think we the expert with the perfect answer. We like the small chil' in a candy store whose mama say, 'No, chil', you cain't have that Tootsie Roll,' but the chil' don't stop hollerin'. He ain't comforted. He stomp his foot and shake his little fist. We like that, Will. We just tell the Lord what we want, when we want it." Mr. Byrd shook his head.

Ripples of fear spread their way up William's spine. The muscles in his shoulders tightened. "Mr. Byrd," he said with a shaky laugh as he stood, "thank you for the water. I believe I'll be heading on back home now. I know you really need your day of rest when you're battling something like arthritis."

Mr. Byrd's wiry eyebrows shot up. "Don't you be worryin' about me and my arthuritis, son. I been dealing with this for years. Please, sit on back down."

Reluctantly William sank back onto the hard wooden seat. He drew a deep breath, waiting for what, he didn't know.

Mr. Byrd closed his eyes for a moment. Then he slowly lifted his jar of water to his lips and took a drink. At last he gave a nod, opened his eyes, and began to speak again. "I know you done heard most of the stories from my chil'hood, Will."

William nodded.

"About how I be born sometime 'round the year of 1859 and how my folks be former slaves turn sharecroppers. How most of us ain't go to school."

William nodded again.

"You heard 'bout how I fell in love at sixteen, with a beautiful gal name o' Hattie Johnson." Mr. Byrd twirled a scarred wedding band on his ring finger. "Those days be the most beautiful I ever seen." He closed his eyes briefly, his lips in a blissful smile.

"Well, after we marry, we stay out on a cotton farm near my fam'ly. Beautiful life. Simple and plain, but beautiful. Up with the sun, to bed with the moon. Eatin' off the land and enjoyin' each other. Couldn't dream up no more perfect life."

William could feel both wonder and love pouring out of Mr. Byrd.

"Well, twelve years pass with jes' me and my beloved, but then Hattie be in the fam'ly way. We be happy on account of it bein' our dream to have us some chirren. You ain't never seen a more devoted mama when our twin sons be born in 1887. Two strong healthy boys, Abraham and Isaac. Handsome boys."

William smiled because of Mr. Byrd's huge smile. "They look like you?"

"Mmhmm, sho' did. Like lookin' in the mirror." Mr. Byrd chuckled. "Ever'day, I still be thankin' the good Lord He let me enjoy my chirren for goin' on two years. Some folks don't never get no chirren at all."

William's heart sped up and a short stretch of silence fell. "What happened?" he asked at last.

"Well, ever'day come and ever'day go. Things be good. You know, just ordinary livin'. Life ain't perfect, I have to say. Ain't never a hundred percent perfect down here, and we be havin' those regular hassles a body go through, but I ain't had much to complain about. Had me the woman of my dreams, two strappin' sons, plenty o' food, roof over our heads, and work I enjoyed doin' with these two hands. When I look back now, I know I ain't realize what a precious gift each of those days be while I still have my fam'ly on this earth with me. I took too much for granted." He grew quiet again, looking at William with an urgency in his eyes.

For a bit, it seemed Mr. Byrd went far away. William began to feel a palpable presence in the cabin with them, and he searched the room, turning to look around and behind him. There was nothing he could see besides Mr. Byrd, sitting with his eyes closed in intense concentration, his hands lifted slightly off his thighs, palms up and his lips moving silently.

William's heartbeat began to accelerate. Something was telling him he was on the brink of entering into some sacred place that not very many were invited to go. By and by, he noticed small drops of perspiration forming on Mr. Byrd's forehead, his lips still moving in that silent speech. He wondered how long this would continue, at the same time glad for the break.

At last Mr. Byrd let out a soft sigh, opened his eyes, and shifted his weight. "December of 1889 come, and me and Hattie be busy folks—me with my farmin' and her with two rambunctious boys goin' on two years. They was all over that place." He smiled, shook his head, and William spied a glistening tear in the corner of one eye.

"Bet that was a handful," he said softly. "Two of them."

Mr. Byrd took his time in answering. "Yep, a handful. But a joy, you understand?"

William nodded.

"Well, that winter," Mr. Byrd continued, "along come a flu bug. You may know 'bout it from yo' hist'ry class. Believe it had a scientific name o' the Russian Flu. I ain't care what they call it or where it come from, that stuff be evil. Done kill a million folks worldwide."

"Wow," William exhaled, shaking his head.

"The outbreak where we stay at be ferocious," Mr. Byrd said. "My Hattie, she be the first one in our fam'ly get sick. Had the dysent'ry and a fever so high she be burnin' up. I kep' wet washrags by her bed to try an' cool her down."

Again William saw Mr. Byrd fondling the wedding band on his finger. He didn't say anything for a bit, then he swallowed a deep breath and continued. "She still be nursin' Abraham and Isaac, but when she get sick, her milk dry up. They be eatin' solid food, too, but they be hollerin' for they mama. I work like a dog to keep my boys happy, but they ain't able to understand what goin' on. My old mama come to stay and help out. She sit by Hattie's bed with a cup o' water, tryin' to get her to take sips and spongin' her forehead. Long as my wife able to respond when I aks her a question, I believe she gonna pull through. They was some folks who beat that flu, you know?"

Will nodded.

"But, my Hattie, she never get up out of that bed. Just kind o' shrunk up into herself. Her eyes glaze over, and came the time she ain't answer me or my mama when we be talkin' to her. Didn't have no doctor, and I did what I could, you know. I got down on my knees. I pray and pray."

"You prayed," William echoed.

"Mmhmm. I pray to God He won't take Hattie. I stay on my knees till they hurt so bad I thought I ain't never gonna walk again. I kep' telling the Lord, I say, 'Get my wife well. I need my Hattie.'"

Mr. Byrd lowered his voice. "Folks be droppin' like flies in our little town. I kept beggin' the Lord, I say, 'Just let my Hattie get well and please don't let my boys get the virus.'"

He slumped down a bit now, turning his head to look out the window and taking a long, deep breath. "But it seem like heaven ignorin' me when Abraham and Isaac got the fever too. Come down with it within a hour o' each other. I feel the heat risin' up off they little bodies as they be laid up in bed. We fought it, William. I ain't lyin'. Fought it hard, mama and me. Spongin' Hattie an' then spongin' Abraham, then Isaac and back to Hattie. But…" His voice trailed off.

William's mind was whirling as he considered what Mr.

Byrd was saying. He shook his head. He wanted to reject what he knew was coming next.

"My boys pass on 'fore they mama," Mr. Byrd said in a soft voice. "I ain't believe it. Ain't able t' accept it. I remember jest shakin' my head, sayin', 'No, no, no. Not my boys. They jest asleep. They sleep hard, you understand.'"

William leaned forward and put his hand on Mr. Byrd's calloused hand.

"I jest wasn't able t' comprehend it." Mr. Byrd shook his head. "I mean, I done prayed and tol' God He need to heal my wife and keep my boys healthy." He paused and looked at William.

William couldn't swallow.

"Well, like I say, Hattie ain't take in nothin' more'n a sip o' water here and there, an' she be totally out of it when our chirren pass. Believe they call it a coma. But she be knowin', somehow, when the boys pass. I remember she flinch, open her eyes and her mouth, for a little bitty minute. She look up at me and my mama with terr'ble sadness. Then she close her eyes and a tear squeeze out. Still ain't got no idea where that tear come from, her being practically dried up then, but it trickle down into her hair, and it ain't long 'fore I could tell she was fixing to let go herself. I put my head on her chest. I beg her. I say, 'Hattie, don't leave me.' But she ain't hearin', I could tell. She pass on, her fingers grabbin' hold o' the sheet so tight I got t' work t' wrench it away. I climb into bed with her, into our marriage bed, but I know I be alone. More alone than I ever been in my life. Had three bodies, three empty bodies, need to bury."

William managed a deep, quiet breath as overwhelming grief filled his chest. He could not believe the horrors this man had endured. It seemed everything around them was frozen until finally he saw Mr. Byrd rise to open the cabinet and get down a sleeve of crackers.

"'Bout supper time," he declared, setting the crackers on the table with a tin of sausages and a wedge of cheese from the icebox.

William glanced down at the food and looked back up at Mr. Byrd in surprise.

"You realize it be six o'clock?"

"No," William said, his eyes traveling to the window. Darkness was falling outside so that he could barely make out the shapes of the trees.

Mr. Byrd's knife clinked on the saucer as he sliced the cheese.

William felt the rumblings of his empty stomach, but he didn't think he could eat anything. However, to be polite, he took two crackers and a slice of the cheese and put them on the chipped saucer the old man set in front of him. He couldn't think of a single word to say. He was stunned at the peace in Mr. Byrd's face, at the genuine smile he wore as he refilled William's water jar.

"How in heaven's name did you *survive*?" William finally managed. "Your beautiful wife, your sons...*gone*?"

"My faith," Mr. Byrd answered without hesitation.

It sounded too simple. William felt a flash of frustration, or was it anger? "Didn't you get *mad* at God?"

Mr. Byrd took his time making a cracker sandwich. "Son, my emotions be all over the place," he said at last. "I be shocked, scared, standin' way down deep in a black pit o' despair, and I sho' be mad. Fact, I be fightin' mad. From down there in that pit, I hold my fist up and I yell at God. Accuse Him of bein' unfair and tellin' Him to get out my life."

"Yes," William said, nodding hard. He understood this with every fiber of his being. If he had lost his true love like that, if Maggie had died in his arms, he could definitely see himself mad at God.

"Lookin' back, I know I be a baby when it come to my faith. I ain't sayin' I wasn't saved 'fore that, 'cause I believe I had me a genuine faith, enough for *savin'* me, but it be small and weak— sho' weren't no seasoned faith—kind a person get from stayin' with Jesus in the tough times."

William took a sip of his water but found it hard to swallow.

"I'm glad I had me a stubborn preacher. Reverend Gates come to the house day after day, bringin' food, sayin' prayers, and insistin' on reading the Word t' me. He read Romans 8:39 so many times I say it in my sleep. He want me to know, down deep, they ain't nothin'—nothin', not even losin' my beautiful Hattie and my chirren—could separate me from the love of my Jesus. But I still be furious. Still ain't want nothin' to do with nobody who gone let me go through sufferin' that way."

William stared as Mr. Byrd forked up a sausage and ate it in one bite.

"Reverend say t' me that the Lord know I be havin' a hard time down here, and He ain't take it lightly, that He gone bring beauty from ashes." Mr. Byrd shifted in his seat. "But Reverend also say t' me that attitude be everythin' when it come t' turnin' ashes t' beauty. Some folks just turn bitter after a hard time, he say, but the Bible all about surrenderin' to the Lord, and that I needs t' get t' the place where I surrender in my fight 'gainst Him 'fore He could use my sufferin' to change me and make me a better man. But I just look at Reverend Gates and shake my head. I still be furious."

"Yeah," William said, feeling his own anger rising hot at the injustice.

"He kep' on, saying. 'Tyronious, please let the Lord use yo' sufferin' t' make you into a new creation.' Kep' on quotin' Philippians 1:6, 'bout how God be committed t' finishin' the masterpiece He begin in a person."

William sat like a statue as Mr. Byrd crunched a bite of cheese cracker.

"But I ain't studyin' that yet. Still I be walkin' in a evil place fill with empty, sad tears ever' time I realize I ain't never gonna hold my wife in my arms again, ain't never gonna see my boys grow into men." William gazed down at his plate. "Several months pass and still I ain't even want t' leave my house. But Reverend Gates, he keep on. He say, 'Get yourself up out o' this lonely house, Tyronious. Get back t' church. Sing those hymns. Pray those prayers. He'p folks. That's what yo' Hattie would want you t' do.' He also say when 'nough time done pass I might want to find me a woman and get married again, but I tell him I ain't studyin' on that."

Mr. Byrd took a swallow of his water. "By and by, I raise up my head and go out my house to kneel down at the altar of my church t' pray, and when I finish, I look up and my eyes land on the wooden cross sittin' on the pulpit, and a light come on way down deep in the middle o' my heart." He was nodding now. "Will, our Lord know it scary to be down here, and that be the reason He send us Jesus. An' Jesus ain't no stranger t' pain. He know what it is t' suffer. He know what it is t' surrender when He hung there alone on the cross and endure both death and hell for our salvation. And because He been there, He able t' comfort us by His presence. That knowledge fill me up, and that be the instant I feel Jesus kneelin' right there beside me. I know fo' sho' He gonna lift me up above anythin' threaten t' clobber me, and I know He gonna go with me through the valleys, and also He gonna lead me home when it be time—time to reunite with my Hattie and my Abraham and my Isaac."

William stared at him. His brain was going crazy trying to wrap itself around everything.

"Now I ain't gonna lie t' you, son. Sometime the nights still be lonely, and some days seem t' go on forever, 'specially in December, but even then I been able t' find a peace and joy I ain't never experience before my valley—on account I feel Jesus, the Presence, walkin' beside me." Suddenly Mr. Byrd was on his feet walking around the cabin. His eyes grew darker and he began waving his arms heavenward.

William gazed incredulously at him. There was absolutely no evidence of his arthritis now.

"I be testifyin' t' you now 'bout the Presence, son. I am convince that my supernatural peace and my joy go as far and wide as they do *because* of my sufferin'. I got things a happy, carefree life ain't able to give a person—gifts like compassion and a deeper faith. These things be mine *because* of what I been through. From that dark valley I stumble through, the Lord put more of His strength and His love in me. The Presence."

He waited for William to acknowledge this, and at last, William managed a small nod.

"Son," Mr. Byrd said, pausing to place his hands on William's shoulders, "life down here be hard, and what you want may not always be in the plans, and so you got t' place yo' life and yo' dreams in God's hands. Surrender. Hold on t' things loose, and realize maybe somethin' better out there fo' you. If God has a different plan, you need to accept that. Ain't nowhere it say a believer got immunity from the hard times…until he walkin' in the eternal realms, that is. Mmhmm, one day the Lord gonna wipe ever' tear away from the eyes o' those who trusted Him, and ain't gonna be no more dyin' or cryin'."

William felt like he'd been walking through a forest where somebody chopped a tree down and it fell on his head. If it was supposed to make him feel better, it didn't. He knew he ought to set his sights on eternity, but he couldn't do that, not in the midst of his fierce love for Maggie and his desperate worry for Ernie. Mr. Byrd's story was no real comfort after all. "I better be heading on back to the house," he said, his heart booming so hard it shook his ribs.

"Wait. Hear me out, son," Mr. Byrd said as William reached the door.

Something compelled William to stop. Was it the Presence Mr. Byrd talked about? He turned his head.

"It ain't wasted. All that pain."

"Is that a fact," William answered wearily.

"Mmhmm. Now God use me t' comfort others who done lost somebody they love, 'specially these days when so many be losin' folks t' this war. Sometime I be call to help those just startin' out down the road o' sorrow. They he'p me and I he'p them when we cry and pray together. We share sweet memories an' encourage each other. I let 'em lean on me, an' I tell 'em all 'bout what I been through and how Jesus done hold me up. These tears o' mines use to gush up outta raw place. I'm tellin' you they flow gentle now. Soften by the healin' that come with time and the Presence." Mr. Byrd raised his hands again, closed his eyes, and murmured a soft "Amen."

William couldn't get the door of the cabin open fast enough. Sucking in great breaths of crisp evening air, he hurried down the steps and along the pathway. Reaching his truck, he yanked the door open, jumped in, and gunned the engine.

Racing along the highway, William rolled the window down to get even more of the cold air blowing across his face. He was totally confused. He'd been praying to God with all his might, asking Him to bring Maggie home to him and Ernie through this war alive. Now he didn't know what to think, what to pray. His poor brain was spinning with doubt as he connected all of the dots in Mr. Byrd's story.

CHAPTER TWELVE

"This is a really fun tune!" Helen smiled as she bopped to the jazzy trumpet of Louis Armstrong echoing off the cinder-block walls of the rec hall.

Maggie nodded.

"Now aren't you glad I pulled you out of our barracks tonight, girl?"

"Yeah, thanks," Maggie answered over the music coming from a speaker not five feet away from them. "I mean, I know I should come to more dances on base, but you gotta understand, after working ten days on, I need a little time to do laundry and catch up on my letter writing."

A smirk crossed Helen's face. "Ha," she said, "I don't believe that for a second. You always seem to have plenty of energy if *Brent* wants you to do something."

"Stop it, Helen." Maggie eyed her friend. "We're just two career-minded buddies who enjoy discussing our jobs."

"Stop kidding yourself, girl." Helen clucked her tongue. "You didn't even make it to see Bob Hope, because Brent wanted a cup of coffee with you at Rocky's, and Bob Hope's the biggest thing to hit this base since—"

"Hush!" A hint of irritation rose in Maggie. She wished Helen would cut it out with the constant ribbing about Brent. He had not so much as kissed her on the lips, and she didn't ever expect him to. Maggie had only endured Helen's nonsense this long because she knew Helen couldn't help it if romance was uppermost in her mind all the time. That's just how the girl was wired.

In fact, every single female in the Feminine Club but Maggie seemed to be wired that way. They all assumed Maggie was unhappy, that it was a bad thing she wasn't officially going steady. Maggie tried to tell them there was nothing wrong with being a single person. That she chose to be alone. But they simply could not understand.

Her eyes skimmed the crowd of folks lining the walls and sitting at several tables set up on the basketball court. Maggie knew practically every person at the dance. WAVES with shining faces, Navy men who worked side by side with the WAVES, and the marines who guarded the base, because it was on the coast.

There was the scent of various colognes and eau de toilette waters. All the girls had on face powder, their bobbed hair curled in alluring heaps at their foreheads and on their necks. Since Maggie avoided the salon on base, her own hair was not styled, just freshly washed and hanging loose in natural waves to her collarbone.

There was one girl on base, Joyce Dunlap from Ohio, who could have been Betty Hall's twin sister, and whenever Maggie looked at Joyce, her heart sighed just a little at the thought of William dating Betty. She wished erasing William totally from her heart and mind was just a little bit easier than it was turning out to be. But she was afraid he'd always be there, lurking in some corner of her consciousness.

She shook her head to banish those thoughts and made her way over to the refreshment table. Plates of ginger cookies and some kind of orange-colored punch in three long lines of cups was not very enticing, but Maggie knew one thing—it would be a nice distraction from her thoughts of William. She lifted a cup and took a sip of watery punch.

"Hey, Mags," she heard Helen's excited voice behind her, "I heard they're having a jitterbug contest tonight." Helen munched on a cookie, smiling at Maggie in a meaningful way.

Uh-oh, Maggie mused. *Knowing Helen, she'll try and force me out there, no matter that I've got two left feet, no matter I couldn't jitterbug to save my life.* "I'm not staying long," she informed Helen.

"In the Mood" began to pulse from the speakers. A new flock of dancers hit the dance floor, and Helen bopped up and down, snapping her fingers, keeping time with the beat. Maggie fancied she could feel Helen's imminent command to dance with her. It wasn't unusual for two females to dance together. Many WAVES resorted to dancing with one another when men were in short supply.

Maggie smoothed her skirt, trying to think of a reason to excuse herself, but in the same instant Helen looked at her and said, "I had a dream about my Jasper again last night, Maggie. You know, the one where I see him stepping down from the plane, and I have my wedding gown on, and I'm heading toward him, and…"

Maggie kept her eyes focused on Helen's face during the recitation of this recurring dream, nodding and patting her friend's hand, while all the time her own mind was working on coming up with some encouraging words. She'd never mentioned to Helen what Brent told her regarding Peleliu Island— about the fact that they'd lost ten thousand men there.

"Sounds like a beautiful ceremony, Helen." Helen's innocence, her faith, made Maggie bleed from a wound deep in her soul. It really didn't sound promising for Jasper after all this time with no word from him. Maggie believed he was one of the "unknowns," but tonight she managed to stop that thought. "Hey, girl," she said, "I noticed you got your new issue of *Photoplay*. Anything good in it?"

"Absolutely!" Helen gushed. "You can read it after me, but when you're done, I'm planning to bring it to the Feminine Club to let members check it out. You know, like a library?" The very notion lit her face up, and her body visibly relaxed. "Know what else I've got planned for Tuesday's meeting?"

Before Maggie could ask what, Helen was going into detail about how they could use cherry Lifesavers to make lipstick in a pinch.

Maggie listened with a smile, until the rollicking notes of "Boogie Woogie Bugle Boy" began to grab even the wallflower

WAVES leaning against the wall. Maggie was thankful Helen didn't seem to be in a dancing mood tonight. She was planning to quietly slip away once she'd finished her diluted punch.

But before Maggie could take a second sip, she noticed Brent entering the rec hall. He smiled and waved when his eyes lit on her. To divert any more ribbing from Helen, Maggie feigned nonchalance. Turning her head away from the door, she tried to strike up a conversation with Helen. "What's this about cherry Lifesavers and making red lipstick in a pinch?" she asked, saying the first thing to pop into her head.

Helen didn't answer. Her eyes were on the door. "Brent's here," she said, her eyebrows high and a smile on her face. "He never comes to dances with us peons. Must be because somebody *else* is here."

Maggie turned her head just a bit, and from the corner of her eye, she could see that Brent was clearly making his way over toward her. She froze.

"I think we need to show them how it's done, Maggie," said his deep, playful voice behind her, and though she was expecting this, still Maggie jumped.

She turned to see Brent's smiling face, his arm reaching for her. Before she could say, "But I don't know how to jitterbug," he was pulling her out into the center of the dance floor.

She protested. "I've never jitterbugged. I'm not a good dancer."

"Yes, you are, Margaret," Brent said, using his left hand to enclose her right. "Whenever we dance at Rocky's, I can tell you really feel the rhythm. So, just let yourself go. Let yourself feel the beat and let yourself go."

Maggie didn't want to let go. But she had no choice except to draw a shaky breath while the Andrews Sisters sang, "He was a famous trumpet man from out Chicago way," and Brent swung her out, a smile on his face.

She moved her left arm, raised her left leg, and worked to feel the beat of the music. After the first few awkward steps, Maggie was surprised to find she was no longer self-conscious. The beat of the song did grab her. To move this way excited her, as did the approving faces of the other WAVES and soldiers gathered around. They were clapping! This lifted her up, buoyed her above any self-consciousness, and the steps of the dance began to come as naturally as if she'd been doing the jitterbug all her life.

She twirled and whirled and jittered around Brent, at times finding herself almost nose-to-nose with him. As the music sped up, he danced faster, the taut muscles of his legs moving with the rhythm, his broad shoulders bopping while his piercing eyes rested on Maggie.

Was that a different glance than usual? A gleam, maybe? Something pulsed through Maggie, making her feel a bit shaky. *Brent's only a friend*, she lectured herself for the umpteenth time as he swung her body in an arc. *You're just having fun here, Maggie. Ignore Helen's smirk over there. It's silly of you to think William's unopened letters can talk to you and tell you that Brent Lawton is bad news.*

The crowd began whooping as Brent gyrated even more

soulfully. He shone beneath their adulation, circling and twirling around Maggie. The hardest thing for Maggie to follow was the hip motion. She tried to sway, forward and backwards, with a controlled movement of her hips, while keeping her shoulders level and her feet gliding along the floor.

But she was holding her own as the Andrews Sisters wound down, singing, "And when he played the boogie woogie bugle he was busy as a bzzz bee."

"You were fabulous, Margaret," Brent whispered in her ear when the song was over and they were sitting on folding chairs, catching their breath and sipping punch.

Maggie only smiled. Her mind grasped for straws from her collection of war bits. "Know what General Eisenhower said?" she asked, pulling back from Brent.

"What's that?"

"He said, 'There's no such thing as a soldier getting used to combat.'" Maggie's heart clenched and she grimaced, remembering how innocent and idealistic she'd been before she joined the WAVES. She took a great big gulp and continued. "'Psychiatric casualties are as inevitable as gunshot and shrapnel wounds,' is what he said." She stared at couples out on the dance floor moving to "Blueberry Hill."

"Well," Brent said, one eyebrow raised, "American morale in Europe is sinking. The men at the front, along with their commanders, expected the war to be almost over by now, and I imagine it's extra hard seeing their comrades getting blown to pieces."

Maggie shuddered. "It's so sad, isn't it? Here it is, almost

Thanksgiving, and those poor soldiers won't be at home eating a nice turkey dinner."

Brent gave a grunt, nodding his head. "I'll tell you one thing," he said as he leaned in so close to Maggie she smelled the cigarette smoke lingering on his clothes, "I'm glad you're not going home for Thanksgiving."

Did she imagine it, or did he give her a sly wink on the last word?

* * * * *

Maggie opened the door and stepped outside the crew's room, shivering as she walked toward the barracks through biting winds. Temperatures had been in the low thirties all day long and she still could not believe how cold New Jersey was in November. She wondered if she'd ever adjust to her new state. Georgia had been a totally different affair; most days she was fine in just a simple blouse.

Her body ached from jitterbugging last night, and to make things worse, she'd tossed and turned all night with thoughts of the war and all its casualties swirling through her mind like leaves in a windstorm.

Working usually numbed her mind, and today she'd poured herself into a line of Avenger Torpedo bomber planes that came from the nearby General Motors plant. During wartime, the plant had ceased making civilian vehicles and was producing these bombers for the Navy. One of Maggie's jobs was to make sure there were no problems with the planes that came from the factory. She and the other sailorettes in the hangar went over them with a fine-tooth comb to make sure they were absolutely perfect before they went to the fleet.

Most days they gassed the planes up, oiled them, and checked their brakes, but test pilots were coming tomorrow to take the planes up, to fly them out over the bay. Then they'd bring them back so that Maggie and the other WAVES could check them a second time.

Only when the pilots gave the okay could the planes leave Mercer Field. They were flown to a base, such as the one in South Carolina, and then down to Florida, and then on to the fleet.

Today's job was checking and fixing brakes. Planes from the factory needed to be absolutely perfect in order to land on very small areas. If one wheel pulled more than the other, the task of landing was impossible. Maggie focused all her energy into this, and when four o'clock finally arrived, she was bleary-eyed. She didn't feel like going to chow, or to the lounge, or even to the showers for her evening routine. All she really wanted to do was go straight to her bunk and crawl in.

Maggie was on her way to do just that when she heard Helen's enthusiastic, "Hey, Maggie, come here!" Her hopeful smile beamed out from the group of girls waiting at the desk for the postmistress to appear with today's loot. She waved Maggie over beside her to wait. Mail-call was the highlight of the day for Helen.

Maggie knew it shouldn't surprise her anymore to get frequent fat letters from William. But something in her always felt sad and a little guilty about the amount of money she knew he was wasting on postage, and even more, the time he was wasting on writing. Her father's and Genie's letters stirred up enough twinges of homesickness for Maggie to deal with, and even her pity for William was not enough to make her break her resolve to ignore his letters and to stash them unopened in her footlocker. It was purely a matter of self-discipline, she liked to tell herself whenever she grew sad about William's inability to release her.

"What'd you get?" Helen gushed when all the mail had been distributed and Maggie had something in each hand.

"One's from my father, and the other's from Genie," Maggie answered. She opened Eugenia's letter as she stood in the hallway. A piece of legal-sized paper was wrapped inside Eugenia's monogrammed stationery, and Maggie unfurled it, squinting at the familiar writing.

"What's all that, Maggie?" Helen leaned over, peering hard at the sheet, full, front and back, of William's spidery script.

Confusion twisted Maggie's mind a moment before an inward cringe gripped her. Her face blushed so hot she knew it must be nearing fuschia. Eugenia was dead meat! *Well, I'm sure not going to read this letter from William.* Maggie stuffed everything into her coat pocket. *I may not read Genie's either! It looks like my very best girlfriend in all the world has betrayed me. Someone I trust—well, trusted!*

"Come on, Mags," Helen urged. "What's his name?"

Maggie scowled. If her roommate's smile got any wider, her face would crack in half. "It's private, Helen," she muttered, heading toward the stairway.

"Hey, want to go to the commissary with me, Maggie?" called a voice. It was Phyllis, Maggie's friend from three doors down the hall. She was a pleasant, kind girl from Philadelphia, and as a rule, Maggie enjoyed talking with Phyllis as she smoked her Camels outside the commissary.

"No thanks," she managed over her shoulder. "I'm so exhausted, I'm even skipping chow tonight."

"You skip chow too much, Mags," Helen chastised.

Maggie shrugged, trudging up the stairs, musing on the three letters practically pulsing in her pocket. She opened the door to her room and flopped down on her bunk. She closed her eyes, willing sleep to come and carry her away. But it was like the letters were alive. They were practically calling her name, and she knew she was not going to be able to ignore them out of existence, knew she wasn't going to be able to get a bit of rest.

Didn't she owe it to her father to at least read his letter? Sighing, Maggie sat up and reached into her coat pocket to pull her father's letter out.

November 3, 1944

Mr. Robert Culpepper
Watkinsville, Georgia

Dear Margaret Jane,
 It sounds like you're working hard there at Mercer Field. Your Aunt Marie reads your letters when she

comes by the house to check on me. She's still mad at me for letting you go off and join the Navy, but I told her I really had no choice, that you're a headstrong woman.

Maggie paused and smiled as the deep baritone of her father's voice floated up from the page.

You say the weather in New Jersey is cold. The temperatures here in Watkinsville are still fairly warm. We don't even need to have a fire but perhaps once or twice a week yet.

Maggie shivered, unfolding the wool blanket at the end of her cot and pulling it up around her legs.

It is my understanding you aren't coming home for Thanksgiving. This is regrettable as it will get mighty lonely here during the holiday season without you and your mother. However, Miss Jo found your mother's stash of family recipes, and she assures me she can fix a Thanksgiving feast the way I'm used to. Miss Jo also claims her green thumb will come in handy when spring comes around. She knows roses as well as your mother did.

Maggie's eyes rolled along these sentences, her heart plunging with every word.

I'm looking forward to seeing you at Christmas.
I must sign off now as it is late.
    Love,
    Father

Maggie's teeth chattered as she refolded the letter and slipped it back into her pocket. She stared numbly at the ceiling, pulling the blanket higher, tucking it around her neck. Her father's words had caught her off guard, and with eyes wide open, she lay still as waves of sadness and longing began to crash without mercy.

They began with a memory of Maggie kneeling beside her mother in the garden, her face buried in the center of a peppery-sweet rose as her mother hummed while snipping spent roses from the vines. Then came a beautiful vision of a slice of her mother's famous pumpkin pie—wafts of nutmeg and cinnamon so real Maggie could smell them. She thought she had safely buried her memories.

Her eyes tingled with tears and a longing filled her heart so that it physically hurt. She yearned to return to that place in her life, to the little girl she'd been, basking in the love and attention of her mother. To the little girl who believed in a good and loving God who held them all in the palm of His hand.

No, Margaret Jane Culpepper, she scolded herself. *That girl is gone forever. You're a grown woman who has found herself at last. You don't need Watkinsville, and you certainly made the right decision to stay here at Thanksgiving and Christmas if this is what you get just by reading a letter.*

Even this self-admonishment didn't totally subdue the hurt Maggie felt inside when she thought of her father's admission of loneliness. As much as she longed to see him, to bring some joy to his holiday, she couldn't risk going back to Watkinsville. She decided she would keep in touch better by writing him more frequent and longer letters, making him a special Christmas card, and phoning him on Thanksgiving and on Christmas day.

Maggie checked her wristwatch. It was chow time, but instead of heading to the mess hall, instead of gathering her hygiene items and heading down the hall to shower, she slipped off her bunk, hung her coat in the closet, turned off the light, climbed back into bed, set her jaw, and prepared to sleep.

The room was dark and quiet, but instead of sleeping, Maggie tossed and turned until almost nine. Helen was still not back, and with curfew at ten, Maggie figured she'd be gone for another hour. Lying on her bunk, still as a stone, she could find no peace.

Her mind turned to thoughts of her high school literature class and Edgar Allan Poe's story "The Tell-Tale Heart," where a murderer hides a body beneath the floorboard then hallucinates that the dead man's heart is still beating. She understood that tale now. She could feel the presence of those two unread letters still in her coat pocket, in the closet.

It was hard to believe Genie had betrayed her. It was bad enough that in her last letter Genie had written about William and Betty Hall dating. Images from that had been following Maggie around like her own shadow.

Wait a minute! Those images were uncomfortable, yes, but weren't they necessary? Confronting thoughts of William dating another girl was definitely a part of leaving the past behind. Maybe Genie was doing what a best friend should do. Maybe she was being loyal and true, helping Maggie move forward.

As soon as this realization sank in, Maggie had yet another epiphany, which made her spine tense up so hard and sudden that she gave a little cry, followed by a nauseous feeling rolling through her. She knew, inside, in that deepest part of her, that William was writing to tell her he'd fallen for Betty Hall. This was his announcement, declaration, whatever she wanted to call it, that he'd found love. William loved Betty Hall and he was just the kind of person who would feel it was his duty to personally write and tell Maggie. What if he were writing to say he was marrying Betty?

Maggie jumped out of bed. She stood at her closet, running her fingers along the seam of her jacket pocket, tracing the outline of the letters. Of course that was it. Why had she taken for granted that it was a love letter to her? She was a fool, a vain fool, to think it was all about her.

She slumped down onto the cold floor. Why was she feeling so torn up inside? After all, she'd been the one to tell William good-bye. Wasn't her deepest desire to remain single and pour herself into serving her country? *Of course it is*, she thought, convincing herself the tension clenching the muscles in her shoulders couldn't be fear or disappointment as she reached into her pocket for the letters.

Dear Maggie, she read in Eugenia's curly hand, *I miss you so much. I wish you were coming home on leave for Thanksgiving, but I totally understand.*

Bless Eugenia's heart, Maggie thought, pausing to let out a big sigh of relief before she read more.

The days are short now and the goldenrod is blooming. There are acorns galore and I know that's why the squirrels are so fat. I'm kind of fat, too. Been drinking a lot of Coca-Colas. Laney's fine. I am working at the grammar school, in the office, part-time. I hope you are staying warm. I am so proud of you, helping our country the way you are. I'm sorry if I fussed at you about going. Guess that was selfish of me, but I sure do miss my best friend.

Maggie let out another huge breath.

Speaking of friends, the Haygoods have gotten no word from their Ernie. Please Maggie, I know you're mad at God and don't think He cares, but would you please, pretty please with sugar on top, lift our Ernie up in a prayer? His parents are sitting on pins and needles waiting to hear from him. Well, guess I better sign off and get this in the mail.

Much love,

Genie

With a frown, Maggie put her chin on her chest, closed her eyes, and said a hasty prayer for Ernie. Not that she believed God would listen but just to get that request off her conscience. She began to re-fold the letter to slide it in the back cover of her journal with all her other Eugenia letters.

But wait a minute. What was this teeny-tiny P.S. written in pencil at the very bottom about? Maggie shook her head, bent closer to squint at the words, her mouth opening in a startled O as she read:

I have to tell you something because I promised William I would. He's not dating Betty Hall. In fact, I'm the one who talked him into asking her out in the first place. It was all to make you jealous. But then, when he did go out with Betty, she said he told her he only loved you.

Maggie bit her lip so hard she tasted the metal of blood. She crushed the letter into a ball and threw it across the room. Eugenia was nothing but a two-faced liar! First, she'd lied about Betty Hall and William dating, and then, then, she'd slyly enclosed William's letter with her own!

Well, Maggie wouldn't read it. That would show them. She climbed back into her bunk and lay in the dark, eyes shut and wide awake.

Maggie heard Helen come in at 9:40 then leave shortly after. Soon she returned and knelt at the edge of her bunk, prayed out loud, climbed into bed, and fell instantly asleep, her soft snores sounding positively serene.

Maggie clenched her blanket. She gritted her teeth. The nerve of Eugenia! After a long, restless stretch, Maggie flipped over onto her stomach, but things were no better in this position.

So much for sleeping tonight, she thought, allowing her mind to travel backward to that day at the recruiting center. She mused on her impulsive decision to join the Navy, to leave Watkinsville, to journey alone all the way up here to serve her country. Hadn't she begun with only her fierce determination? Surely that would be enough to carry her through.

You're strong, Maggie clucked to herself, *and nothing William has to say in that letter can get to you and crumble your resolve so that you go running home, your tail tucked between your legs. May as well face the music.*

With a resolute breath she climbed out of bed. Tiptoeing across the freezing floor, she opened the closet, removed William's letter from her coat pocket, and slipped into her chenille bathrobe.

She made her way to the bathroom down the hall. It was quiet and still at this wee hour of the morning, and as she sat down, a little jolt of coldness from the closed toilet lid hit her even through her PJs and her robe. Ignoring this she unfolded the letter and began to read.

My Dearest Maggie Jane,

I am so thankful to God that you're reading this letter.

Maggie had an impulse to crumple the letter up and stuff it in the wastebasket beside her. She drew a very deep breath, clenched her teeth together so tight they hurt, and continued to read.

I haven't been able to sleep for two nights running because I keep remembering that night at the Varsity Drive-In.

Against her will Maggie recalled the sound of William's sweet Southern drawl speaking her name as he professed his undying love. She recalled the way his soulful brown eyes lit up at the sight of her wearing that reindeer pin he'd given her. The one sitting right now at the bottom of her sock drawer.

The feelings I expressed to you that night have not changed. In fact, they've gotten stronger. I love you more than life itself. I'm sure you know by now that I had a date with Betty Hall. But please let me explain. In the beginning, it was only to get you jealous so you'd want me back, and that was stupid, I fully admit. I've got to tell you that Betty doesn't hold a candle to you, my love. I felt absolutely zero for the girl.

Maggie studied these lines for a long moment, let them wash away all those ugly images she'd had of William with Betty. It was calming to have those mental pictures destroyed, though she was loath to admit it.

Anyway, I'm writing you for several reasons other than confessing my sins. This letter's also an invitation to you to come home to decorate the most beautiful, pick-of-the-tree-farm Virginia pine on Christmas Eve. I'll play our song. You know, Bing singing "I'll Be Home for Christmas."

Maggie Jane, we haven't missed a Christmas Eve together since we were seven years old, and it breaks my heart to think you won't be here for Thanksgiving. Please know that it would mean the world to me if you came home for Christmas. I'm not asking you to stop being in the WAVES or to leave your Navy career. If that's impor-tant to you, then it's important to me. I'm just asking for a little time at Christmas so I can hear your sweet voice and see your beautiful face and just be near you. Please don't cut me out of your life. I really don't want to live without you, even though Mr. Byrd says I'll have Jesus by my side no matter what you decide. I have times when it hurts to pray. Literally hurts.

Maggie drew a sharp breath. "Drat!" she said so loud it star-tled her. The boy sure did know how to make her feel guilty, didn't he?

Well, anyway, that's what this letter is all about—inviting you to come home for Christmas. If you don't want to do it for me, then do it for your poor, lonely father and for your best friend, Eugenia, and oh yeah,

Mr. Byrd. Mr. Byrd really misses you, and December is a hard season for him to get through because of some things in his past.

Unfair! she wanted to yell. She bit her lip, pulled her knees up, wrapped her arms around them, and sat in a cold little lump on the toilet seat, every atom of her tense body straining to block the memories.

So much for being strong, she thought as the tears fell like rain. She reached a trembling hand out to grope for a few feet of the scratchy toilet paper to catch them before she read William's closing lines.

Let me know what you decide, Maggie Jane. Either way, know that I'll love you forever with all my heart, and that I'll love no other, and I'll leave this world loving only you. I adore you, my beautiful darling soul mate.
    Yours forever,
    William

* * * * *

The next morning, Maggie was out of bed, feet on the freezing floor, before her alarm went off at five. She hadn't slept a single wink, and instead of her usual routine of a hot shower first thing, she pulled her uniform on in a daze and trudged toward the chow hall through bone-chilling darkness.

When she stepped inside, not even the aroma of coffee or the overhead lights warmed her. Like a robot, she moved along the serving line, her raw eyes barely seeing the eggs, the potatoes, and the toast she placed on her tray.

She sat down at a long Formica-topped table and poured a third of a glass of milk into her coffee. Tipping her head back, she guzzled this down and set her mug down with a loud, unintentional *thwack* on the table.

"Hey, you okay?" Joyce, who was sitting across from Maggie, rose slightly in her seat.

"Yep."

"Really?" Joyce asked a bit later, leaning forward to touch Maggie's wrist. "Are you really, truly okay? You look terrible. Maybe you ought to go to the infirmary. You're all pale and your eyes are sunken in."

"I'm fine," Maggie said tersely. She hunched her shoulders up, ducking her head down. The shock of William's letter, mixed with pure exhaustion, had all but robbed her of her manners. Tears of frustration burned just behind her eyeballs, and she shut her eyes to stop them from coming here in public.

The background murmur of a dozen conversations began to fade into nothing as Maggie felt herself slowly slipping into a hazy kind of sleep. At first, she determined to fight it, but then, from somewhere, came the notion that if horses slept standing up, she ought to just give in and let the Sandman come. Her last cognizant thought was the hope that she would not flop face forward into her food.

She did, indeed, remain upright, but along with sleep came the firm, real yearning to be with William. This desire trickled to life inside her in the form of a dream she couldn't will away. Maggie entered the dream, actually the memory, of a place she'd been time and time again, her senses filled to overflowing.

First, she saw a fire crackling in a brick fireplace. It cast a soft glow in the Doves' living room. Then she took in fragrant gulps of air laced with clove and cinnamon and pine, her eyes traveling to the spot where William stood. She noted his shape, strong and handsome, standing just in front of the impressive Christmas tree between two floor-to-ceiling bookcases full of books.

Moving closer, William smiled and held out one end of a long string of popcorn kernels for Maggie as he secured the other end to a branch near the top of the tree. Once that was done, he beckoned to her to drape the strand around the tree.

This was so familiar; a scene she'd lived year after year each Christmas Eve, that beautiful sense of holiness mixed with expectancy. She reveled in the warm kiss of the fire on her legs, the mugs of steaming mulled cider waiting as they decorated the tree, tree lights glowing in the dark, and with every breath the vivid knowledge that here was happiness and security and beauty in a world that could sometimes seem scary.

"Maggie, Maggie! Wake up!"

Maggie blinked. She turned her head and looked into Joyce's face. Joyce was standing beside her now, holding her by the shoulders, an expression of surprise mixed with fear on her face.

"You fell asleep hard, girl. You really scared me," Joyce said. "Took me awhile to get you to wake up."

"Uh, uh, I—" Maggie felt the coolness of a bit of saliva at the corner of her mouth as she tried to think of an answer. She shook her head, but the specter remained, that image of herself and William.

"Margaret, I really think you ought to stop by the dispensary and at least let them have a look at you."

Maggie didn't answer. She rose and walked to the shelf where trash and dirty trays went then strode through the door, holding herself together until she was outside.

* * * * *

Maggie pulled the bed sheet off her face, opened one eye, and watched Helen enter and pull the door to their room closed behind her.

"Hey girl," Helen said, smiling as she tugged a muffler from her neck. "Whew! It's so cold out there I feel like an icicle. I cannot wait to get some good old balmy South Carolina air next week." She plopped down on a chair to unlace her shoes. "I heard you're feeling poorly today, Mags, and I hope you'll be feeling better for our Feminine Club meeting tomorrow. I brought you some crackers from the chow hall." Helen reached into the pocket of her coat and pulled out four saltines wrapped in a napkin. "I'll put them right here next to your pillow, and you be sure to eat them, because you need to get your strength back. I wouldn't want you to miss our meeting for the world."

"Thanks," Maggie said, smiling. Helen had a motherly quality it was hard not to respond to.

All day, since her embarrassing moment in the chow hall, followed by a trip to the infirmary, then lying in bed, Maggie's passion for William lived on in her consciousness. It felt like a giant magnet pulling her toward him, and the most horrible thing of all was that, because of her exhaustion, she couldn't trust herself to work on the planes. Because of this, there was absolutely *no* distraction from her thoughts.

Part of Maggie had wanted to lie to the nurse and tell her that her dear, dear friend had been killed in battle, so that she might get some kind of I-don't-care drug. But then she'd gotten scared this might jinx Ernie, or Jasper's return to Helen, so she didn't.

"Are you feeling any better at all, hon?" Helen was saying, a concerned look on her face as she petted Maggie's forehead.

Maggie nodded. "I'm sure I'll be fine, Helen. Just some kind of little bug that rest and crackers ought to cure." *The William Bug,* she ought to say, but there was no confiding about William to Helen. To say it aloud was to give it reality.

"Poor, poor baby," Helen said. "I'll go get you a ginger ale from the lounge if you want, Mags. That's what helps me when I get a bad stomach on account of fretting about my Jasper." She sighed and shook her head. "Whenever I start feeling all urpy, I go get me a ginger ale and give myself a rousing little pep talk, and everything's all better. I mean it, girl. Then I just laugh at myself and my silly worrying. I know Jasper's coming home to me, and I start planning the wedding again and naming the babies we're going to have. I'm planning on at least four."

Maggie watched as Helen's face softened.

"Don't you want yourself a whole houseful of babies?" Helen hung her coat in the closet. "I want two girls and two boys. Caroline and Annabelle, then Jasper Junior and Henry. So, what do you think?" She spun around, waiting for Maggie's answer.

Maggie felt a horrible sinking feeling in her chest. Helen's hopes were far too high. Who knew what the future held? She shook her head, remembering how it felt to have her mother ripped from her grasp like a favorite blanket from the arms of a child in need of its comfort and security. "Nope," she said in the next breath. "No children for me."

"Oh, Maggie, hon." Helen wrinkled her nose. "You keep saying that, but deep down I bet you want a passel of babies. Every woman wants babies. It's our natural instinct." She paused for a moment to take Maggie's hand in hers for a squeeze. "Well, you do need a man first." She giggled. "Speaking of that, who was that letter from you got yesterday?"

Maggie could feel her jaw tensing. "Helen, I don't need children and I don't need a man. I told you, I've got the life I always dreamed of. I am blissfully happy."

Helen gave an indulgent sigh, as if to say she knew Maggie wasn't in her right mind at the moment.

Just as quickly, Maggie's own words began to trouble her just a little. Was she happy? Before the letters yesterday, she'd been proud of her self-control, her discipline. Now she was afraid there was a crack forming in the dam. Reading her father's, and then William's, words had taken her to some painful places in her heart.

Helen released Maggie's hand with a final squeeze. "Guess I ought to scoot, hon. My bridge game starts in five minutes. You eat your crackers, and after my game, I'll bring you a nice cold ginger ale. We've got to get you well before our meeting."

"Bye," Maggie said, swallowing hard.

Helen shut the door behind her and the room grew silent. Maggie missed Helen's compassionate face and the feel of her warm hand. She tried to put her thoughts on work, picturing herself on a day there'd been ice on the runway and she'd had to go out at 4 a.m. to chip it off.

This strategy worked for a good fifteen minutes, but then Maggie felt a little bud of want and longing beginning to unfurl inside. "Stop it!" she cried, disgusted with herself. She told herself she was so exhausted that she was only feeling nostalgic for the kind of life she'd lived in the past. A life that no longer existed, no longer was possible. Time was moving on, and time was her friend. If she could just hang on, keep up her disciplined life in the Navy, time would eventually work its magic. It would soften the edges of the past until she'd totally forgotten both William and her mother. She'd already forgotten God, hadn't she?

Maggie smacked the bed with her open palm at this realization. This surge of energy seemed to rejuvenate her. She sat up, ate the saltines, patted down her frazzled hair, and climbed out of bed. She was determined to keep her defenses up, her thoughts and her emotions under strict control.

* * * * *

The next evening, Maggie reluctantly made her way to the lounge. When she pushed the door open, she saw a billowing cloud of cigarette smoke hanging over six girls who were seated at a table, chatting and giggling at the top of their voices, until Helen spied Maggie and stood up.

Helen banged a makeshift gavel made from a broom handle on the table. "This meeting of the Feminine Club will now come to order!" she belted out.

Instantly, the girls hushed. Maggie noted that Helen's blond hair was freshly washed and curled into a perfect sculpture, her lips a red so shiny they reflected the overhead lights.

"Now that we're all here"—Helen looked pointedly at Maggie—"let's say our creed."

Maggie squeezed herself into the empty folding chair between two of the girls. Glancing down at a piece of paper on the table, she saw a recipe for squash casserole written in Helen's curlicue letters. Glossy copies of *Photoplay* and the *Saturday Evening Post*, along with a Whitman's box of chocolates, were the centerpiece.

Maggie winced at the thought of the creed, a creed she didn't agree with at all. But swallowing hard, she joined in the enthusiastic chorus of voices by only mouthing the words.

"I promise to remain a civilized lady at all costs, to aspire to our ideal of a Christian woman who is virtuous in character, feminine in action, to maintain my femininity in a world of combat and aggression. To be modest, sensible, chaste, domestic, kind, and submissive to our husbands…reverent in behavior…"

"Okay, ladies," Helen said, sitting down when they'd finished, "let's join hands and pray. Now remember, when I get to the point where I lift up our servicemen and I pause, each of you say out loud the name of whoever's on your heart. Okay?"

The girls all nodded, except for Maggie, who mentally rolled her eyes. *Here it goes again*, she thought to herself, *another useless ritual.* Dutifully, she dipped her head so that her chin rested on her chest, her eyes still open as a hand on either side reached for hers.

"Oh, gracious Heavenly Father…" She listened to Helen's soft, reverent voice, and she had to admit it was a soothing sound that seemed to chase the chill out of the room. "We come before You to ask You to help us live our lives so that they reflect Your love to others every day.

"Especially, Lord, since we are Navy ladies, military ladies, we lift up our military men. We lift up those men who have been wounded in action, and we ask that You bind up their wounds. Heal them, Father. And Lord, be with the families and the loved ones of those who have been lost to us. Comfort those left behind to grieve. Strengthen their hearts. And You know, Father, that some soldiers are haunted by what they saw, or what they had to do on the battlefield. It's not their bodies that are hurting. It's their minds. Lord, heal those emotions, and when they bring the ones who are wounded, in body or in mind, to the Navy hospital, help us ladies who are volunteers there to be bearers of Your love and Your healing. At this time, Lord, we lift up these names especially." Helen paused, drew in a quick breath, and said in a trembling voice, "Jasper McCartney."

A cascade of other names fell from the lips of those in the Feminine Club, and Maggie felt her muscles tighten like steel as she listened to each member asking God to keep a certain man safe.

Maggie knew that these girls in the circle with her only believed God was listening because they were afraid, but still, her heart ached at the pain she heard in each syllable, in the lingering sniffles. Suddenly this ache turned into fury. A fury that grew so strong Maggie wanted to spit. She was angry at the loss of lives from the war. She was angry at this useless ritual of prayer.

Part of this anger washed over into thoughts of Helen and Jasper. Wasn't Helen being foolish? Hadn't she brought this possible grief on herself? Why get involved with a man in a dangerous occupation? Losing your fiancé in the line of duty was not exactly unheard of. Should Maggie even allow herself to feel sorry for Helen, after the girl so knowingly allowed this risk?

The thing was, love always involved risk. Someone could get hurt, and Maggie was the only one here with any brains. Her goal was to steer clear of any relationship. She didn't care if he was 4-F and working on a Christmas tree farm in Watkinsville,

Georgia. She didn't care if he was thousands of miles away from the bullets and bombs of enemies. There was still a chance William Dove could get hurt, could die. Shoot, eventually everyone died. Nobody made it out of here alive.

Maggie's face grew hot as she listened to more names being lifted up, and as she thought of what Helen often said. Just like a parrot, she'd say, "God drew me and Jasper together, and God will work things out." So simple-minded! Maggie fumed silently as the names continued to be called out amidst tears.

Her fury grew as she thought about her ex–best friend's deception. Two times! Just to show Eugenia, Maggie vowed as she sat there not to read any more of her letters either, and not to write her anymore. Her mind shifted to William's invitation for Christmas Eve. He'd asked that she answer him one way or the other, but hadn't she made herself clear that night in her mother's rose garden?

If William couldn't realize that, or accept it, then that was his problem. She would never allow herself to be a victim again. Listen to these girls. Who needed love anyway? The WAVES were enough for her.

At Helen's "Amen," Maggie snatched her hands away from her seatmates so abruptly that they both flinched.

"Okey-dokey, girls," Helen said, "it's time for our sewing lesson." She began talking about ironing in a fold before beginning to use your needle and thread in a hemming job, and Maggie felt her attention fading once again. Helen's voice was only a steady, indiscernible background noise as she fixed her mind again on how furious she was at Helen, at God, at Eugenia, and at William.

Vaguely she heard Helen moving on to the subject of the squash casserole recipe and then to her lesson on beauty, the same thing she'd already shared with Maggie about how to use cherry Lifesavers for lipstick. Then came a Bible lesson from Psalms, some verse about children being a heritage of the Lord.

"All right, ladies," Helen said after this, "time to pass out our refreshments and have sharing time. And what goes better with love than chocolate?" She pulled the Whitman's box to her place, removed the lid, and presented the neat rows of chocolates to the group. "I'm in the mood for coconut," she said, selecting a piece and passing it to the girl on her right.

When the box reached Maggie, she chose a caramel and settled it on her tongue, closing her eyes in pleasure as the creamy chocolate coating began to melt.

Helen smiled over at her. "Who wants to go first? Maggie, are you ready to reveal a love hookup, a romantic rendezvous, be it by letter or by phone—or *by person*?"

Maggie scowled and was thankful when Della, a tall brunette from Ohio sitting across from her, raised a hand. "I do, I do!"

Helen nodded at Della.

"Okay," she said in a breathless voice, "the last letter I got from Zeke, he opened it with the words, 'How's my girl?' and he closed it with, get this, '*Love*, Zeke'!" Della paused to run her hand through her hair. "So see? I think he's finally ready to admit his feelings. I think he's moving toward commitment, which means he's through with being a bachelor. I wrote Mama that when I'm home for Thanksgiving, we should go to the fabric store and look at silks and satins." Della was smiling so hard her eyes were slits.

Maggie stared hard at her. She could see vulnerability in the girl's face as plain as day. Della was falling hard and fast and blind. *Hold on to your heart, Della!* she wanted to warn her, *because Zeke is a fighter pilot in the Army Air Corps, and that's a risky job.*

"Well, that certainly sounds promising!" Helen clapped her hands together in a little flurry. "Do keep us informed, Della. Carmen?" she said, turning to the slim girl on her left, "what's going on with you and Franklin?"

"No letter since our last Feminine Club meeting," Carmen said quietly.

Maggie saw tiny lines of worry on Carmen's forehead, and even Helen seemed to sense that she should step lightly.

"I understand," she said, patting Carmen's wrist. "I'm right there with you, hon. Anyone else?"

Several voices chimed in at the same time, one bubbling a pitch higher than the others about meeting some boy's family when they'd come to Trenton for a long weekend.

Maggie bit her bottom lip, fervently willing her thoughts elsewhere. She might feel cynical about love, marriage, the whole commitment thing, about all these hopeful hearts, but that didn't mean she felt strong enough to declare it aloud right now. She certainly didn't want to utter William's name or tell about his letter. She wished the meeting were over and she were in her bunk with the covers pulled over her head.

"Okay, girls, our next meeting will be in December," Maggie heard Helen saying. "Hope all of you have happy trips home for Thanksgiving—hugs from your families, delicious food, and warm kisses from your lovers." She giggled here and looked at Maggie. "And remember, bring back one of your favorite family recipes for Christmas goodies to share at our next meeting."

Della turned to Maggie. "You're staying here in New Jersey, aren't you, Maggie?"

"Yep." Maggie gathered up the little brown wrapper her chocolate had been in, along with her recipe for squash casserole, and stood up. She thought she was safely out of the room when Helen called out to her.

"Maggie may be staying here, but she won't be *a-lo-o-o-ne!*" Helen drew out the word so it had three long syllables.

"Hush, Helen," Maggie said, flashing an irritable glance. "I mean it. I'm staying here to *work*, to serve my country."

Helen looked at Maggie with what seemed like a smirk.

"Brent and I are just friends!" Maggie yelled, feeling something like fire rising up inside.

Helen began to laugh so hard she doubled over. "Hey, calm down, hon," she said when she finally got her breath. "Okay, okay. You're just friends. Did you know your freckles get darker when you're mad?"

Then they ought to be black, Maggie thought to herself,

crumpling the recipe up into a ball and shoving it in the waste-basket on her way out the door. She heard the other girls calling out their good-byes and goodnights and sleep wells as she hurried down the hallway.

* * * * *

There was still a while till curfew, and Maggie decided to take a walk around the base to clear her muddled mind. Stepping out of the barracks, she was momentarily stunned by the sharp slap of a freezing November night. She wondered if she would ever get used to the cold here. Lifting her eyes, she saw that the sky was clear enough, stars winking down on her, the moon hanging full and orange.

But she returned her gaze to the ground, the gravel, the dirt, and the few patches of grass as she stomped along past the commissary, as thoughts of what she mentally referred to as "those two tricky letters" tried to barge their way in. What she should have done was to follow her impulse and not read them. No one needed a two-faced friend like Eugenia.

Maggie began to walk faster, practically race-walking, and as she rounded a corner of the building that housed the dispensary, a sharp wind lifted her hair from her neck and she shivered so hard her teeth clacked. Pulling her coat closer, she hugged herself. It was almost cold enough at this hour to force her back inside, but she set her jaw and continued.

Maggie kept this brisk pace up until she approached the

chow hall and felt a stitch form in her side. The most irritating thing about it all was that she was as full of turmoil as she'd been when she first stepped outside. Peace was no easy thing to get your hands on. She decided to jog, see if that would help.

A quarter mile later, she approached the chapel. Narrowing her eyes, Maggie turned her head sharply to look in the opposite direction. She'd not darkened the doors of the chapel once since setting foot on base and she did not plan to. She lifted her chin and blew out a sharp "Hmph!" that created white clouds of breath. A wave of grief hit her as she recalled the last time she'd been in a church—that cloudy afternoon of her mother's funeral.

She shook her head at the memory of her saintly mother lying in that coffin up front. Only her father, sitting beside Maggie on the pew and holding her hand tightly, kept Maggie from jumping up and running out of the church as Reverend Peterson preached on the beauty of heaven. What were all those folks thinking as they sat, nodding and amening at the Reverend's words, with her mother lying up there stone-cold?

Maggie shook thoughts of that awful day away. The faith some folks were able to embrace in the midst of life's difficulties amazed her. She pictured Helen's face as she prattled on and on about her wedding plans. The poor girl had detailed descriptions of her dress, the flowers, and the music, as well as the food for the reception. She'd even gone so far as to take Maggie's measurements so that her aunt, a professional seamstress, could begin work on the bridesmaids' gowns.

What really bewildered Maggie was Helen's mantra, "God

drew me and Jasper together, and God will work things out." Every time she said this, her face literally *glowed*. Besides that, when Helen knelt each night beside her bunk to say her bedtime prayers, which Maggie couldn't help but listen to, she was always struck by the pure faith, the fervency, and the familiarity she heard in the words. It always sounded like Helen was having a conversation with a close friend. She'd talk in this intimate tone, pausing every now and again like she was listening to someone reply. Then she would say things like, "Thank You, Lord," and, "Yes, Father," and, "Amen, so be it. I believe."

Maggie realized it was the exact same way William talked to God. A memory of him on his knees at the altar rail during last Christmas Eve's church service weaseled its way into her thoughts. She tried to distract herself, tried to focus on anything else but this image, but it was impossible.

She remembered the way a forelock of William's hair fell forward, the candlelight giving it a sheen, and his voice as he prayed for Maggie's mother. Wasn't William's voice her absolute favorite sound in this world? His palm touching hers so tender and warm? His scent one that awakened her senses? She shook her head in wonder. He'd surely been her entire world back then, in that short window of time between that magical night at the Varsity and her mother's passing.

As she thought about that night, the sad, lonely places in her heart filled with pure sweet love for just a moment, followed by a longing to be near William that was so strong she actually felt a physical ache.

How in tarnation did William Dove do this from so far away?! Her every sense was tuned to a boy who was way down in the state of Georgia, probably sitting at his desk writing her another one of his long, pleading letters. Thinking of this was like rubbing salt into a wound, and it stung so much Maggie stopped walking and stamped her foot on the ground hard and yelled out, "No!" Now pain shot up through her leg along with a huge ripple of annoyance.

Here she stood, Margaret Jane Culpepper, aircraft mechanic in the U.S. Navy, every lonely puff of white breath magnifying the emptiness inside her as the image of William's smile danced larger-than-life on the screen of her mind. There was the gorgeous dimple in his left cheek and that endearing cowlick. Here came the remembrance of the way his hand felt in hers that day they'd discovered they had what some call chemistry between them.

Even long distance, William Dove was making her have feelings she vowed she would never let herself experience again. Oh, it hurt inside. Maggie began to jog again, going faster and faster, pushing her legs toward the runway and the hangar. When she reached the crew's room, she leaned against the glass, holding the stitch in her side and breathing hard. Through the window she spied her chair, the place from where she watched "her" planes, when the test pilots came and took them up and out over the bay. The Avenger Torpedo bombers that were helping her country fight this war.

Always, when she was at work as an aircraft mechanic, when she poured herself into performing her duties to the best of her abilities, she was able to shut out her personal turmoil. She'd gotten good at that, hadn't she?

Biting her lip, nodding, Maggie knew what she needed to do. She needed to get herself back to her bunk, get some good sleep, and then morning would come and she could work on her planes again. Her job required top physical and mental condition, and it was her duty to make sure lives were secure.

Morning light, her hands at work—this would clear her tortured mind.

This realization softened her anger and strengthened her resolve. Now she pictured her mother's coffin descending into that red Georgia clay, then her usually stoic father as his grief consumed him, and nothing in the world seemed more logical than her plan to pour herself, heart and soul, into the U.S. Navy.

As long as she stayed here with her tool box, as long as she didn't come face-to-face with William Dove, she could fight off the pesky swirling emotions. Yes, if she could make it through Thanksgiving and then Christmas without seeing William or Watkinsville, then time *would* be that healer. She would hang out with Brent and apply the self-control, the militant determination that made him such a successful Navy officer.

* * * * *

When Maggie made her way to the chow hall on November 23, the sky was low and overcast. It was a depressing steely gray day and numbingly cold as well. She stepped inside, surrounded by the unmistakable smell of bacon, but not until she'd had her second cup of scalding black coffee did it register that today was Thanksgiving. Thanksgiving in Trenton, New Jersey. Well, she didn't really feel like giving thanks for much at the moment anyhow.

Then she recalled Helen's words from just a few days earlier. "Mags, this'll be my best Thanksgiving ever! I have so much to be thankful for I can hardly stand it!" This was several minutes after receiving word that Jasper McCartney was not a casualty of the battle against the Japanese on Peleliu Island.

Maggie smiled at the memory of Helen's beaming face as she ran up and down their hall, announcing to everyone that Jasper was now safe and sound in a military hospital, recovering from severe dehydration, an infected cut, and a dislocated knee. "It's proof God answers prayer," Helen had said to Maggie later that night as they were brushing their teeth.

Of course, Maggie did not say to Helen that there were plenty of other men who fought on Peleliu Island, ten thousand in fact, whose loved ones' prayers were *not* answered. And that realization—instead of making Maggie want to thank God for saving Jasper—angered her.

Now she forked up a bite of egg as she pictured Helen in Florence, South Carolina, in the bosom of her family, enjoying warm, sunny weather, chatting endlessly and excitedly about her wedding plans, eating homemade yeast rolls and scuppernong jam for breakfast, while smells of a roast turkey and cornbread stuffing drifted in from the kitchen—dishes being prepared for their Thanksgiving feast later on that day.

At the Culpepper residence in Watkinsville, Georgia, Miss Jo had most likely been in the kitchen since before dawn, studying Maggie's mother's treasured recipes and working her hardest to fix a holiday meal Mr. Culpepper would be thankful for. For dessert, there would be a pecan pie and a pumpkin pie, and Maggie's father would polish off a slice of each then spend an hour napping on the divan in the front room, a half-smile on his face.

Maggie stopped that train of thought in its tracks as she scanned the dining hall for WAVES she knew. She didn't see anybody she was particularly close to, so she focused on thoughts of the day's work.

To her, the prospect of a day spent in the hangar putting wing rockets and gun racks on aircraft was satisfying. She enjoyed thinking of herself as an independent woman. A lifer in the U.S. Navy. In fact, she finished her breakfast and sat for a minute, staring into space, fighting the impulse to cancel her evening get-together with Brent.

* * * * *

It was almost six, and Maggie's feet were getting tired as she waited in the lobby for Brent. She'd been waiting since five-thirty, coiffed and dressed in civilian clothes for their Thanksgiving dinner together. She'd brushed her hair to a high sheen, even rubbed a cherry Lifesaver on her wet lips, not so much for Brent's sake, but in honor of Helen's good news about Jasper.

"Don't you look nice," he said when he finally strode up.

"Thank you."

"You're welcome." He paused. "Am I late?"

"Yes."

"Oh, sorry. Some things came up earlier today that I had to tend to, and so I didn't get a chance to cook our feast, and I had to hunt up a buddy of mine who owes me a favor. Took me awhile to locate him and get him to say he'd do it."

Maggie gave Brent a quizzical look.

"It's James, fellow who works in the mess hall," he said. "It was his day off, but he talked to his boss and got a couple Thanksgiving dinners boxed up for me."

Disappointment flooded Maggie at Brent's words. *Thanksgiving dinner from the mess hall?* Maybe she misheard him. Maybe he'd actually said something about how *awful* that would be if that *were* to be their celebration. Her imagination could be pretty strong at times.

"The mess hall?" Maggie questioned, trying not to wrinkle her nose.

"Yep." Brent gave a brisk, businesslike nod. Did she only imagine it, or was the look he gave her one of chastisement, as if he thought she didn't share the unifying spirit of sacrifice on the homefront while soldiers were being machine-gunned in Germany?

"I'm sure it will be tasty," she managed.

Brent chuckled. "I'm sure it will be. You ought to feel especially honored, because I did take a minute to clean my place up."

"Great," she said in a tone that sounded like a question to her own ears. She was still not sure there wasn't some mistake. Could Brent really mean something so unappetizing, and even more than that, at his place, alone?

Alarm filtered through Maggie, because being alone with a man was something her mother warned her about repeatedly, something a nice girl didn't do. Here on base, if a female were in a male's room, the door had to be left open, and at least one foot of each person had to remain on the floor at all times. "Uh, alone?" she managed to ask as Brent held the door open for her.

"Of course alone," he answered, impatience, or was it irritation, dripping from his voice.

Her mind whirled. Well, he was an officer, she decided after a moment, and he did have the authority to override this rule. Plus, he was the kind of man she could trust. She knew Brent Lawton to be a man of complete self-control.

"Is it always this cold in New Jersey in winter?" Maggie asked in a playful tone as they walked past the tennis courts and then the marine barracks, toward the officers' quarters, their hands stuffed into coat pockets, chins tucked into scarves.

"Yep," he said. "If you think this is cold, just wait till February."

"Brrr" Maggie shuddered against the thought.

"Oh, you'll get used to it," he said, chuckling. "You're a tough one. All these other WAVES scurrying home, and here you are, serving your country."

Maggie couldn't stop the wide smile that came from Brent's

compliment. She liked the fact that he was in his uniform this evening. Something about the immaculately pressed trousers he wore made it seem like a real celebration.

When they reached his apartment, Brent turned the key and led her inside. Closing the door behind them, he removed his coat and scarf and hung them in the closet, crossing the short entranceway and turning on the light in a tiny kitchen. Maggie followed suit with her coat and scarf.

"Sure is nice and cozy in here," she said, walking in behind him and looking at two chrome chairs tucked beneath a Formica-topped table.

"Please, have a seat," he said, pulling out one of the chairs. "Make yourself comfortable and I'll heat up our dinner."

Maggie watched as Brent padded about, removing a boiler from beneath the tiny stove, a handheld can opener and a wooden spoon from a drawer, and a cookie sheet from an overhead cabinet. Everything looked brand new, like he'd just peeled the labels off. He opened a can of peas, dumped them into the boiler, and set this on a burner. Next, he opened a big, oddly shaped, paper-wrapped package of food she assumed came from the mess hall. From this he pulled a lump of meat-product out with a fork and set it on a cookie sheet. He added two pale rolls, a slab of something brown and crumbly she decided was dressing, and a congealed yellow mass that must be squash, and slid it into the oven. This done, he set out two plates, two forks, and two spoons. While the peas were simmering, he poured coffee into a percolator and turned on another burner beneath it. Soon the kitchen filled with the smell of warm peas mixed with coffee.

"The coffee sure smells good," Maggie said, admiring the fact that the interior of Brent's apartment was so orderly, tidy, and no-nonsense. Just like he was.

"Glad you think so," he said, lifting the lid on the peas and stirring them with the wooden spoon.

"I adore coffee, any kind of coffee. Even Navy regulation coffee." Maggie laughed. "Sometimes I think I could live purely on coffee."

"That right?" Brent said, as the final bit of water in the percolator gurgled through the grounds. He poured two cups, setting one in front of Maggie.

"Thank you," she said, wrapping her cold palms around the cup.

"You want cream or sugar?"

"Black's fine."

"Won't be long on our meal," Brent said, sitting down across from her.

"Great," she said, though she felt she could wait a long time for the smelly peas. The look and smell of green peas had turned her stomach since she was a little girl. Cup to her lips, eyes closed, Maggie let the hot liquid linger on her tongue.

"Busy day on the job?" he asked after a bit.

"Yes," she said. "But nice. I like my work. No, I *love* my work." She watched his face for a response but could read nothing.

The lid on the peas burped and Brent hopped up to turn the

burner off. He peered into the oven. "Looks like our Thanksgiving feast is ready," he said. He found a slotted spoon, grabbed the black handle of the boiler, and scooped a small mountain of peas on each of two plates waiting on the counter. Next he slid his hand into a blue oven mitt and pulled the cookie sheet from the oven.

As Brent meticulously placed slices of hot meat-product and lumps of dressing and squash on the plates next to the peas, Maggie felt anything but thankful. He set the plates on the table with a flourish, sat down, raised his fork, and said, "Okay, let's dig in." It didn't sound like an invitation. It sounded like an order.

"Okay," Maggie said, looking down at an unappetizing forkful of squash. In her mind she'd already determined to enjoy it. After all, those soldiers in gloomy foxholes would probably love to have a hot meal like this. She ate her squash then aimed a spoonful of mushy peas into her mouth, chewed, and swallowed. "Mm," she said, working hard to stifle her gag reflex. "This is mighty good." She took a gulp of bitter, not-quite-hot-anymore coffee to wash it down.

They ate in silence for a few minutes. Then Brent cocked his head to one side and said, "So, you don't have a boyfriend anywhere who's pining away for you? Nobody you had to race home to eat Thanksgiving dinner with?"

Brent's question caught Maggie off guard. But, after a moment, she gathered her wits together enough to say, "No. When I told you earlier that I wanted no romantic entanglements to distract me from my service, I meant it." She was proud of this response. Her words were calm and sure, straight and to the point.

She was hoping Brent would move on to another subject, but he leaned forward with a glimmer in his eyes. "You planning on becoming a nun?" he asked.

"No, of course not," she said. She thought she'd made it more than clear to him that she was a lifer in the Navy.

"No wedding vows?" he pressed on. "No husband or brood of children down the road?"

She shook her head firmly.

"Sounds like a lonely life if you ask me."

Maggie sat up stiff and straight. "I told you, Brent. I'm a lifer."

"A true Navy woman, yes, you did tell me that." He arched one brow, smiling at her.

Her appetite was completely gone now. She pushed her plate back and laid her fork and spoon in an X across it. She crossed her arms over her chest.

"Hey, hey," he said after several moments of silence. "I can certainly understand being a lifer in the Navy." Nodding, he scraped up the last of the peas on his plate onto his spoon and shoveled them into his mouth. When he'd swallowed, he cleared his throat and said, "What you mean is the Navy is your family. You're deeply committed to the U.S. Navy."

Maggie smiled and let out a long breath. "Yes. That's exactly what I mean. The only vows I'm making are ones to serve my country." She'd made other vows in the past, personal ones. Not for marriage, but against it.

"Care for seconds on anything?" Brent asked as he rose and began loading up his plate with more dressing and peas and meat-product.

"A bit more coffee would be nice."

He poured the last of the coffee into her cup. "Don't have any dessert, I'm sorry to say. I do have some Beeman's chewing gum if you're interested."

"Oh, no thanks," she said, taking a sip of the fresh coffee. "This is fine."

By the time Brent had cleaned his plate after seconds, Maggie was still nursing her coffee along. He kicked back in his chair, pulled a pack of Lucky Strikes from his pocket, and lit one up, watching her intently all the while. "Know what?" he said, blowing out a precise line of smoke, one eyebrow raised. "You've got the creamiest, purest looking skin I've ever seen. I believe you could even be in commercials for soap or lotion, things like that."

Maggie blushed. She cleared her throat. "Uh, thanks. So, what do you think about what's going on in the Pacific?"

He didn't answer and she looked up from her plate. Now he was staring at her as if she were Thanksgiving dinner and he was a starving man.

"Let's move to the sofa," he said, stubbing out his cigarette onto his plate. "It's much more comfortable in there."

Maggie's heart was beating double-time. "I like sitting here just fine," she said, fumbling at the handle of her coffee cup with her thumbs. "In fact, I'm getting tired. What with working all day." She managed a weak laugh. "I don't want to sound rude, but I better turn in, Brent. Thank you for dinner. It was delicious, but I've really got to get my rest so I can do a good job for our soldiers." She laughed again.

"You didn't eat enough for a five-year-old child," he said, nodding at her plate. "You didn't even eat your roll."

"I'm sorry. I told you I'm not a very big eater."

There was a long moment when neither of them said a word. Maggie held her breath. Friends didn't look at friends the way he was staring at her.

"Well, good night," she said, getting to her feet. "Thank you again for dinner. I'll walk myself home so you won't have to get back out into that freezing night." She was certain Brent could hear the hard pounding of her heart as she scraped back her chair and stood on shaky legs.

She'd almost made it to the door when she heard him spring up. He was behind her, his hands on her shoulders, holding her in place, hard.

Maggie drew a quick, shocked breath. "Let me go, please. I—I want to go home."

Brent didn't answer. He turned her around, and for several heartbeats, they just stared at each other, his hands encircling her waist now. Then he moved in closer, so close she felt his breath on her forehead, smelled the Lucky Strikes.

"I want to kiss you," he said finally. "I need to stop this

pretense and show you just how much I love you, Margaret Jane Culpepper. I dream of you every night."

Stunned by his words, his tone, his intensity, and his hands traveling upward, she tried to pull away. What a fool she'd been to let herself think she could be just friends with any man. Hadn't she learned her lesson with William?

"If you knew what you do to me…," he said, grabbing her even tighter.

"No! Stop!" she demanded now, fury at herself and at Brent making her bold. "I told you, I'm going home."

"Home?" he mocked, burying his fingers in her thick hair. "You didn't want to take leave to go home. You chose to stay here with me."

"I did not!"

"Yes, you did." Now he sounded even more determined. "I love your fire, Margaret. I've often, late at night, pictured you with that red mane down out of the head scarf you wear while you're working on some plane. I imagine it tumbling down around your bare shoulders, those bronze freckles across your silky cheeks."

"Don't," she spat. "Don't think of me that way."

But Brent only laughed. "One thing I love to think about," he said, stroking her jaw line, "is that night we were dancing the jitterbug together. I remember the way you moved, that smile you had on your face."

Maggie stood, mute. *The eyes are the window to the soul* flashed through her mind. Brent's eyes were intense, steely, and she realized she couldn't see inside him at all. She did see his nostrils flare as he looked her up and down, determination evident in the set of his jaw.

"You know we'd do each other good," he said.

She stared at him open-mouthed.

"You know you want me too," he added, and the sureness, the commanding tone in his voice, made Maggie's mouth go dry.

"I'm the reason you stayed here for Thanksgiving, and I'm ready to take our relationship to the next level. I think you are too." Brent's fingers bit into her upper arms and he moved his head toward hers.

He expected her to *want* this? Shock, followed by fury, helped Maggie summon all of her energy and duck down so quickly it even surprised her. This put him off-guard, and she was able to spring away, shaking her head, hugging herself.

Huddled against the wall, too embarrassed to look Brent in the eye, Maggie was able to pull herself together a little bit. She sucked in a breath and said in a weak, trembly voice she despised, "You're wrong. I don't want you. Also, that so-called Thanksgiving meal was absolutely disgusting. If I'd known you were serving mess hall fare, I could have saved myself the trouble."

* * * * *

Maggie ran, eyes wide open, taking awhile to realize she'd left her coat behind. Without hesitating, she sprinted on, somehow with superhuman strength and resistance to the cold, shoving open the door to her barracks.

She flew up the stairs and into her room and jumped into bed. After a moment, she realized she was absolutely freezing, her teeth chattering together noisily, and her extremities so numb she could hardly feel a thing. Pulling the covers up, she rolled herself in them like a cocoon, staring blankly into the dark quietness.

She lay there, hardly even thinking, gradually regaining feeling as she thawed out. Her brain must have thawed out, too, because at last it resumed its annoying spinning. There were so many thoughts and emotions at once, it put her in mind of a kaleidoscope.

Finally, her thoughts focused on Brent Lawton. Brent was definitely not the kind of man she thought he was. Helen had been right. Desire was there, though Maggie had been pretending it wasn't, and the man was a strategist, a military strategist who'd been waiting till just the right moment to make his move. Well, she had to give him that. Brent certainly had fooled her with his military-man-who's-in-control façade. Even the Navy's infamous discipline couldn't make a man what he wasn't, and there was no way she would forgive him after what he'd done to her tonight. No way she could ever trust him again, even to discuss their careers.

But it wasn't just Brent's sudden improprieties that rankled her. There was her own naiveté, her vulnerability. Was she really that clueless that she hadn't seen it coming? Hadn't her mother warned her about men like Brent? As her mother's face came into her mind's focus, Maggie's throat tightened and her breathing came in ragged little gasps. She worked to force down the burden of her sorrow, the grief that was yet too big for her to handle.

How unfair it was to lose her mother—a woman who had tried to raise her properly, to warn her about the opposite sex. Strange, though, Maggie realized, her mother had trusted William implicitly, often referring to him as "part of the family." She admired William's work ethic, his kindness, his humility, and that funny, self-deprecating sense of humor he had.

Indeed, there was something innately good, almost noble, about William. Maggie wasn't blind to his good qualities. She saw them in the gentle respect he had for small creatures they happened on at Dove's Tree Farm. She saw strength of character and honesty clearly in his eyes, those windows to the soul. She felt it in the tender restraint of William's kisses. All traits Brent Lawton did not possess.

For a moment, it felt as if the world had stopped spinning on its axis. As if time stood still then rolled back just a bit. Just like that she was *there*. In Athens, Georgia, on that December day, kissing William with the radio on low as Bing Crosby crooned "I'll Be Home for Christmas."

"That's our song, Maggie, baby," William was saying in that soft Southern drawl that sent tingles up and down her spine.

The longing she felt for William now unnerved her. Longing for his soulful brown eyes and the pure love that moved across his guileless face. There was the craving to be near him, to have him hold her and reassure her. He knew her. He loved her.

Struggling out of the cocoon of covers, Maggie groped her way through the dark, breathless, turned on the desk lamp, sat down, and began a note. It read:

> *Dear William,*
>   *I'm answering your sweet invitation. I'll be home for Christmas.*

But before she could sign, *Love, Maggie*, she paused to run her fingertips over the line *I'll be home for Christmas*. Taking a great gulp of air, she closed her eyes and tumbled headlong into a painful vision of herself in Watkinsville, Georgia— a place full of tender memories and reminders of unanswered prayers.

Her heart seized up, so that the recent image of her and William together disappeared like dew on a sunny day. What in the world had come over her? Why on earth was she glancing back at the past? Maggie shook her head. She needed to focus on her Navy career, her patriotism. Hadn't she been doing just fine ever since that day in her mother's rose garden when she'd officially closed and locked the door to her heart for good? No divided loyalties for her!

She crumpled up the first letter and began another on a fresh sheet of stationery:

Dear William,

I'm going to stay on base for Christmas. I wanted to let you know so you can find someone else to decorate your Virginia pine with.

Sincerely,

Maggie

After she'd sealed the note in an envelope and put William's address on the front, Maggie thought about Virginia pines and the tree farm and then dear Mr. Byrd. She remembered William's comment about December being a difficult month for him to get through. She'd never known, because he always seemed so jubilant—wasn't that a funny word? It described Mr. Byrd to a T—when they were there playing at the farm. Whatever it is was that haunted him, she admired his ability to be so happy.

"Mr. Byrd," she said with a sigh, "I'd give anything to know your secret."

CHAPTER THIRTEEN

William waited just inside the front door, staring at the mail slot, trying not to look hang-dog, which was something Mr. Byrd had accused him of as they ate lunch together earlier.

"You had a tail, it be tucked 'tween yo' legs," Mr. Byrd said between bites of cheese and saltines. " 'Sides lookin' hang-dog, I didn't know better, I be thinkin' you ain't nothin' but a ol' man like me, way you been limpin' 'round out here, rubbin' yo' ankle and all."

William hadn't said anything in response to these concerns. In fact, since Mr. Byrd's confession of his soul travail, William didn't talk to the old man very much. He preferred not to hear any more stories.

He worked around the tree farm, unwillingly cradling the knowledge that God's answers weren't always what a person wanted, and occasionally he stepped into such soul-wrenching puddles of doubt he felt he might be drowning. He had a hard time encouraging himself with the knowledge that by this time Maggie had surely read his letter, his invitation. He wasn't walking on air or smiling with anticipation as he breathed in the scent of cedars and pines, of *Christmas*—which he used to think was one of the best smells in life.

Days were busy at the tree farm now that it was December 5, and William gazed wistfully at families, the children galloping ahead of parents down rows of trees, stopping to finger a particular tree here or to smell one there, then finally to find Mr. Byrd or himself, to say they'd found "The One." Then there was the ever busy Yule-Tide Shoppe, which Mr. Byrd handled on his own for the most part, occasionally needing William to fill in.

Often during the workday, William made a side-trip over to stand near the stately Virginia pine, willing the dream to come and lift his heart for a moment, his faith for a bit, so that he could go on with his tasks. But it seemed futile, like he'd been zooming down the highway of confident expectation happily and then suddenly smashed into a huge boulder sitting smack-dab in the middle of the road. His vehicle was wrecked and he could not go forward or backward or even to the sides. That was where William had come to. A great impasse.

Waiting for the sound of Fred bringing the day's mail, William let his eyes fall on the glossy magnolia boughs his mother had arranged on the mantel. Red velvet ribbons were artfully woven in amongst the dark green leaves. Bright oranges pricked with cloves sat at both ends of the mantel and left a spicy fragrance.

However, the tree stand placed between the bookcases was empty as William had decided not to cut the Virginia pine until he'd heard from Maggie. Though there was a nice, full cedar his brothers had decorated standing in the foyer, it was a pale shadow of what William envisioned and failed to put him in a Christmas mood.

William tried not to look at the empty tree stand as he stood listening intently for the distinctive sound of Fred's engine, his happy-go-lucky gait coming down the walkway. At last he heard Fred as he walked toward the house whistling "Santa Claus Is Coming to Town."

William had the door open before Fred's foot hit the bottom step.

"William, my man!" Fred raised his free hand in a salute, a bundle of mail clutched in his other.

"Anything for me?" William asked, realizing he was already holding out his hand.

"Well–l–l–l." Fred drew out the word torturously, his eyes twinkling. "May have a letter or two here for one William Dove."

William felt a rapid acceleration of his heartbeat. "Don't play with me, man," he fussed. "Give it here."

"Say please. Say pretty please."

"Please," William said through clenched teeth.

"Well, now," Fred said, still holding the letter a few inches from William's outstretched hand. "That sure is a fine howdy-do. Here I am, trudging through rain, sleet, and snow to bring you your mail and I can hardly get a please."

William was in no mood for funning around. He snatched the letter from Fred, and seeing Maggie's return address, he caught his breath. *Maggie* touched *this*, he thought, feeling weightless for a moment.

"So you finally got a letter from her." Fred didn't phrase it like a question.

William blinked. He hadn't realized Fred was still there, leaning against the doorframe now waiting, he supposed, for William to open his letter. William felt his muscles tense. "Don't you have more mail you need to deliver today, Fred?"

"Boy howdy, I guess," he said, chuckling to himself as he turned on his heel to go.

Gently William closed the door, leaning his back against it as he opened the letter.

"No–o–o–o–o..." A low wail left his mouth. He felt like someone was kicking him hard in the ribcage, over and over again, his life ebbing with every whimper. If there was anything left worth living for, he didn't know what it was. William felt himself shrink inside his own skin, but maybe it was that his dream had finally fully died, the last vestiges of a dream that used to fill out the cells of his body, that used to pump him up with hope and joy and anticipation.

Dragging his gimp leg, he climbed the stairs to his bedroom to get the wedding ring quilt still sitting on his chest of drawers. After putting it away in the linen closet down the hallway, he returned to his room and fell on his bed, the exhaustion from his day's toil at the tree farm settling over him like a shroud.

* * * * *

The Yule-Tide Shoppe was packed. It was a cold, rainy day, so there were no customers wandering about the choose-and-cut acres of trees, and William was inside the cabin helping Mr.

Byrd. William knew nearly every person in there. He saw Eugenia, who was with her mother, holding an armload of silver
garlands.

William was busily straightening a row of snow globes, trying to avoid eye contact with Genie. Luckily there were shelves
near the rear of the cabin, where he could work with his back to
customers, out of the line of sight of all those people who were
bound to be saying hello and inquiring after his family. In the
week since he'd received Maggie's letter, William tried to keep
to himself as much as possible, not so much licking his wounds
as just managing to exist.

He was thankful Mr. Byrd's festive presence filled the little
store. The old man wore his best pair of overalls, the ones without a fraying cuff, a mended tatter, or a stain. His shoes were
polished to a high sheen, and he wore the first Santa hat William
had ever seen him in. Beneath the hat his grin was even wider
than usual, his eyes twinkly and serene, with no trace of fighting
painful memories or the aching joints of arthritis that rain usually meant for him. He was the picture of health and happiness.

"Got so much to celebrate at Christmas," Mr. Byrd was saying through his chuckles as he punched the adding machine
stationed on the counter. "Mmhmm. Got these pretty baubles
and got parties and got fam'ly gettin' together. Time off from
our labors. But mostly we get t' celebrate the greatest gift of all,
don't we, Miz Fairfield? Our Lord and Savior, Jesus Christ."

Mrs. Fairfield's response caroled loud and clear. "Why,
yes indeed, Mr. Byrd. Speaking of parties, I made my famous

coconut cake, and my James is coming with his wife and my two lovely granddaughters."

"I know you proud," Mr. Byrd said. "Enjoy yo' beautiful fam'ly."

William heard Mr. Byrd telling some whiny kid that all the Rudolphs were gone, that there were some toy Frosty the Snowmans that were just as fun. The kid started bawling until Mr. Byrd told him he could have a peppermint stick if he'd hush.

William worked on, arranging and rearranging little decorations. Eugenia was being uncharacteristically quiet. He could almost feel a presence, something palpable in the shop with her. Maybe it was time to go check the tree lot, he thought to himself. See if some brave souls were out there and ready for their tree to be cut.

Before he could get outside, he heard Eugenia's sniffly voice. "William?"

It made him freeze. It made him want to stop up his ears, all those places within his soul that were already so painful. He ignored her. He focused on various customers' voices, the distant sound of a car's engine coming from the parking lot.

Finally she spoke again. "William?"

He turned. Eugenia's eyes were sparkly with unspilled tears.

"I'm sure you've heard about Ernie by now," she said, her lip quivering, "and I almost feel guilty buying anything to celebrate Christmas after the telegram his folks got today."

William simply stared.

"My mom went over to the Haygoods' to play bridge," Eugenia continued. "And Mrs. Haygood's housekeeper told Mother that Ernie was gone. He was killed two days after Thanksgiving, in a German air attack near Belgium."

This was a moment, a scene straight out of one of William's hellish nightmares. Grabbing Ernie's letter jacket, he stumbled out the back door of the cabin.

* * * * *

William usually left the tree farm around eight on evenings in late December, long after the last shred of daylight had disappeared, along with most customers, leaving Mr. Byrd to tidy up and shut everything down.

This evening he was still there at ten. He'd filled the time by raking up needles along rows of cedars, in the dark and on wet ground, no less, then checking the oil in the small tractor used to transport trees from field to checkout, and finally, by sweeping up the floor of the Yule-Tide Shoppe. As soon as Mr. Byrd had pulled the shades on all the windows of the cabin and shuffled out to the road to shut the gate, William gathered up the cash, counted it, and wrote it in the ledger, something he usually did in the early mornings.

Mr. Byrd had asked him a couple of times during the afternoon if he didn't want something to eat, didn't want to sit down for a cup of hot coffee and a conversation break. But rather than unburden himself, rather than say aloud the news he'd heard about Ernie, William would just point to whatever task he was on and shake his head.

"You ain't et a bite since 'leven, son," Mr. Byrd said, setting a plate of pimiento cheese spread on thick slices of bread and a steaming cup of coffee on his small table. "Here some supper fo' you."

"I'm not hungry," William said, in the next heartbeat realizing it was probably past the old man's bedtime, and maybe he was trying the polite way to get rid of William. Mr. Byrd had removed the jaunty Santa hat, along with his brogans, and he looked tired, leaning against his sink while rubbing the back of his neck.

"Uh, no thanks, Mr. Byrd," Will said. "Guess I better be heading on home."

"Don't leave on my account. Want you a Coca-Cola instead?" Mr. Byrd reached for the handle of the icebox. "Some cold water?"

William shook his head. "See you in the morning." He turned and headed toward the door, dragging his bad leg.

He was shocked when Mr. Byrd quickly slid over in his sock feet, wedging himself between William and the door, standing there quietly for a minute and studying William's face hard. "Somethin' be eatin' at you, son," he said at last, his voice full of concern.

"Uh, I told you," William managed. "Maggie said she's not coming home for Christmas."

"That ain't all."

Mr. Byrd's ability to see inside William amazed him. "I'm just tired," he tried again, making a feeble attempt to get around Mr. Byrd and out the door. This wasn't a total lie. The prior weeks of not enough sleep, of nights spent tossing and turning, were catching up with him. He truly was exhausted, weak, his game leg gone from bad to worse, his hand acting up at times. But the news of Ernie's death, the realization that his best friend was no longer on this earth, was staggering, and William was doing his best not to break down in front of Mr. Byrd.

"Ain't nobody keep they strength up if they don't eat." Mr. Byrd took hold of William's arm. "Now, sit down and eat you a bite of supper 'fore you get on the road."

William looked past him to the table set with food. There was no use arguing with Mr. Byrd. When he was seated, Mr. Byrd sat down across from him and quietly watched as he ate several bites, chasing each one with a gulp of bitter black coffee.

"I see a shadow hangin' over you," Mr. Byrd said after a bit.

"You do?"

"Mmhmm. There be trouble in your spirit."

William cleared his throat. "Uh, today while I was working, Eugenia Peterson was here buying some things with her mother, and she—she said that... What she said was that Ernie's folks got a telegram and he's—" William lowered his head and pressed his forehead on the table. The words clotted in his throat. He could only roll his forehead from side to side, grinding his teeth in disbelief.

Mr. Byrd rose from his seat, came around the table, and

bent over to stretch one arm across William's shoulders like a wing. Grief, overwhelming grief, surged through William at the warmth of this touch. It shattered him. He'd been trying not to look the news of Ernie's death squarely in the eye, not to feel the loss, feel anything, and now it was staring at him.

"Oh me, oh my–y–y–y," Mr. Byrd began to moan. "I ain't heard 'bout Mr. Ernie's passin'. Oh me, oh my–y–y–y." He stood and raised his hands, still sounding deeply sad as he continued to wail the words, "Oh me, oh my–y–y–y." But then, it was like something in his spirit changed suddenly, and he made a complete U-turn.

He began to pray, to sing a prayer, rich and strong. "Oh, our gracious Lord, our Heavenly Father, hold Mr. and Mrs. Haygood close to Yo' heart. Let them feel Yo' arms 'round them as they grieve for they boy. You know how it feel t' lose a son. You know how they hearts be breakin'. Use me t' comfort them, Father. Jest let me know when I be needin' t' go visit with Ernie's folks. In our Lord and Savior Jesus' name, amen."

Memories of the best friend he had lost were scattered thick as pine needles across the ground of William's consciousness, and as he confronted them, the sadness came so deep it was like quicksand pulling him down. There was no use fighting it any longer and William closed his eyes and allowed the tears.

Mr. Byrd placed his hand on William's shoulder. "Now, Father, I be liftin' up Yo' chile, William Henry Dove. Hide him 'neath Yo' wings. Thank You, Father, for carin' 'bout ever' tear fall from this man's eyes. Let Yo' tender mercies cover him."

After a bit, Mr. Byrd removed his hand and William heard him sitting back down in his chair. William deliberately avoided opening his eyes, avoided meeting the intense gaze he felt on him. Futility sat like a stone inside his chest, and finally he put the back of his wrists on the edge of the table, buried his face in his hands and let it pull him down, down, until the dark closed over him and he hung in the valley of no light, tears running down his nose and dripping onto the floor.

The shrill *brriinngg* of Mr. Byrd's telephone yanked him back to awareness of his surroundings. He heard Mr. Byrd saying, "Yello?" then pausing. "Yes, yes, Miz Dove. He right here. Been workin' so hard I convince him stay and eat some supper, rest a spell 'fore he get on the road. Yes, yes, ma'am. Been a busy day with the Christmas crowd. Don't you worry none. I tell him."

William lifted his head and rubbed his swollen eyes, blinking at Mr. Byrd, who was putting the phone back on its cradle.

"Yo' mama worried 'bout you. She save some ham biscuits fo' you in wax paper in the breadbox." Mr. Byrd watched William with a question on his wrinkled, brown face. "You want me t' he'p you cut yo' pretty Virginia pine tonight?" he asked at last. "I know this place in the dark good as in the light." He gave a little chuckle.

"Nope," William said impassively. "That would be a waste of time. Maggie's not coming home for Christmas." William winced as he felt the sharp edges of that recently shattered dream.

"Ain't Christmas yet, son."

"Mr. Byrd," William's voice was weary, "I've been trying. Truly, I have. After our last little talk, when I told you about Maggie's letter saying she's not coming home for Christmas and you told me to still keep the faith, I've been trying. I've honestly been working at fanning the flames of my faith." He shifted his feet. "I've been praying and dwelling on positive things, like you said. But this, *this* today is the final nail in the coffin of my faith that she'll ever come home."

Mr. Byrd closed his eyes, raising his face heavenward. He murmured something, his lips only a silent movement to Will. "Don't throw in the towel on yo' love," he said at last, his eyes back on William.

"Why not?" William shrugged. "Why would a beautiful woman like Maggie want to marry a cripple?"

"Because she love him," Mr. Byrd said simply, with absolute, unwavering conviction. "Trust the Lord, and be patient, son. He patient with us, and we got t' be patient with Him. On account o' we know His answers and His timin' be better'n ours."

"Answers? Timing? Hah! Maggie's not coming home for Christmas, and Ernie's not ever coming home again! *That's* what I get for having faith." The bitter words shriveled William's tongue.

"Trust me, Will. Surrender. God know what He doin'."

William stood abruptly, limped over to where Ernie's jacket hung on a peg inside the door, and punched his arms into the sleeves.

"Hang on to yo' faith, son!" Mr. Byrd called, right on William's heels as he stepped out into the night.

* * * * *

Dove's Tree Farm was buzzing with the coming holiday. Crowds were surging in during daylight hours now that fathers had time off from work. Mothers were chasing their flocks of children who were out of school, yelling, "Better be good, for goodness' sake!" while the children were fairly obedient as they dreamed of Santa Claus and his elves paying a visit to them. Mr. Byrd seemed to overflow with the holiday spirit, passing out peppermint sticks and Scripture verses with a wide smile. He was the picture of health and happiness, with no morning stiffness and no painful joints.

From his earliest memories, William had awaited this holiday with the breathless anticipation of a young boy holding his first fishing pole. He loved the special church services, the decorations, the food, the gifts he gave and the ones he received. He loved the extravagant rush of Christmas.

But now, all he felt was an empty coldness and a physical exhaustion that made his work at the tree farm just something he had to get through each day. Lingering weakness in his muscles from the polio had worsened so that he was never without his cane, so that his right hand often failed to obey him.

One afternoon during a lull in business, he limped out to the rows of Virginia pines. Up and down he walked, thinking of all the soldiers who wouldn't be home for Christmas. Here he was alive, feeling the kiss of sunshine on his cheeks, moving along the trees, when Ernie Haygood was not on this planet to breathe and to work and to *feel*.

"Why?" he yelled, holding a fist heavenward and dragging his shriveled leg, using powerful strides from his other. He came to the foot of the splendid nine-foot-tall tree he had chosen for Maggie and himself to decorate, and just as quickly Maggie's words from long ago circled through his brain, *"I wanna help beat the Germans."*

William blew out a long breath as he reached up and pulled the ribbon-marker from the tree and stuffed it into his pocket. "Okay, God," he said, aiming more words upward and breathing in the sharp scent of pine, "I surrender. If that's the way You're going to be, then somebody else can have it!"

CHAPTER FOURTEEN

Maggie eased herself into the steaming shower stall, letting the hot water cascade over her head, her torso, then down to pulse on her grateful toes. She stood beneath the scalding flood, raised her face, closed her eyes, and pictured herself rising along with the white clouds of steam, carried away to finally evaporate somewhere—her body gone and her soul floating gloriously free.

The water, hot and steady, felt like heaven. Maggie smiled and exhaled slowly, thankful for the space around her, the solitude. This early morning shower, this dream of evaporating was her escape, the best part of her day. Sometimes it was hard to turn the water off and climb out. Sometimes she wouldn't mind standing in here permanently.

Another glorious thing was that in here she could get warm. Trenton, New Jersey, was absolutely freezing in December. A cold that went right down to the very core of a fair-skinned Southerner. Sometimes, if Maggie wasn't careful about exercising her diversionary tactics, she fantasized about summer evenings back home in Georgia—hot, balmy nights with the noise of the cicadas' *skreee* a heavenly backdrop.

But in the shower she kept herself together. In here, nothing could touch her. Here, there was bonafide escape. This morning she let the burning water numb her until she could feel absolutely nothing, spending several minutes in abandoned bliss.

Yesterday at the commissary, she'd purchased a pale green bottle of shampoo, and now she absentmindedly reached down to get it from the corner of the shower stall. Squeezing a blob into her palm, Maggie luxuriously massaged it into her scalp, reveling in the mini-massage, the wonderful feeling of it until the smell reached her nostrils and a flash from the past blindsided her.

"Dove's Tree Farm!" Maggie gasped. Shock filtered through her and she stood frozen for a moment, beneath the running sheets of hot water. Dove's Tree Farm, with its rows of stately and fragrant pines. Maggie drew in a shaky breath, inhaling whiffs of the shampoo as childhood images of herself running through Dove's Tree Farm with William materialized. Here he was laughing, swinging her by the arm for a game of Statue in the section full of Virginia pines. She was laughing too, solely caught up in the fun of the moment, the absolute happiness of it all.

Looking down, she blinked water droplets from her eyes and saw that the bottle bore some fancy script saying Pine Paradise. A label she had failed to read when she purchased it.

This is absurd. Just calm down and remember to breathe. Focus your thoughts on other things. She shook her head, hard, but the images were still there, sticking like chewing gum on the bottom of a shoe. Here came a vignette of when they were older, maybe fourteen or fifteen. There she stood, in the Doves' house, with William's eyes on her as they decorated the tree they'd chosen together. She twirled a rope of popcorn around the boughs, looking to him for his reaction, and he nodded, smiling with those curvy lips and soulful eyes.

Suddenly, with water cascading over Maggie's head, the truth of William's love hit her like a piece of shrapnel. She felt a huge, ragged wound rip open in her chest at the realization of all they'd had together. "No!" she wailed, sudsy, pine-tasting water running into her open mouth and startling her tongue. Quickly she spat and rinsed the shampoo from her hair.

Stepping out, Maggie used uncoordinated motions to dry herself, and she discovered she was still damp all over as she struggled into her work clothes. They clung to her skin, but she didn't care. At the sink she brushed her teeth in a daze.

Her next move was spontaneous and impulsive, almost autonomous. When she'd rinsed her toothbrush and put it back in her ditty bag, Maggie pressed a fingertip into the thick steam on the mirror above the sink. A shiny curved line took shape beneath her index finger, and she drew another mirror image of the curving line, joining it to the first one.

A heart.

In the center she made a cross and wrote the letters W.D. on the top cubes formed by the cross, then M.C. on the bottom. Stepping back and looking at what she'd done, Maggie felt a jolt of surprise. *Oh! You are so childish, Maggie Culpepper!* She fumed, yanking off the towel she'd wrapped turban-style around her head, swiping it furiously across the mirror.

In a huff, she gathered up her things from the shower and from the wooden bench just outside of it, throwing the bottle of green shampoo in the wastebasket on her way out the door.

* * * * *

"Ten days till Christmas!" Helen's sparkly eyes and wide smile said everything. She was settled on a couch in the lounge, a cola in one hand and the latest issue of *Life* magazine in the other. "Merry Christmas to my favorite roomie!" She held her cola out in the gesture of a toast to Maggie.

Maggie managed a small smile and lifted her cup of black coffee in acknowledgment.

The lounge filled early on these cold, wintry evenings. Groups of card-playing WAVES; girls drinking sodas, smacking gum, and gossiping; girls bopping and singing along to songs on the small Philco radio, which was constantly on, tuned to a station in Trenton.

"White Christmas" was currently playing, and a group of four WAVES was standing in a line, arms linked, singing along at the top of their lungs. There was a long strand of red tinsel running along the far wall, and a small, artificial tree in one corner, covered with crude paper snowflakes.

Maggie shivered when she sank down beside Helen, a chill caused not so much by being in a cold hangar working all day but by the episode from her morning shower, and even more so by the news in a letter from Eugenia she'd finally opened in a weak moment. Ernie Haygood had died in service.

"Hey, you're shaking, Mags." Helen reached out to pat Maggie's knee. "Maybe you should cut back on the coffee, huh, girl?"

Maggie shook her head.

"Don't you just love Christmas?" Helen asked, practically dancing in her seat with enthusiasm.

"Sure," Maggie said, without an ounce of conviction. "It's just great." She wished she could see such a happy and beautiful future as easily as Helen could. Her thoughts kept going over Eugenia's news about Ernie, and in the two hours since she'd read it, it still had not soaked in as real yet. Maggie felt dazed, as if what Eugenia shared was just some story in a book, something that had happened to an imaginary character.

"You okay?" Helen was nudging Maggie in the ribs with her elbow.

"Tired and cold, that's all."

"I know something that'll pick your spirits up." Helen smiled broadly, waving the latest issue of *Photoplay* magazine in Maggie's direction.

"Have I ever read a single *Photoplay* since you've known me?" Maggie asked, running her fingers through a tangle of hair behind her ear.

"Sorr-ee. I just want you to cheer up, Mags. I'm worried about you. I hate to think of you staying here again during Christmas."

"I'll be fine."

"This is nowhere to be at *Christmas*!" Helen shook her head. "While all us other members of the Feminine Club are at home, in our nice warm beds, with home-cooking and presents and our own private bathrooms and pretty clothes and—"

"I told you, Helen!" Maggie saw red now. "I've dedicated my life to my Navy career! You more than anybody should know that."

A silence settled between them as Helen read and Maggie sipped her coffee. Bits and pieces of conversation laced with giggles drifted over with strains of "White Christmas" coming from the radio.

"Well, Mags"—Helen turned to her—"guess you lifers will have to celebrate together here. I heard that Brent Lawton's fixing a nice Christmas dinner at his place."

Maggie felt her mouth go dry. "That's not funny."

Helen stifled a giggle. "Okay, okay. You're right. Sorry. I shouldn't have said that. But I actually did hear he's staying here."

Maggie shrugged, though she felt her skin tighten and her heartbeat speed up.

"Listen, girl." Helen's kind eyes studied Maggie. "Maybe, well, maybe you'd come home to Florence with me? I mean, since Jasper's visiting with his folks and not coming to meet my family till the day after Christmas, it would be so much fun to have you to travel all that way home with me." She raised her eyebrows, tilted her head, pleading. "It's not too late to put in for a leave. What do you say, Mags? Come home with me? Please? My aunt can fit your bridesmaid dress on you while you're there.'"

Maggie licked at lips so wind-chapped they felt like sandpaper. "I appreciate your offer, Helen, honestly, but..." She fumbled for words. "But, I think I ought to—"

Her words were cut off by the abrupt ceasing, mid-note, of Frank Sinatra singing "Have Yourself a Merry Little Christmas." The radio crackled a moment before an announcer's grave voice began: "We interrupt this broadcast to bring you news that deeply saddens all of us. We have just received word that we have lost one of our greatest jazz musicians. Glenn Miller's plane went down today over the English Channel as he was flying to Paris. We mourn a selfless man who performed for our troops and at war-bond rallies. We will deeply miss this forty-year-old legend, who will live on in our hearts and minds and especially in his music. Here is Glenn Miller's beautiful 'Stairway to the Stars.'"

Maggie's heart—already ripped open and tender from her experience in the shower, then from the news about Ernie—stopped. There was a moment of surrealism, as if time were standing still.

Then Helen, bless her, broke the silence, the stillness. She threw up her arms and began to weep loudly. Then she wailed, "O Lord God, no–o–o–o! Not our Glenn Miller! No–o–o–o–o—"

This opened the floodgates, and it seemed to Maggie as if every WAVE in the lounge was trying to outdo the rest in volume. The soothing, disarming notes of "Stairway to the Stars" were drowned out, and Maggie hung her head, feeling somehow guilty for not crying with them.

The wailing continued until a new Glenn Miller song, "Little Brown Jug," came on. Still stunned, still a bit numb, Maggie watched as the women settled down, crying quietly and hugging one another, murmuring in words that sounded like baby-talk. Helen's hand reached for Maggie's. Her hand was warm and soft, comforting, and Maggie squeezed it gratefully.

"Our Glenn Miller is dead," Helen murmured, shaking her head.

"My friend and classmate, Ernie Haygood, is dead too," Maggie said. "A boy I've known since kindergarten, a boy I sat next to in third grade, who pulled my ponytail, who loved to fish and play catch—" She didn't add the words "with his best friend, William Dove."

"Oh, darlin'," Helen said, looking over at Maggie with tears streaming from her blue eyes. "I am so, so sorry. I knew there was a cloud hanging over you. Please come home with me. You don't need to be here alone at Christmastime. Not after this. I'm not taking no for an answer."

"Okay." The word tumbled out of Maggie's throat almost by itself.

"You will?" Helen lifted her tear-stained face. "Really? Promise, Mags?"

"Promise."

"Oh, thank you, thank you, thank you! You know we'll have fun! I've been praying you'd say yes. And now look! We'll bake gingerbread men with raisin eyes, and we can go downtown to the courthouse in Florence to see the big wreath. Oh, we'll have so much fun! I want you to be happy, Mags!"

"Tuxedo Junction" came on and the mood in the lounge lightened a teeny bit as Maggie shook her head in disbelief at what she'd just promised Helen.

* * * * *

Maggie knelt on the cold floor of the barracks, her suitcase open at her knees. She looked down at her wristwatch. Fifteen minutes had passed and she still had not packed one thing. In fact, days had passed since that moment in the lounge when she'd agreed to go to Florence, South Carolina, for Christmas, and she still wasn't mentally ready to leave Trenton.

Time is ticking on, she thought. She wished time would tick on faster, that this trip, Christmas especially, would be over and done with so she could be back here at the naval air station, safe at work.

She'd been insulating herself fairly well from painful memories and mentally steeling herself from dividing her loyalties with things like love, until Helen had come along and made a fairly large crack in her insulation. Maggie didn't want to, but she cared deeply about what happened to her friend. She longed for Helen to have her happy dream. She wanted Helen to have love, marriage, and a pile of babies.

Struggling to her feet, Maggie opened the drawer that held

her civilian clothes, placed a pair of brown loafers on the bottom of the suitcase, then two sweater sets and a tweed skirt on top of that. Pajamas and a robe and bedroom slippers came next, then she absentmindedly made a scoop of the whole layer of her underthings, deciding that it was a lot less trouble just to pack everything in that category.

Something glinted in the corner of the empty drawer, and Maggie bent over closer to peer down at it. Her heart was hammering in her ears as she lifted the glittering reindeer-head brooch William had given her that momentous night at the Varsity a year ago. The pin she'd buried when she arrived here on base. The pin she'd just as soon forget.

She held it in her palm and stared at it for a full beat. What an intent boy William had been that night! Clearly Maggie saw his eyes, felt his touch as he pinned the brooch to her sweater. She stood transfixed as sweat beads formed on her forehead, her throat began to constrict, and she felt as if she were standing on the edge of a steep cliff, looking down, too terrified to even swallow.

Maggie had a fleeting impulse to fling the reindeer pin into the trash can. She sank back down to the edge of her suitcase, biting her lip, mentally struggling to convince herself that her allegiance to the Navy was stronger than any silly emotion.

At last she gave a satisfied nod, swiping her hands together in victory. As far as the brooch went, she would keep it, but only as a memento of those moments she'd once shared with William. Times that were no more and would never be again.

She pressed the brooch firmly into one corner of her suitcase, beneath a pile of socks.

When everything from her chest of drawers was neatly tucked in, Maggie turned to her closet. She pulled her heavy coat from its hanger, wincing briefly at the memory of retrieving it from Brent, then gathered her thick wool scarf and lined gloves from the shelf, laying these items on her bed to wear as they left the base.

She needed all the insulation she could get, because several days earlier a snow had fallen, a pure white powder that lay like diamonds beneath her boots. Maddeningly, as soon as it came, she couldn't help thinking of William's dream to see real snow with her, and there came this tiny mental image of their holding hands, with crystalline flakes falling all around, a vision so real it made her stomach ache.

Not even her iron will could totally blockade thoughts of William from her conscious as long as the snow remained. He was right there at the heels of her mind, following her to work, to chow hall, and back to the barracks, making her catch her breath as unwelcome emotions balled up in her throat.

Well, she smiled, *that would certainly stop now.* She sure wouldn't see any snow way down there in Florence, South Carolina. Why, Florence was no more than a hop, skip, and a jump away from balmy Watkinsville, Georgia.

* * * * *

Maggie gave in to a huge yawn, snuggling down into the luxurious embrace of a civilian mattress and satin sheets. She watched as Helen readied herself for her nightly prayer, kneeling in a puddle of lamplight beside the twin bed next to Maggie's, a pink lace canopy stretching above her blond head.

They'd been here in Florence for two days now, in the La-Motte home where original oil paintings dotted the walls and Oriental carpets iced hardwood floors. Things were so different than in the barracks back in Trenton, yet so much the same.

Maggie never failed to be awestruck by the sounds of Helen's nightly prayer. She talked to God in that *familiar* way of hers that she always did. Her head bowed, her fingers entwined beneath her chin, she spoke with a simplicity, a purity, and a faith that unnerved Maggie and made her cast her eyes at Helen as if she might actually see God right there, listening, answering, His arm across Helen's shoulders.

Maggie closed her eyes, looking forward to exploring the fifty acres of land that comprised the LaMotte's estate tomorrow as Helen had promised. Not to mention the real Columbian coffee with real cream Mrs. LaMotte insisted on for breakfasts. Maggie hadn't had this much carefree fun in months. The days had been mild and sunny, the lowest temperatures in the evenings only in the fifties, and the LaMottes were gracious, relaxed hosts who didn't pry and who made Maggie feel totally at ease as they rolled out gingerbread for cookies and shelled pecans for tarts.

"Well, Father," Helen was saying, "guess we're to the part where I lift up the hungry people and the cold people and the children who are scared. Please hold them all beneath Your wings and take care of them. I want to thank You for taking care of my Jasper and for our upcoming wedding and thank You for my dear friend Maggie being here with me for Christmas. Let us have a good night and a happy day tomorrow, and I'll talk to You tomorrow evening. Good night and amen." Helen climbed into bed and reached over to turn off the bedside lamp.

"Night, Mags," she called through the darkness.

"Good night, Helen." Maggie thought she would fall asleep quickly, but her thoughts kept going over and over the day—walking down to the small catfish pond at the edge of the La-Mottes' property, the scratchy yet fun task of trying on her brides-maid gown, eating fudge and drinking iced tea out on the veranda as Helen's two younger brothers wrestled in the grass below.

"Helen?" she ventured into the quiet. "Thanks for inviting me. You were right. You've got a wonderful family."

"Well," Helen murmured sleepily, "they love having you here."

"Um," Maggie said, her heart speeding up a bit, "I brought a gift for your mother. You know, a hostess gift."

"You didn't need to do that, Mags. She adores having you here. That's your gift. Get it? Your *presence* is your present?" Helen giggled softly.

"I get it, but I want to." Maggie's mind raced. "The way I was raised, we always brought a hostess gift, something for the ones putting us up. And your mother's been wonderful to me." Her mind flitted to the tall, plump, kindly Mrs. LaMotte, who had red hair and freckles just like Maggie. She was a humorous, down-to-earth woman who'd wrapped Maggie in a big hug the first time she laid eyes on her.

"Okay. If you put it that way. Anyway, I know how stubborn you are."

"Thanks."

"You're welcome. What is it?"

"A pair of wool socks." Her heart clenched up a teeny bit as she recalled opening the package from her father containing the gray-speckled socks along with several other small gifts and some cash. A note tucked in read, "Merry Christmas, dear daughter. I'll miss you. Keep warm! Love, Father." She'd not removed the tags from the socks, and she decided Mrs. LaMotte would love them as much as she did.

"Oh," Helen said, a smile in her voice, "Mama can wear them at night when she's sitting on the veranda. She always says her feet get chilly. She truly does. Can I see them?" Helen's lamp came on and she was sitting up in bed, waiting expectantly.

Maggie climbed out of bed and crossed the room to the window seat, which held her suitcase. She unfastened the latches, lifted the lid, and snaked her hand down through the corner, searching for the socks.

She heard Helen get out of bed and felt her presence beside her as she rifled through, still hunting. All of a sudden Helen caught her breath, her hand reaching into the suitcase to draw something out. It was the reindeer brooch. Cradling it in her palm, she turned it this way and that.

"Ooo-weee, girl," Helen breathed at last, an expression of wonder on her face. "This is gor-ge-oussss!"

"It's pretty enough," Maggie said with a shrug, trying to act as if there were nothing extraordinary about the pin. She found the socks and she dangled them in front of Helen, who didn't seem to see them.

"Pretty enough? Girl, this is exquisite! Where in the world did you find this?" Helen stroked the reindeer head and looked into Maggie's face.

Maggie's chest drew up tight.

"Please tell me where you got this beautiful brooch."

"An old friend gave it to me."

"Friend?" Helen's eyebrows were raised high. "Boy or girl?"

"Why does it matter?"

"Oh, come on, Maggie, hon. Just tell me who."

"Nothing to tell."

"Promise?"

"Helen, the person who gave it to me, we're not even friends anymore."

"You serious?"

"Yes." Maggie tried to sound like it was no big deal, but her voice cracked. "Of course I am."

"It was a boy," Helen said. "Sure must have been a *good* friend." Suddenly her eyes widened and her playful voice turned into a whisper. "Oh, honey," she said, draping an arm across Maggie's shoulders. "Did he die? And it's just too painful to look at this? Oh me, oh my. I bet that's it. He's the one who died in combat. No wonder you've been walking around under a black cloud! You're hurting so much and you can't talk about it." Tears glistened in her eyes. "Poor, poor girl. Your heart is broken, isn't it? Oh, bless your heart."

Maggie knew she should correct Helen's assumption, but she couldn't find the words, and she didn't want to shut out the comfort of her friend's touch. Anyway, she really was grieving. Her heart was heavy. Constantly she saw the faces of the dead— of Ernie, of Glenn Miller, of the countless other men who'd given their lives in the war. She let that reality be what kept her silent now.

"Well," Helen said, teardrops trembling on her jaw line, "definitely you need to wear this." She pressed the pin into Maggie's palm. "Wear it in his honor. You can do that much, I know. He gave his life, Maggie! That's not something to sniff at. Wear it and remember this man who gave his life for our country. And on Thursday night we'll go to the Longest Night service at my church, and we'll honor him. We'll honor his sacrifice. Okay? That will help you, I know."

Helen's soothing words and her gentle touch clouded Maggie's thoughts. She couldn't think to ask about the meaning of a Longest Night service, nor could she summon up her usual resistance to anything God-related. "Okay," she murmured, "yes," tucking the pin back into her suitcase, out of sight.

* * * * *

"That looks so pretty on your sweater, Mags," Helen said as they lingered at the long dining table after breakfast.

"Thanks," Maggie replied, feeling warm spots appear on her cheeks. There was no choice but to wear William's gift to her. She tried not to look at the sparkling pin or at Helen's sympathetic eyes. She tried to focus on the cut-glass bowl full of oranges in the center of the table.

"I know it's hard to lose someone you love." Understanding colored Helen's soft words. "Death is so final, and understanding the whys is not easy. That's exactly why our church holds the Longest Night service every December."

"Oh, really?" Maggie said, feeling her heart begin to pound. "What is this thing again?"

"Well, the Longest Night is a special service for people who've lost someone during the year. Reverend Turner says Christmas is especially hard for those folks, and because of that, he holds this service every year on December 21." Helen paused, sipped some water. "Maybe it's called the Darkest Night service. Anyway, we went last year because my Granny Truett had passed away over the summer. Reverend Turner lit a whole bunch of candles, and folks in the pews had candles, and we lifted up the name of our loved ones who'd gone on to their heavenly home. Mama said it was so nice to go honor her mother like that, to receive the peace that passes understanding."

Longest night, darkest night—whatever. Church was the furthest thing from Maggie's mind. Cynicism about this peace Helen gushed about was all she could wrap her mind around.

This is going to be hard, she realized. This certainly wasn't the way she'd imagined her Christmas to be.

At last Maggie took a hot, rich swallow of Columbian coffee. By sheer force of will, she'd just turn off her mind and her memories until all this was over and she was back on base in Trenton.

* * * * *

"Be time to bathe and dress for the service before too long," Helen told Maggie later that day as they stood in the front room admiring the Christmas tree lights. "I know we want time for our hair to curl."

"Yeah, sure," Maggie said, her hands wrapped around a warm cup of cocoa Mrs. LaMotte had offered her when the girls came in from an afternoon walk.

"I'm going to wear my burgundy velvet dress," Helen said. "What are you going to wear?"

"Oh, I don't know," Maggie replied, managing to stop herself from shrugging. She felt bad for her lack of enthusiasm. It was hard to fathom Helen's excitement about this church service tonight. She guessed maybe if she worked really hard she might could remember feeling that way...back when her mother was still alive.

Oh, I miss you so much, Mother. Maggie brought the cup to her lips and took her first sip of the fragrant cocoa. It was warm and silky and sweet, laced with wafts of cinnamon that reminded her of home so much that the creamy rich liquid formed a clot in her throat. Tears sprang to her eyes.

"What's wrong?" Helen turned to look at Maggie.

"Um..." Maggie shook her head, trying to think of something to say. "Nothing. I'm fine."

"You don't look fine. Come on, let's go upstairs and start getting ready."

Maggie trudged along behind Helen. When they reached her bedroom, Helen pulled her dress from the closet and settled it with a flourish over the chenille spread on her bed. "Why don't you go ahead and get the first bath, Mags," she said over her shoulder. "I need to polish my pumps and do my nails anyway."

Maggie nodded, searching through her luggage for something suitable. She pulled out a silky cream-colored blouse, half-heartedly shaking out the wrinkles, taking this, along with a navy skirt and some clean undergarments, into the bathroom adjoining Helen's bedroom. Setting her clothes on a wicker table, she turned on the water in the huge, white claw-footed tub that reminded her of a princess's bath. Leaving the door cracked so she could talk back and forth with Helen, she undressed and climbed into steaming water that felt like heaven.

"Hey, girl, I think I'll turn us on some music," Helen called after a bit, and Maggie smiled as she remembered seeing the small black radio on a bookshelf in Helen's room.

"Now here's a little music that's guaranteed to rejoice the soul." The deejay's voice threaded its way into the bathroom. "Recorded October of 1943, by our own Bing Crosby, this is a song that touches a tender place in the hearts of all Americans, both soldiers and civilians. All of us who are in the depths of war. Last year, in 1943, this song joined 'White Christmas' to become one of America's most popular holiday tunes. This recording by Bing Crosby shot to the Top 10. So hold on to your hats as we bring you, 'I'll Be Home for Christmas.'"

Maggie flinched as the notes from Helen's radio shattered the sanctuary of her bath. "I promise you, I'll be home for Christmas," sang Bing, as she heard William saying in his soft, Southern drawl, "That's our song, Maggie Jane." A voice laced with incomparable sweetness on that night he confessed his undying love to her.

Suddenly she felt her world ripping apart even more than when she was downstairs sipping cocoa.

I don't have to take this! Maggie shut her eyes and submerged her head so that she was totally enveloped. Wrapped in her beautiful watery cocoon she could hear nothing, and she stayed this way until her lungs began screaming for air. When she popped up, Bing was on the final strains, "I'll be home for Christmas, if only in my dreams."

"And now we extend our Christmas greetings to each and every one of you listeners out there," the deejay was saying. "May the joy of Christmas and its peace and beauty be yours."

"Ha!" Maggie said to him. "You don't know a thing. I'm just going to get myself through this church service tonight, get myself through Christmas, and then I'll have joy and peace when I'm back home in Trenton."

* * * * *

"Girls night out!" Helen said. "We're going to have such a good time, and we couldn't ask for a prettier night, could we, Mags?"

Maggie was not so sure that a church service constituted a good time, but she noticed the night was pretty as she climbed out of the LaMottes' car. A full moon and a zillion stars twinkled in a velvet-blue canopy.

Mrs. LaMotte and Helen were talking in low voices as the three of them walked toward the front doors of the church, while Maggie was quiet, glancing at the spire rising majestically toward the heavens. They were a bit late and Mrs. LaMotte hurried up the brick steps, through the vestibule, then between two heavy wooden doors that led into the sanctuary, Helen and Maggie right on her heels.

Maggie drew in a breath as they started down the center aisle. The dark pews, stretching from side-to-side, gleamed softly in the light of a row of flickering candles in tall silver holders along a tall, narrow table at the front. Stained-glass windows shimmered in shades of wine and emerald.

At the front of the sanctuary, a tufted cushion for kneeling stretched the length of an altar rail carved with intricate designs. Carpeted steps led to a raised platform holding the pulpit, and behind that was the choir loft and a grand piano with holly and a thick candle inside a hurricane glass on top of it. It had been a long time since Maggie'd been in a house of worship, and she felt an overwhelming sense of awe descend upon her.

"Helen? Margaret?" The gentle voice and hand of Mrs. LaMotte startled Maggie as she reached out to pull both girls into a pew about halfway down the aisle. Maggie sank into her seat and noted that everyone was sitting expectantly as from up front came soft piano notes, the beginning strains of "Silent Night."

Maggie's breath caught in her throat at the sense of holiness the music brought. It seemed a million years ago when she'd believed in a benevolent God who listened to her prayers. *I will not let this music have an effect on me!* She ground her teeth together.

When the hymn ended, a tall, skinny minister in a dark suit climbed into the pulpit. "Brothers and sisters," he began, "welcome to this special service of hope and consolation. The season of Christmas is upon us. A time when we celebrate God incarnate, God made flesh.

"Yet this joyous time can be hard for some of us. When we experience a loss, a death, profound grief, Christmas can be soul-wrenching. Both spiritually and emotionally. Because of this, we hold our annual Longest Night service.

"Tonight, December 21, is the Winter Solstice. It's that night of the year with the longest period of darkness. But, and this is important to remember, it is also the *beginning* of that part of the year in which the amount of daylight each day increases gradually, up until June 21." He paused to sweep his left arm out toward the row of flickering candles.

"We are gathered here in God's house tonight to claim the

promised return of joy, of light, into our wounded lives. To claim the healing. My prayer is that the healing love of our Savior, Jesus Christ, will be with each of you in this coming year. Each one of you who has lost someone dear to you."

A choir of hushed amens rose and fell as the congregation murmured their agreement. Maggie was quiet, shifting uncomfortably in her seat.

"Jesus said, in John 8:12, 'I am the light of the world.'" Reverend Turner lifted a flickering candle high. "Isaiah 9:2 tells us, 'The people walking in darkness have seen a great light.'"

The woman directly in front of Maggie began weeping softly, hugging herself as she rocked back and forth. Mrs. La-Motte reached up to pat the woman's shoulder.

"The ushers will begin passing out candles," Reverend Turner continued. "When you receive your candle, hold it upright. An usher will give the first person in each pew a light. Pass that light along until all have their candles lit."

Maggie inhaled the scent of hot wax drifting through the sanctuary. She wondered if she could quietly refuse to take a candle, a light. No, she decided just as quickly, as her hand closed around the cool end of a candle Mrs. LaMotte passed to her.

"As we turn more and more toward the Light of the world, toward Jesus," Reverend Turner said, "we can release our burdens and become a people set free from our grief. I ask you tonight, do you have the peace that passes understanding in your life? That comes from knowing God is in control of our universe?

"Life is difficult." He leaned forward now, his voice pleading. "We will all face difficulties and heartbreak along the way. But we know we are not just wandering aimlessly in some desert. There is order and there is purpose because our God is in control.

"He sent Jesus, our Lord and Savior, and come what may, Jesus will be with you. He will comfort you. I tell you tonight that He has the power to save you from your grief and your despair. Even from *death*. He will lift you above your sorrows, uphold you in His everlasting arms. Charles Wesley said it like this when he wrote this beloved hymn." The Reverend nodded at the plump older woman perched on the piano bench, her hands poised above the keys.

Maggie tensed yet again as the beginning notes of "Hark! the Herald Angels Sing" poured forth, wondering what it was about songs that put such huge cracks in her defenses. The music continued, and when it was to the last half of the last verse, Maggie found herself clenching her teeth so hard they ached as the congregation sang:

> *"Mild he lays his glory by,*
> *Born that man no more may die,*
> *Born to raise the sons of earth,*
> *Born to give them second birth.*
> *Hark! The herald angels sing,*
> *'Glory to the newborn king.'"*

Maggie held her candle with shaking hands. The song was over and a flame from the tip of Mrs. LaMotte's candle was dancing in her line of vision. Miraculously she managed to hold her candle still enough to receive it and then pass it along to Helen's waiting candle.

The room filled with tiny flames, and each jewel in the reindeer head at Maggie's shoulder caught and reflected the lights so that it appeared as if the brooch were on fire.

Maggie held her chin high, looking toward the front of the church where the reverend stood, holding his candle with a serene expression, waiting for something she was not sure of.

When at last he did speak again, his voice startled Maggie. She was so caught up in the expectant hush of the congregation. "Many of you have lost someone dear to you over this past year." The reverend's voice was like honey poured in hot tea. "I invite you now to lift your candle high in honor of that person. You may lift their name up, call it aloud if you so desire, and if anyone would like to come forward and share words about the person you have lost, please feel free. Or you may come up front and kneel at the altar rail for special prayer. Tears are welcome here at this service. Our Lord knows every tear you cry. Give your pain to Him, to the Light of the World."

The weeping woman rose from the pew in front of Maggie, her jet black hair gleaming in the candlelight. She moved to the front of the sanctuary and Maggie saw the shiny tracks of her tears when she turned to face the congregation. She cleared her throat. She held her candle high. "This is for Henry James

Lumpkin," she said, dipping her wet cheek to dry it on the fabric at her shoulder. "As many of you know, I lost Henry James, my nineteen-year-old son, in the war this year. I had to pray for strength to bear my grief. While my grief has not gone away, it has become bearable. I know for certain that my Henry is with God. And although my world feels like it's falling apart sometimes, God has given me peace that is beyond my understanding."

A smile broke through her tears. "In spite of my loss, I still have my cherished memories. Memories of nineteen years with my Henry James. He was—is—a gift from God. I tell you, people, I am so thankful I had my son for nineteen years. A boy, a man, who was willing to die for our country. To fight against the evils on this globe. He told me sometimes, in those days before he left for Germany, he would say, 'Mama, don't cry for me if I die, because some things are worth dying for.'

"Still today, even when I cry because I cannot have him here with me, because he's not here for Christmas, I am comforted in that deep, deep part of me—knowing for certain that my Henry James is held safe within the loving arms of God.

"So, don't you see?" she asked, her plaintive voice filling the sanctuary. "He *is* home for Christmas. He's home with his Father in heaven, and I will see him again. We will be reunited when I reach my eternal home." She bowed her head, cupping one palm around her candle as she moved back to her pew.

Maggie had been so transfixed by the woman's words she hadn't noticed the hot wax trailing over her knuckles and down her wrist. Now she looked at the hardened trail in surprise as

Reverend Turner cleared his throat and began to speak once again.

"Thank you, Mrs. Lumpkin, for sharing your heart with us. I knew Henry James, and I know so many more of you, personally, who have lost someone to this war. My heart is crushed over the number of men who won't be here with us for Christmas, who won't be home with their loving families. We should learn to live every day as if it were our last. We should tell our loved ones often that we love and appreciate them. We should praise God that one day He will wipe away every tear from our eyes, and there will be no more death or crying or pain. The old order of things will pass away and we will possess eternal peace and joy."

The reverend's words fell on Maggie like a shaft of morning sun. Light filled her dark, wounded soul so that her crushed and buried dreams began to climb out of their graves, to fill with optimism, with faith. She caught a glimpse of the old Maggie, the hopeful, faith-filled, and joyful Maggie who'd been trapped deep inside.

Oh, Mother, I'm sorry. I'll embrace my memories of you. I won't fight them any longer. I know God's in control and you're with God, and I know I'll see you again one day.

Maggie felt her heart beating steady and strong. She felt her insides rearranging, the fortress she'd built around her heart crumbling. The faith, the peace that passes understanding was hers again. Those things she thought had died with her mother were resurrected like the daffodils in spring, pushing up, all light-filled and beautiful and strong.

She didn't have to keep running away. She knew exactly where she wanted to spend the holidays and the rest of her life. The word "love" seemed insufficient to describe what she held in her heart for William Dove. The power of it filled every cell and nerve ending in her body as she touched the reindeer head.

The service wasn't over, but Maggie leaned over to whisper to Helen, "May I make a long-distance telephone call from your house tomorrow?"

Helen's eyes grew large, questioning, but she whispered back, "Yes. Of course you may."

Maggie sat, only vaguely aware of the other worshippers as the service drew to a close. There was only one thing she could think about right now.

Please, please, Lord, she breathed. *Please let William still want to spend his life with me.*

* * * * *

Early morning light spilled in through the window of Mr. La-Motte's home office, illuminating a black telephone on the corner of a large mahogany desk. Maggie's hand shook and her finger trembled as she dialed then spoke to a switchboard operator and waited, breathless, as it rang once. Twice. Three times. Then, right before the fourth ring, someone picked up.

"Hello?"

"Father?" she said. "It's me. Maggie."

There was a sharp intake of air, followed by a pause. She listened to the sound of the line crackling with interference at some point between South Carolina and Georgia.

"Are you okay, sweetheart?" he asked at last. "You sound funny."

"Um, yes, I'm fine. I'm absolutely wonderful." Maggie took a deep breath before continuing. "But, Father, I've decided I really want to come home for Christmas."

"You do?"

"Mmhmm. More than anything."

"Well, this is certainly a surprise," he said. "But it's wonderful, sweetheart! You'd make my holiday."

"Do you think you can come get me?"

There was a momentary silence, and Maggie's heartbeat accelerated. She hadn't told her father she was going to spend Christmas with Helen's family, and she was worried his feelings would be hurt. "I'm not in New Jersey," she ventured. "Actually, I'm not very far from Georgia. I'm in Florence, South Carolina, where my friend Helen LaMotte's from, and if you have enough gas stamps, I mean, I know it's asking a lot, but do you think it would be poss—"

"I've got plenty of ration stamps, sweetheart," he interrupted, his voice like music to her ears. "Give me their address and I'll be on my way right after I finish my coffee."

* * * * *

As her father drove past the courthouse in downtown Watkinsville, then up Harden Hill toward their house, Maggie thought she'd never seen any place so beautiful. She rolled her window down, drawing in great gulps of air, inviting everything to welcome her home—Georgia pines, the homes of old friends, neighborhood dogs, festive wreaths fastened to front doors, the carcass of an old tractor in a shed beside Miz Webster's house.

They had scarcely gotten parked and carried her luggage inside before Maggie was out the back door, down the steps, and halfway along the path to the Doves' house. It was dusk and, as she got closer to the Doves' back porch, she could see William's unmistakable silhouette. He was sitting in the swing, reading something by lamplight. How much more perfect could things be?

Though things did appear perfect, Maggie was suddenly bombarded with such a complex weave of remorse, anxiety, longing, and love that she could barely think. She froze in a patch of straw in the Doves' backyard.

Help me, Lord. Please give me strength and help me with my words here because I really do love William Dove. I'm sorry for running away, from You and from him. Can You please just reach down here and put Your hand in this moment?

Maggie felt herself moving up the steps toward the swing. She found herself standing before William with a smile on her face so wide it was hard to form words. "William Dove, I love you," she managed, "and I want to spend my life with you."

She heard his indrawn breath, saw his startled face and his hands grasping at the book that fell from his lap as he stood up.

"Maggie Jane?" William blinked. He shook his head. "What are you doing here? When did you decide you loved me?"

"I didn't have to decide it. I've known it for a long, long time. But getting to this point is a long story. Guess it happened mostly when I was at a church service last night."

"Did you just say *church*?"

"Yes. God cleared up some stuff for me, and I realized I want to spend the rest of my life with you."

"Are you sure?" William's words were falling all over each other. "I thought you weren't interested in God anymore."

"Well, I got mad at Him when Mother died."

"I know," Will said, his eyes closing. "I even understand a little better now. You know we lost Ernie, don't you?"

"I do, Will, and I'm so, so sad about it. I really am." She reached out to touch William's arm. "The old me, the me who was mad because I thought God couldn't care if He took my mother, was furious about Ernie dying too. There were things I just didn't realize."

"Like what?" William looked into Maggie's eyes.

"Um, let's see how I can put this." She paused. "You remember that old saying we learned in English class, something along the lines of 'Better to have loved and lost than never to have loved at all'?"

"Yes. Tennyson."

"Well, I see now, William. I see how true that is, and how important love is. Letting people love you, loving them right back. I mean, I *could* make it on my own. I've proven that to myself. I know from my work with the WAVES that I could stand on my own two feet. I could make it without you. But I don't want to. I see clearly now that without love, without you, William Dove, there's going to be a great big gaping hole, an empty spot in my life."

She heard William gulp. "I can't guarantee you a perfect, pain-free life, Maggie Jane," he said. "A life without risk. You know *I'm* not perfect."

"What are you trying to say?" she asked after a moment, her heart in her throat.

"I'm saying that I'll always have a limp. I'll always struggle with this hand of mine." William's voice was measured as he held up his hand, then his foot. "The effects of polio aren't going to just disappear, and besides that, I'm certain we'd have our share of other hurts along the way."

"I know that," she said, taking a tentative step closer to him. "But no one has a happily-ever-after kind of life except story-book people, and I can't see my future without picturing you, William Dove. Do you think it would be possible for us to decorate that beautiful Virginia pine together on Christmas Eve?"

"Am I dreaming?" William sounded incredulous. He started pinching himself and said in a sort of joking voice, "I think this is what they mean when they say 'A little bit of heaven on earth.' You're my one and only, Maggie Jane, and never in my life have I seen anything more wonderful than you standing here on my back porch, telling me you love me and want to spend your life with me. I couldn't ask for anything more. Of course we'll decorate that Virginia pine together."

"I'm not home for good, William. Not yet. I need to fulfill my duty and serve until this crazy war is over—plus a bit of time after that—until they give us gals the go-ahead to leave. But, then I'll be home forever and for good."

"Well, I'm so glad you're home for Christmas." William stepped forward and enfolded Maggie in his arms. She felt his warm neck resting on the top of her head, his heartbeat against her cheek.

Exactly the words Maggie longed to hear. She smiled, shaking her head in wonder that, come Christmas, she would not be in Trenton, New Jersey, or in Florence, South Carolina. She would be right here in Watkinsville, Georgia, where she belonged. In the arms of William Dove, the man she loved. She'd truly be home.

ABOUT THE AUTHOR

 Julie L. Cannon is a multi-published author as well as a speaker and entertainer who travels across country serving up helpings of down-home humor and warmth described as "Southern-fried soul food." She lives with her husband and three children in Watkinsville, Georgia.

summerside
PRESS™

When I Fall in Love™
ROMANCE WITH A NOSTALGIC BEAT

Available Starting September 2010

𝒟𝑜 you remember the song that was playing during your first kiss? Can you still sing the lyrics to the tune you and your first love called "our song"? If so, you are going to love Summerside's newest fiction line—WHEN I FALL IN LOVE. Each book in the WHEN I FALL IN LOVE romance line, to be set in the 1920s through the 1970s, will carry the title of a familiar love song and will feature new, original romance stories set in the era of its title song's release. Watch for six new releases in the WHEN I FALL IN LOVE romance line in 2011.

Love Me Tender
BY JANICE HANNA

As *"Love Me Tender"* plays in the background, Debbie Carmichael determines to salvage her family's restaurant, Sweet Sal's Soda Shoppe, after her father's health fails. Teen heartthrob Bobby Conrad, agrees to perform at a fund-raiser concert. But just two weeks before the highly publicized event, Bobby backs out of the benefit. Enter...Johnny Hartman...a young, unknown singer. Debbie soon realizes the twists and turns leading up to the concert have been divinely orchestrated. And it isn't dreamy Bobby Conrad who has stolen her heart—but the tender Johnny Hartman.

ABOUT THE AUTHOR

Janice Hanna (also published as Janice A. Thompson) has published more than thirty novels. She has also written three devotionals, more than fifty magazine articles, and several musical comedies for the stage. Janice is proud of her four daughters and four grandchildren, and makes her home in the Houston area. Read more at www.janiceathompson.com.

summerside
PRESS™

Soul-stirring romance...
set against a historical backdrop readers will love!

Summerside Press™ is pleased to announce the launch of our
fresh line of historical romance fiction—set amid the action-packed
eras of the twentieth century. Watch for a total of six new
Summerside Press™ historical romance titles to release in 2010.

NOW AVAILABLE IN STORES

Sons of Thunder
BY SUSAN MAY WARREN
ISBN 978-1-935416-67-8

The Crimson Cipher
BY SUSAN PAGE DAVIS
ISBN 978-1-60936-012-2

**Songbird Under a
German Moon**
BY TRICIA GOYER
ISBN 978-1-935416-68-5

Stars in the Night
BY CARA PUTNAM
ISBN 978-1-60936-011-5

COMING SOON

Exciting New Historical Romance Stories by These Great Authors—
Patricia Rushford...Lisa Harris...Melanie Dobson...and MORE!